My Brothers' Keeper

A NOVEL

HARRY D. STERN

Author of *Anemone in a Desert Landscape*

The characters and events portrayed in this book are fictitious. Any similarity to real persons, living or dead, is coincidental and not intended by the author.

ISBN-13: 978-0-9978573-3-7

Cover design by: Juliana Booker
Printed in the United States of America

Dedication

I am indebted to my wife, Aviva, who was always available to listen and offer invaluable recommendations. My daughter, Lora Sommer, applied her remarkable editorial skills, helping to refine this manuscript. Debra Hill of A Novel Edit shaped this work into what I hope is an entertaining read. Michael Jacobs lent his knowledge of regional issues and editorial expertise to improve this novel.

CONTENTS

Cain invited his brother, Abel, into the field, whereupon he slew him.
The Lord asked him, "Where is thy brother?"
Cain replied, "Am I my brother's keeper?"
The Lord said, "Your brother's blood cries out to me from the soil."

GENESIS 4:8-10

1
No Way Back?

Joshua Canaan shouldered open the cab door and raced to Gate 21C of Ben Gurion Airport. Weaving through throngs of tourists, he made it just as boarding ended. As the gangway door was closing, he shouted, "Wait! I can't miss this flight."

He was headed to a bar mitzvah in Hungary; his twenty-year career as a Mossad agent left him little time or energy for family. It was tough balancing a normal life with the nasty fight against terrorism. Retirement was the beginning of a new chapter. The attendant opened the boarding door. "Sir, try to get to the gate thirty minutes before departure."

Joshua was surprised that El Al employees were so polite. *The real world has changed in my two decades away.*

The end of World War II found surviving members of his extended family dispersed to America, Palestine, Hungary, and a handful of European cities. He was re-establishing contact.

Budapest's Dohány Street Synagogue was one of the largest Jewish houses of worship in the world. As Joshua sat in the main sanctuary on a crisp Saturday morning, unusually cool for June, the beauty of the Moorish Revival architecture struck him. The stunning, richly colored, stained-glass windows sparkled with slim rays of sunlight. Ornate maple woodcarvings depicting biblical themes were arranged in geometric patterns framing the ark that housed the Torah scrolls.

He marveled at the sculptural realism. The parting of the Red Sea with the Israelites fleeing Pharaoh's forces seemed in perpetual motion; the portrayal of David's slaying and beheading Goliath was exquisite in its detail. How comforting to luxuriate in a friendly setting, his extraordinary attention to detail taking in the beautiful surroundings rather than tracking terrorists.

Joshua was told that the robust attendance was unusual in this depleted Jewish community. More than two hundred men, uncomfortably seated on frayed cushions, attended the bar mitzvah. Several elderly synagogue members appeared agitated. Their furrowed faces spoke of Nazi occupation and crushed revolutions. Thirty or so preteens, friends of the bar mitzvah boy, fidgeted in their seats and continually poked one another.

About thirty feet above Joshua, the women's gallery arced around the sanctuary. Figures engraved on the balcony's underside aesthetically and colorfully intertwined Byzantine, Gothic, and Romantic elements. The synagogue was designed with the thriving prewar Hungarian Jewish population in mind. This Saturday found only about seventy-five occupied seats in the women's balcony, leaving fourteen hundred eerily vacant.

Gilda, Joshua's distant cousin and proud mother of Alexei, the bar mitzvah boy, sat surrounded by family and friends and a smattering of service regulars. She reveled in her son's mellifluous chanting of the *haftorah* prayers.

A rear aisle seat gave Joshua an unimpeded path out of the sanctuary. Twenty years of checking out his surroundings and looking over his shoulder left an indelible mark. He headed to the restroom before Alexei's *dvar Torah*, when the thirteen-year old would thank everyone under the sun and beyond for making the day so special.

Joshua made his way toward two eight-foot, ornate glass doors, which opened noiselessly, as he entered the smartly carpeted vestibule. The brilliant sun shone through the rose window above the main entrance. Signage in Hungarian, English, and Hebrew directed him down the hallway.

He never got that far. A few steps before he reached the men's room, a deafening explosion rattled the building.

The bomb blast was thunderous. He was hurled against

a wall lined with shattered portraits of the synagogue's past presidents and board members. Glass shards littered the gray carpeting. Screams pierced the yawning gap where the entrance doors had hung seconds before.

Fragments of the ornate window he'd just admired lay all around him. He tried standing, and agony raced up his left leg. Broken or badly sprained, he thought. He pushed toward the sanctuary, suppressing the pain as he dragged his leg along.

Chaotic screams came from all corners of the sanctuary. The ark and the dais where a rosy-cheeked thirteen-year-old stood holding a Torah scroll were obliterated. The bomb had been planted alongside or underneath the podium to maximize casualties. The distinctive, bleach like odor told him two things: TATP was the weapon, and Abu Yusalem had tracked him.

The thick, acrid smoke didn't shroud the bodies, some recognizable, some not. As Joshua stumbled through the haze toward the dais in response to the shrieks and calls for help, he collapsed.

The next forty-eight hours passed in a dreamlike state. Voices tugged him out of a restless sleep. He opened his eyes one at a time, squinted, tried to focus, and turned to the left, crinkling the starched white sheets of a hospital bed.

A gaunt man with pallor from too many hours indoors and a stocky brunette nurse, triangular cap slightly askew, stood near the door. The nurse scribbled on a worn clipboard. Joshua quickly scanned the room. Two windows just behind him; the draft told him that one pane was cracked and probably faced the front of the hospital. The door was about six strides away with its window curtain drawn. The orange throw rug to his right might be slippery if he needed to move quickly. His mind, though still a blur, was an instinctual calculator.

He noted his visitors' pleasure at the unspectacular feats of opening his eyes and tilting his head. Joshua was reminded of his springer spaniel's daily delight upon his awakening in their Tel Aviv home.

"Where am I?" Joshua was surprised at the crackling, congestive sound of his voice.

"Szent Ferenc Hospital in Budapest. You arrived by ambulance after the terror attack at your house of worship." The physician's English was passable; his nurse followed his translation attentively.

"You've had a serious concussion, which we've carefully monitored. The plaster cast on your left leg is precautionary. Your leg was not broken, but you suffered a dislocation of the kneecap. We expect a full recovery after physical therapy. I'll return in an hour or so." He was already halfway to the door.

The doctor nodded toward the nurse. "Sylvia will change your sheets and manage your medication. Later she'll bring you a light meal. She speaks English but is shy about her accent. When you've finished, she'll bring in a visitor."

"What does this visitor look like?"

"In his fifties, graying hair — what's left. Slight paunch. Very European-looking."

"Thanks, Doctor."

The doctor smiled. "Two of your cousins are with him. They're seated on a bench outside your room."

He opened the door, pointed to a chirping monitor to the right of Joshua's bed, shot additional instructions to Sylvia, and flitted down the hallway to his next patient.

The nurse, with a disarmingly sweet smile, seemed ready to experiment with her heavily accented English after the attending left.

"I will help you get up, and you can sit on the chair near your bed while I change your sheets." Her Slavic accent pleasantly rolled her *r*.

Not waiting for a response, she helped him sit up and slowly slide his legs off the bed. The cast weighed on his left leg, but the pain in the dislocated knee was bearable.

Sylvia gently guided him, "Please drape your arms over my neck and shoulder." With surprising strength she led him six feet to the chair. Joshua thought she had the power and the center of gravity of a sumo wrestler.

She changed the soiled sheets and pillowcases, which stank of sweat. The starched, sweet-smelling linens were welcome now that Joshua could appreciate them. Sylvia helped him back to bed, adjusted his IV, and rolled the old bedding into a ball.

Bundle in hand, she smiled and told Joshua, "You can push the call button for any nurse on duty. With your permission I will tell your visitor to enter, but for no longer than thirty minutes. I'm serious." She waved her finger menacingly to match her mock-scolding tone.

Within minutes the door opened, and Zvi Levi entered. He made sure the door closed securely behind him. He approached the bed and whispered, "Thank God you're OK — or almost OK. I'm terribly sorry about the loss of so many family members."

His former boss's words cut through the sedative-induced torpor. The smells, the cries after the explosion came crashing back into his consciousness. Dreading the response, Joshua asked how many were killed and how many were family.

"Ten killed, sixteen seriously injured. Six of your family members were among those killed. I'm so sorry."

Joshua moaned. "My God. Children, women, defenseless old men." He ran his hand through his thick, matted brown hair and almost came to tears. Even a hardened Mossad operative had a breaking point.

For six of Joshua's twenty years in Mossad, Levi had been his boss. They had planned and carried out some of Israel's most audacious counterterrorism operations in Southeast Asia and East Africa. They had great respect for each other. Levi knew that Joshua was a cunning, relentless, often callous field operative, just as he'd been before assuming the director's position.

"Twenty-six minutes," Joshua said matter-of-factly.

"What does that mean?" Levi asked.

"The bulldozer that ushered you in here gave us thirty minutes, and she means it."

"OK, here goes. First, the two cousins sitting outside are part of a contingent from our embassy in Budapest. They're heavily armed and will look out for you 24/7. I'll check you out of here myself in forty-eight hours and fly back to Israel with you. We can get into more details then.

"You'll be helicoptered from the roof helipad to an El Al flight. We'll meet with the prime minister when you're up to it."

He waved a hand. "Joshua, you know and I know that this was the work of Abu Yusalem. It looks like he wanted you out of the way so you couldn't interfere with his plans."

Levi leaned close. "We've had reports —" He glanced at the door and took a quick survey of the room. "He's been highly active recently, showing up in intel from a handful of sectors. He's up to something. We believe it'll be major by the look of it. I know you just retired and have been through a trauma, but I need you. Israel needs you."

Levi reached into his attaché case and handed a 9mm Beretta and a fifteen-round clip to a bleary-eyed Joshua. "It's not your Beretta, but keep it under your pillow anyway. It should help keep away bad dreams."

"Twice I almost had the fucker," Joshua grumbled. "Once in the West Bank and even closer in the Czech Republic. He still has my slug in his left shoulder from our last encounter." Joshua pushed to sit up higher. "Zvi, I've had it. I'm not sure if there's anything left in me. The screams, the blood, the devastation —" He looked away from Levi. "Let's just say that this attack got to me in a way that I haven't experienced before. And if Abu Yusalem doesn't kill me, Anat will."

2
The White Supremacists Of Birmingham

The red Ram pickup pulled into the crowded Stormfront headquarters parking lot. Its dinged-up muffler produced the raucous and blustery entry music relished by Charlie "Red Tide" Tabor, the violent white supremacist group's leader.

"Red Tide" had little to do with University of Alabama football and a lot to do with a history of bloody and often deadly attacks on African-Americans and Muslims.

Tabor backed into his parking space near the exit. His was the only reserved spot in the sea of pickup trucks. The proximity to the exit and his face-out parking were elements of a rapid-escape drill that had been cultivated over a crime-riddled career.

Tabor was a big guy, over 6-2 and 250 pounds. He looked like the kind of monolith a high-caliber slug would have trouble penetrating.

Today's meeting was important, as evidenced by the full parking lot of the former commercial printing company. The industrial area was conveniently deserted after 5. A number of small businesses had relocated, wanting to be nowhere near this locus of racist activity.

The final straw for the Bates paint supply warehouse, about 500 yards down the road, was Stormfront's signage. When racist posters and signs began to adorn the headquarters, the Bates family moved far from the warehouse that had been their legacy for decades.

Those signs grew bolder when it became clear that local police wanted no confrontation with the lethal organization—or sympathized with its cause.

Tabor slid out of his pickup, checked out the thirty or so trucks jamming the lot, and headed toward the entrance. He proudly passed under the recently hung sign that read, "Stormfront Headquarters—if you are WHITE, you are welcome." The older and yellowed poster on the front door shouted: "Muslims, Black Folk, and Jews NOT WELCOME."

Harsher language for African-Americans would violate a county ordinance and could bring FBI intrusion. They weren't ready for that. Not yet.

Opening the front door took some elbow grease because of its double steel-plated panels. Inside, Tabor passed through a metal detector. Stormfront regulars knew that weapons needed to be sidelined during meetings. Sometimes they needed reminding. He paid little attention to the alarm's clanging. It stopped blaring after twenty seconds.

Forty young men in their twenties and early thirties — tanned arms displaying an array of colorful tattoos — sat around a dozen folding tables pushed together. About twenty automatic rifles were neatly stacked against the rear wall. Handguns had been placed on another folding table, clips removed, lest anyone lose his temper.

"Hey, Charlie," a sunburned, muscular wiseass muttered, sitting with six buddies. "Late to the party."

"No concern of yours," Tabor answered acidly as he placed his loaded .357 on the table, muzzle aimed at the joker. No one seemed to care that only "Red Tide" remained armed.

"No harm intended; just happy to see ya," the young man answered, suddenly aware he was treading on thin ice.

The room stank of cigarette and cigar smoke and cheap beer. The cloud of vaporized tobacco hung heavily; the group had been there awhile.

"Let's push these tables closer so we can see each other,"

Tabor offered in a slightly more congenial tone. "Pass me a beer. Good to see all y'all. I think we got some actions on our agenda. I wanna hear from y'all."

He waited until the racket of rickety tables eased, then said, "Let's get right to it."

He pointed to a wiry thirty-year-old whose skin was paying the price for years of farming in the Alabama sun. "Billy, why don't ya lay it out for us?"

Billy Townsend wore a backward University of Alabama baseball cap. He generally sat to Tabor's right, the symbolic arrangement lost on no one. Billy spent a fair amount of his youth in and out of jail and work camps. He was a petty thief with a mean streak. His history of crime and punishment made him an exemplary comrade in arms and a longtime ally of Tabor's. He was one of the few Tabor trusted in this barrel of bad apples: ex-cons, gang members, and other deviants.

Two empty beer bottles sat in front of him. He asked for a third. He twisted off the cap, nodded to his lifelong buddies, and spat out his comments with a sneer.

"We got some Jew holidays comin' up in a few weeks."

He met the eyes of several men. "These Jews are gettin' to be a real pain in the ass. We got Jew civil rights attorneys, three Jewboys who went and got elected to Birmingham councils, and now we got one of them kikes gonna run for Congress.

"We've let those kike pussies run our businesses while they pressure the police to come after us. Soon they'll be runnin' everything. I think we teach 'em a healthy lesson on their Jew holidays."

A murmur of approval penetrated the tobacco smoke. Several cronies volunteered fictional examples of Jewish corruption in business and arrogance in politics.

Tabor looked around and asked what they had planned for the Jews of Birmingham.

"I'd like to suggest a different approach." The speaker, a slim six-footer, had no trace of the sunburned, prematurely wizened faces of the thugs around him. He stood slowly and with a hint of drama smoothed back his hair and stroked the back of his neck. His taut lips and smirk conveyed a vibe of volcanic malevolence. Without raising his voice, he often intimidated the intimidators.

"While I like the target, I think we should delay action on the Jews. My understanding is they have many holidays we can help them celebrate by reducing their population in Birmingham."

"Speak your mind, Peter," Tabor said.

Abdul Hazian, a hunted terrorist feared throughout the Middle East, stood before his tattooed, sun-scorched, bent-on-evil, unsuspecting comrades. His clean-shaven appearance and unblemished skin were Stormfront anomalies. He'd worked with these men and answered to the name Peter Baron for five months.

Iran had cleverly infiltrated Quds Force operatives into BDS — the Boycott, Divestment and Sanctions movement against Israel — and other right-wing fanatical organizations. On the surface, Quds operatives worked on anti-Muslim, anti-Semitic propaganda or Israel's settlement policies. Their real goal was to amass information on local Jewish organizations and prominent Jewish community members. They aimed to cause catastrophic damage to Jews and their institutions.

He'd served, he maintained, in India as a volunteer teacher, although no one had asked what his subject matter was. Teacher or not, something about his eyes, his demeanor, his calculated way of presenting an idea, and his penetrating stare at anyone he addressed made even these hardened men shudder.

Their respect for him came when he pronounced his anti-Semitism, a loathing exceeded only by his professed hatred of Islam. Muslims, he preached, would weaken America and foment terrorism on a grand scale, just as they had done to Europe.

Hazian couldn't let this ragtag crew of violent amateurs mess up his plans for the Jews of Birmingham. He had to deflect their small-time hit so that twenty-five Quds killers could do a more complete job.

"Thank you, Charles." No one addressed "Red Tide" as Charles. Nobody, that is, but Peter Baron. Hazian's smirk couldn't varnish over the venom that exuded from his pores. Even his dapper apparel couldn't cloak the hair-trigger threat he brought to Stormfront.

"Some of you know" — Hazian glanced to his right and nodded at two thugs with whom he had discussed the Muslim "problem" — "something about my India experience. Why India? Because I was helping the lawful white citizens keep the colored Muslim invasion at bay. Muslims are besieging us in the same way throughout the Southeast. They're destroying the Western world."

He banged the table before counting on his fingers. "Three mosques in Birmingham, one in Tuscaloosa, and two in Mobile. What's next? They overran Europe, and now it's starting here." He slowly swept his right hand across the room. "*We* are the guardians of the white race. *We* are America. The Jews can wait until we're good and ready. I say let's fuck up the Muslim dens."

His fluent English, unblemished pale skin, and black crew cut provided a perfect cover. He revealed nothing of his devout Muslim upbringing in a madrassa in the slums of Beirut.

Hazian shifted slightly when the man almost directly across from him coughed. Their eye contact stayed fixed, neither man willing to shift focus. Perhaps it was simply intuitive self-preservation refined over years of evading Mossad and Interpol that made Hazian feel uneasy when seated too close to Richie Larkin. Even among these vicious thugs, something about Richie worried him.

The wily terrorist would have been only mildly surprised to learn that Richie Larkin was Ron Shavit, an American transplant to Israel. Ron had served in Mossad for six years. He, his wife, and their 8-year-old daughter lived in Kibbutz Oren, just outside Jerusalem.

Shavit had spent the better part of three years living as a community agitator in Nashville, Tennessee. He'd been in Birmingham for six months. His virulent white nationalist, anti-Semitic Nashville website blended seamlessly with the spewed hatred of Stormfront's social platforms. Billy Townsend and "Red Tide" invited him to Birmingham for a "talk."

Shavit was grilled for three hours while Tabor toyed with his glistening .357. Billy glowered at him continually and halfway through their meeting confronted Ron. "You look like a Jew boy. How does that happen? What makes you think you can join us?"

"Who said I want to join you? You asked me to come visit. And, Billy, I don't mind looking like a Jew. They may be shits as people, but they're pretty smart. So I accept your compliment —that I look smart." Ron locked eyes with Billy.

Tabor interceded. "I like you, Mr. Jew-look-alike. Get your ass down here and help our guys with their website and social crap."

Shavit joined Stormfront shortly afterward. Always looking over his shoulder, he still felt OK about staring down the guy he knew as a wanted terrorist in Israel.

Hazian dropped his glare, stretched his shoulders, and gave Richie a sideways glance. The murmur of approval for his redirection of Stormfront's plans and a nod from *Charles* were everything he was looking for.

3
Short-Lived Retirement

Joshua's limp was barely noticeable. The ringing in his ears had subsided in the nearly two months since the blast. What he couldn't erase were the memories of the chaos, the screaming, the acrid smoke searing his nostrils, and the body parts of family members blown across the main sanctuary of the Dohány Street Synagogue.

Six weeks of intensive physical therapy at the North Tel Aviv Sports Rehabilitation Clinic ended on the last day of a blistering July. Israel was experiencing a heat wave that left even the stalwarts wondering whether Iceland was welcoming refugees.

"I can't tell you how happy I'll be not to see your pretty face anymore," Joshua said with a smirk. "This rehab process was harder than my basic training." The enthusiastic twenty-four-year-old physical therapist helped relieve much of the pain in his left leg. Most of the lacerations had healed. The geometric patterns of wounds on both arms and his right leg had also mended. "But, kidding aside," he looked directly at her, "you've really helped me, and I appreciate it."

Even the discomfort of the tetanus booster and the antibiotics that aggravated his colitis subsided. His cast-free left leg felt much better. Nothing, however, had healed the ache of six family members dead, including the bar mitzvah boy, and many others wounded.

He thought about the cool June day when two Mossad operatives ferried him and his creaking wheelchair to the hospital's rooftop helipad. Levi was to accompany Joshua on his return but had decided to take an earlier flight. Just as well. He was still pretty foggy and in no mood to talk. The chopper, with markings of the Hungarian Rendorseg, the country's civil law enforcement agency, kept its rotors at almost full throttle, seemingly eager to take off.

Joshua was lifted into the helicopter. "Where are we headed?" His voice sounded creaky to him.

"Directly to Ferenc Liszt International Airport; it's about a thirty-minute flight," an officer responded. Three Hungarian counterterrorism agents and Joshua's two guards flanked him.

As Levi had promised, the El Al flight was waiting for him. The police cleared his guards; they met with no lines, security checks, or bureaucratic delays.

"Thanks, 'cousins,' for staying with me in the hospital. It made this beaten-up guy feel better." The embassy guards were staying behind.

Despite physical and emotional pain, Joshua managed to ask his chaperones, "Why couldn't the flight have been booked on Swiss International Air Lines? The meals would be so much better."

Now in Tel Aviv, he was beginning to feel fit again. He'd maintained a strict exercise regimen all his adult life. For years, his day began at 5 a.m.; he was in his apartment complex's gym by 5:30 on cardio equipment that he complained about until management reluctantly agreed to update it every three years.

His morning routine progressed to weights after thirty minutes of aerobic exercise. Joshua's bench-pressing awed the young women who made sure that their workouts coincided with his. He often ended his routine with fifteen minutes of sprint swimming in the adjacent outdoor, thankfully heated pool.

He wasn't back to that aggressive schedule yet. That early August morning, already a toasty eighty-five degrees, found him relaxing on one of the lounge chairs placed sparingly around the pool deck of his Ramat Aviv apartment complex. He was summoning up the energy to cool off and try a lap or two when the hinges of the gate announced an arrival with the irksome screech of unoiled wrought iron.

Joshua rarely sat with his back to a door or entry point. Today was no exception. He watched as Zvi Levi, uncharacteristically dressed in khaki shorts and a pale-blue T-shirt, entered.

Mossad operatives were never unarmed in public, so Joshua needed no reminder why Levi carried a small leather bag. His former boss had the sensitivity to stay away during Joshua's recuperation. Acknowledgment of tender feelings had little value in their profession.

"Hello, Joshua. You look fit. I hope you're wearing sunblock; we wouldn't want to expose you to the dangers of the sun."

"Zvi. Nice to know that you're still looking out for my safety."

"Yours, and all of ours. Isn't that what we do? So listen carefully and don't answer a question that I won't ask."

"Sounds like a mental acrostic." Joshua motioned for Levi to sit. "You know I'll listen; I owe you that. You saved my life more than once and helped me return to Israel after Budapest. I won't forget that."

"I'm not here to cash in old debts. But I want you to pay very close attention. Let's move into that shaded area."

"You mean I have to give up my comfortable chair and a clear view of her?" Joshua pointed discreetly across the fifty-meter pool to a shapely twenty-something beauty in as scant a bathing suit as allowed by law. "Her pool schedule often coincides with mine. And I'd hate not showing proper appreciation."

"I'm happy to see that you're back to focusing on important issues," Levi said with only a hint of envy. Levi had covered for his colleague on several philandering exploits.

Joshua had maintained his conditioning at a level that would make most spy chasers-turned-bureaucrats envious. His bronzed body was speckled with the scars of his trade; fortunately, those scars often drew female attention.

At six feet and one hundred eighty-five pounds, Joshua carried no trace of the insidious corpulence that mysteriously appeared on retirees within weeks of receiving a gold watch at a farewell party. He had no desire to slack off on his workouts.

"I thought you'd forgotten me," he said to Levi as they arranged their chairs.

Levi shook his head. "Working literally night and day."

Once seated in the shade under an orange-and-white-striped pool umbrella, Levi looked directly at Joshua and extended both arms, palms out. "Don't say anything yet. Just listen to me, then we can argue."

Joshua smiled and crossed his right leg, careful not to rest it on the healing wounds of his tender left knee. "Zvi, I know that this is important to you, whatever it is. So just go for it."

"First, and this is not a pro forma request, the prime minister wants to meet with you tomorrow at the Knesset. It is a request, but as firm an invitation as one can make short of a directive — 10 a.m.

"We're on the brink of an attack by Iran with the support and active participation of Russia. 8200 has put together a convincing report for the PM. He'll present it to the Security Cabinet on Sunday morning.

"The planned attack is like nothing we've experienced before. It's a little more than three weeks to Rosh Hashana, the date the intel says we'll be attacked. We'll go into greater detail when we meet the PM."

Joshua leaned forward; Levi had his attention. Joshua asked, "How long have you known of these plans?"

"8200 has been piecing together intel; the full picture has just come clear," Levi answered. He stood, paced around his chair, and sat down no more than a meter from Joshua.

"Russia placed a shitload of their most advanced fighter aircraft in Syria and recruited Iranian pilots, who have been training day and night to hit us. To complicate matters," Levi paused, cleared his throat, and looked straight at Joshua, "three Diaspora communities are in the crosshairs of Iran's Quds Force, with attacks also planned for Rosh Hashana. And our latest report confirms that Abu Yusalem has assembled a team to develop a sarin-laced bomb to be detonated in the Jewish Quarter in Paris."

Joshua peered at Levi and hoped that he was hiding the conflict raging internally. He said, "How I would love to track down that bastard and break his neck." But he was silently screaming, *Not again. I retired to get away from this.*

"How reliable are the reports and the data?" Joshua asked.

"8200 says it's their most accurate and extensive report."

"And what do you, the PM, and anyone else expect of this beaten-down, retired agent?"

"Don't rush things, Joshua. For now, I want you to listen to the PM." Levi held his breath, and after a meaningful silence, he continued.

"Joshua, you've for at least a decade been Israel's best asset in fighting jihadi terrorism. Twice you had Yusalem cornered and almost eliminated that dangerous prick. He is Russia and Iran's point man in the asymmetric part of their attack plan. He's coordinating a Hezbollah missile barrage at the time of the air attack planned from Syria."

He paused to gauge any reaction from Joshua. There was none. The recent retiree sat with a practiced impassivity.

"We've been tracking Abu Yusalem on his visits to Moscow and Tehran, and we know that he left his calling card in Budapest. Sorry to bring that up, but we're certain it was his attempt to eliminate you, the one man he believes is a threat to him and to their plans to hurt Israel."

"So what do you want of me?"

Levi felt Joshua was opening the door. Joshua was a racehorse that needed to run; retirement would drive both him and Anat crazy. Levi understood Joshua's DNA, as it closely resembled his own. Love for Israel and a commitment to defeat anything that threatened its existence were imprinted on every chromosome.

"I don't have an answer to your question yet," Levi lied. "Let's discuss all options with the PM tomorrow." Levi stood, took two halting steps toward the gate, turned, smiled, and said, "Bring her if it'll make you feel better." He angled his head toward the tanned beauty who had just emerged from the cool water. She was ever-so-slowly and tantalizingly drying herself with an oversize beach towel.

"I'll pick you up at 8:30 tomorrow morning at the front entrance. Yes?"

"I'll be waiting, Zvi. Thanks for messing up my life."

Levi headed for the screeching gate. He didn't turn back but threw a quick sideways glance at Joshua's pool partner.

Joshua sat back on his cushioned chaise and waved to the longhaired Russian beauty across the pool. "Good morning, Natasha. Haven't seen you here for a while."

In heavily accented Hebrew, she responded, "Three mornings a week, 7 to 8. Monday, Tuesday, and Thursday, to be precise."

It had been weeks since Joshua felt such intense sexual arousal. He was happy that he was seated with a towel draped over his legs. It seemed like ages since he and Anat had sex, not that she wasn't eager and attractive. He continued to be psychologically MIA after the chaos and brutality of the bar mitzvah attack.

Natasha sauntered off, ensuring that her towel didn't obscure any part of her made-for-sex body. She casually waved goodbye and wished him a nice day.

He returned to the less sensual conversation with Levi. He felt he'd been subjected to a subtle command performance. The PM — what could he possibly want to pawn off on a retired Mossad operative?

His former boss avoided hyperbole. Joshua had come to understand that about him after a few brief encounters in his early years in the spy agency. He repeated the conversation in his mind and came back again and again to Levi's assessment that Israel faced an existential threat.

Mossad's raison d'etre had always been to track down and eliminate those planning to harm Israel or Jews. The agency had vast expertise in global intelligence collection, covert operations, counterterrorism, and, in an understood mission, protection of Jewish communities.

Joshua sat back, visualizing the Security Cabinet debating an approach to these challenges. They had faced many threats; living in a hostile neighborhood had compelled Israel to develop powerful military and intelligence capabilities. The inner circle of Mossad more often than not was the arena in which the perennial question was raised: Is Israel the Jewish world's bodyguard?

So many of the country's political and military leaders were the offspring of families traumatized by the Holocaust. For Joshua's generation, it was the 800-pound gorilla lurking in every bedroom and behind every curtain. It was the uninvited gate crasher at every celebration. It consciously and unconsciously influenced much of Israel's public policy.

Joshua received no exemption from the European barbarism that weighed on him like the ancient mariner's albatross. His family was granted little respite from the savagery of Nazism and the complicity of many European nations in addressing "the Jewish question."

He often exchanged bittersweet humor with Anat, joking that they were lucky to have been born in Israel, surrounded by half a billion people vowing its extinction. *At least their intent is unambiguous, and we can protect ourselves* was their joint conclusion.

Joshua's grandparents and European Jewry had no such luck. They'd been powerless against the swirling vortex of nationalistic demagoguery and omnipresent anti-Semitism.

Until the mid-1930s, his paternal grandparents were pillars of the Viennese social and cultural world. His grandmother, Margaret Cohen, was special. All who heard her performances of Mozart and Schubert attested to her virtuosity as a concert pianist, and she rose to fame in Vienna and throughout Austria. Not to be outdone, Paul Cohen, his grandfather, excelled as the choirmaster of the Vienna State Opera and sang lead tenor in many Verdi and Puccini operas.

The Cohens got the message of the rising danger. Unfortunately, many of their family members refused to believe their lives of culture, acclaim, and financial success would soon come to a crashing end.

His grandparents gathered what valuables they could carry, packed up their infant daughter, and beseeched their kin to heed the warnings and flee Vienna before it was too late.

They set out on a labyrinthine path, which they recalibrated daily for two years, narrowly escaping the deadly traps of the Nazis and their all-too-willing European accomplices. They wended their way to a still-friendly Casablanca, Morocco, and ultimately to the United States.

Joshua's father, Jacob, was the first American member of the Cohen family, born less than two years after their arrival on safe shores. Twenty-one years later, the Cohen family celebrated the wedding of Jacob to Andrea, a demure and artistic New York beauty.

Six years later, the Cohen family was not quite as celebratory when Jacob and Andrea announced they were planning *aliyah* to Israel.

Jacob's family was convinced that Andrea had influenced him to immigrate to the frontier country, then barely twenty-eight years old as a nation. Of course, the fingers pointed in a different direction in Andrea's home.

Within one year of their arrival in Israel, Jacob and Andrea Cohen officially became the Canaan family. The name change represented a permanency to their migration. For the Canaans, the name was a symbolic connection to their new country and a distinct departure from the *should I stay or should I return* immigrants who flooded the Ministry of Absorption.

The Canaan family turned out its first local product two years later. Joshua was one of more than a thousand infants born that year at Tel Aviv's Ichilov Hospital.

The loving home life of Joshua's childhood nurtured independence and self-sufficiency. He rapidly developed a craving for daring adventures. His parents took great pride in his increasing physical strength and athletic abilities, and no family member was surprised when at eighteen he announced that he was trying out for an elite brigade in the paratrooper corps.

Throughout his childhood and young adulthood, the Holocaust, pogroms against Jews, and the virulent anti-Semitism of nations either complicit with or feckless about Jewish persecution hung shroud-like over his family history.

The indelible trauma etched into his grandparents' faces deepened with each of their many visits from the States. The effects of their suffering touched him deeply. Seeing them reinforced his commitment to ensure that trauma to the Jews of the world would never again go unpunished.

The national debate on the country's role as the Diaspora's guardian roiled the waters of political discourse. With the twenty-first century now twenty percent in the books and the Holocaust three-quarters of a century in the past, most Israelis hadn't been alive when the Germans perpetrated their "final solution" to the "Jewish problem."

But that hellish era remained the bedrock of their decision-making. Even now, in the early days of Joshua's retirement, protection for the world's Jews consumed him. The rise of anti-Semitic gangs in France and England and the throngs of migrants fleeing war and persecution who flooded Europe worried him. Most, he was convinced, were seeking refuge from real danger and were no different from his grandparents in the 1930s. Camouflaged in the sheer number, however, lurked those wishing to hurt the Western world and Jews in particular.

Abu Yusalem was an expert at navigating the shoals of immigration policies and border security. He was a cunning assassin who certainly played no small part in what the PM was to share with him the following morning. Joshua was committed to terminating the killer of six of his family members at the Dohány Street Synagogue. His grief over their loss had intensified since his return to Israel. He hadn't attended any of the funerals, having been rushed back to Israel. His firm conclusion, however

— and certainly Anat's — remained "Leave it for the next generation of Mossad agents."

4

The Prime Minister Weighs In

Levi called over the lowered window of his dusty green Subaru, "Slight change of plans." The twelve-year-old sedan coughed and sputtered with what sounded like automotive emphysema.

"Zvi, it's 8:25, not like you to be early." Joshua slid into the musty sedan, buckled his seat belt, and girded himself for the ride to Jerusalem. "What's the change?"

"Got a call from the PM himself asking that we come to his residence in Rehavia instead of the Knesset. I'm surprised it wasn't a collect call."

"Zvi, don't confuse the PM with your miserly obsession with your budget."

Both men smiled, and Levi moved on.

"I told him we'd try hard to be on time. He understands the traffic nightmare of entering Jerusalem from Tel Aviv."

"Funny that you should comment on the charge of the call." Joshua returned to one of his pet peeves with his former boss. "You, my friend, are the stingiest person I've ever worked with. I'm surprised that you're not asking me to share the cost of gasoline."

"How do you know I'm not?"

Their trip passed quickly with contemplative silences interrupted by casual discussion not remotely connected to their visit to the PM. As they approached the hills leading up to Jerusalem, traffic started backing up around the Latrun Monastery.

Trucks, packed to the rafters, inched their way up the steep inclines, infuriating the perennially short-tempered Israeli drivers. Passing any vehicle on the winding roads required skill and bravura from the driver and a blindfold for the passengers.

Once they entered the outskirts of the city, they made their way through the charming neighborhood of Kiryat Shmuel toward the PM's Rehavia residence.

"You know, Zvi, I've been to the prime minister's official residence three times in two decades, each time with a new occupant." He'd never met Eliezer Simcha, who had served as PM for only eighteen months.

"I've heard a lot about him and his military background. I hate to say it, but I'm looking forward to meeting him — in a guarded sort of way."

They arrived at the unremarkable building and parked on the street. The modest lot had no room for guest parking. They endured a rigorous security check, during which Levi was asked to relinquish his firearm to the soldier sitting behind a rickety table.

"Even the head of Mossad has to go through this stuff," Levi joked, although he was annoyed.

Most Rehavia buildings were constructed with a pale-gray Jerusalem stone facade and were three or four stories high. A single-family home was rare in this part of Jerusalem. Building codes stressed uniformity; it was unusual to find an apartment building that exceeded a height of four stories. Cacti and succulents, the greenery of choice, needed virtually no watering and were therefore plentiful. The PM's residence was no different, except that his family was the sole tenant; the building had long since been reconfigured to accommodate its unique occupant.

"Coming here," Levi said caustically, "is like running through a gantlet."

An aide to the PM greeted them. The young soldier flashed a disarming smile. "We're heading up the staircase to the second-floor conference room." His accent was familiar.

"Where are you from soldier. That is, your folks?" Joshua asked with a smile.

The soldier was unmistakably of Ethiopian descent: high, arched eyebrows, a narrow face with concave cheekbones, and sparkling eyes.

"Addis Ababa, or just outside of there. A small village," the soldier answered.

Joshua had developed respect for the combat ability and dedication to Israel that characterized most Ethiopian immigrants to Israel. "Thanks," Joshua replied. "Been to the capital but never made it to the villages. Good to see you here."

To their surprise, Maayan Simcha, the PM's portly and attractive wife, greeted them at the top of the staircase.

"Welcome. Good to see you again, Zvi. And you are Joshua Canaan, yes? Eliezer will be so proud that I didn't mess up your names the way I usually do. Becomes embarrassing with visiting dignitaries. I've learned to say, 'So nice to see you.' "

She ushered them into an anteroom just off the conference room and poured coffee without asking whether they wanted it.

"I'll have two sugars please," Zvi requested.

Joshua said nothing. Both welcomed her warmth and spontaneity.

Within minutes, the PM entered. He greeted them, kissed his wife, and thanked her for welcoming his guests. He ushered them into the conference room and told Maayan that they would be a while.

The only detail that distinguished the room as a conference venue was its name. The deep-purple overstuffed couch, the rose-colored loveseat, and the recently upholstered vermillion armchairs took Joshua back to his grandparents' living room in Westchester County, New York. All that was missing, he mused, were the plastic slipcovers.

But they got right to it. Three military men, irrespective of the location, had scant use for small talk and bullshit.

"Thank you for being here today. Joshua, I'm terribly sorry about the loss of your family members in Budapest. I know that you were injured as well; you seem to have healed well." Still a handsome fifty-something, the PM sat upright and looked as fit as Joshua.

"On the outside, yes," Joshua said.

The PM didn't acknowledge the comment. He looked over his left shoulder to make certain that his wife had closed the door, then turned back. "At an urgent meeting with the Security Cabinet Sunday morning, I'll inform the members, which will include the head of Aman in an unusual appearance, that within three weeks a multifront attack is planned on our country — an attack of unprecedented scope."

Joshua started to speak, but the PM, looking at the floor, thrust out his hand.

"I know that Zvi has shared some of this with you. My challenge is to inform you of the danger we face while not breaching protocol overmuch by sharing information that isn't yet one hundred percent vetted and that preempts my meeting with our Security Cabinet."

He paused, took a deep breath, looked directly at Joshua, and said, as emphatically as a tight-assed military careerist could, "Israel needs you now."

Joshua sat back against what was decidedly not his grandmother's armchair, aware that his resolve to continue his nascent retirement was about to face a frontal assault.

"Syria," the PM began, "is the staging ground for a Russian-Iranian-axis attack against us." The "axis" reference to the Second World War Nazi allies registered with Joshua.

"Over the last two years, Russia has introduced its most advanced fighter aircraft into Syria. Russian advisers in Syria have trained Iranian pilots to fly these fighters. There's more," he paused for emphasis. "Iran's Quds Force has infiltrated Paris, Rome, and even the U.S.'s Birmingham, Alabama, with squads of assassins. They're in local BDS offices to pinpoint Jewish institutions, neighborhoods, and activities more accurately.

"Intelligence has informed us that Abu Yusalem is a linchpin in the coordination among Moscow, Damascus, and Hezbollah. 8200 determined that he's close to operationalizing a sarin-laced dirty bomb in the heart of Paris's Jewish District."

"How close is close?" Joshua asked.

"We believe within three weeks. At least three Iranian and Russian chemists have met with him in Paris over the past few weeks."

"Yusalem is a key figure in these plans, but by no means the only one," Levi interjected.

The PM sat back for a moment and let Levi take over.

"Just now," Levi said, "Abu Yusalem is in Suite 406 on the fourth floor of the Minsk Hotel in Minsk, Belarus. We have several operatives trailing him. The hotel has four doormen, three of them KGB agents and the fourth our agent. He keeps an eye on the other three.

"We know that Yusalem is meeting with three foreigners in his suite as we speak. We're reasonably certain that they are Iranians and Russians."

"Why not take him out now? Why meet in Belarus?"

Joshua was engaged. Precisely the response that the PM and Levi were hoping for.

"There are too many moving parts at this point," the PM answered. "We need the rat to lead us to his den. He's in Belarus because it's a convenient pass-through from Moscow to Eastern Europe. He's returning to Syria after meeting with Russian military leadership in Moscow.

"He's their liaison to Hezbollah. Yusalem has also met repeatedly with Quds operatives in Rome and Paris. Visiting the terrorists in Alabama was too risky."

Joshua raised a finger. Before he could speak, the PM added, "We've intercepted his coded and encrypted communications with them." The PM leaned forward and slammed a fist to the arm of his chair. "I'm determined to take them all out at the same time: Russian airpower in Syria, Hezbollah forces if they remain organized as a conventional army in Syria and no longer hiding in civilian enclaves, and the Quds units in Europe and, yes, in the U.S. as well.

"I rarely personalize my positions early in a military action.

War is about facts and opportunities, not personal preferences. We'll debate a course of action at Sunday's meeting at the Knesset. There'll be differing views on a plan forward, but we won't leave the conference room without a unanimous approach. There's no middle road here."

The PM shook his head and inhaled deeply. "We're faced with major military challenges and have less than three weeks to act."

He sat back on the oddly inappropriate embroidered loveseat, lifted his coffee cup, and sipped his now-cold espresso. He slowly turned to face Joshua and slung his right arm over the low back of the sofa.

"Sounds like deep shit," Joshua said, breaking the intentional silence. "I don't think we've ever had such a complex battle theater, not even in 1947 and '48. OK, here goes: What do you want of me? I've retired, started a new life. I actually recognize my son now and have a wife who would picket your residence if I re-engage.

"Why now? What's moved Russia to take this dangerous step? How did they get Iran involved in these catastrophic plans?"

Levi, seemingly involuntarily, banged his fist on his chair. "The Russians are clever. They are striving for Middle East domination. Iran is their means to an end."

"I don't have to repeat the immediate threat to Israel and Diaspora Jews," the PM said. "I know you get it." He stood and began to pace. "You follow Yusalem like a bloodhound. You feel him, you smell him, you can think like him.

"He's the terror coordinator for Russia and Iran. Iran looks to him to train and coordinate attacks on overseas Jews. Yusalem is also working hand-in-glove with Iran's proxy Hezbollah. They plan to hit us with missiles on our coastal cities.

"For now, we want you to take him out just before their planned attack. We can't let on that we have definitive—that is, almost conclusive—proof of every step of their plan. We know that he's meeting in Minsk, but we also believe that he'll be heading to Beirut after Syria, probably through Iraq, within the next day or two. He'll coordinate battle details with Hezbollah leadership and the Russians who've been training Iranian fighter pilots. He'll then return to Paris using some alias to make final preparations for the Quds actions in the Jewish Quarter and his sarin bomb."

Joshua crossed his leg over his sore left knee and peered at his former — maybe not so former — boss, shook his head, and said, "Zvi, Mossad has many operatives. I get the danger we're in, but I'll be honest — I'm spent. Wiped out."

"Joshua," Levi replied with uncharacteristic warmth, "we know what you've been through. In a rough and dirty business like ours, once you're out, the relief is overwhelming. We've lived through it. We've done some honorable and some horrendous acts in defense of our country. But all the marbles are on the table now; we need the best if we're to come out on top.

"Yusalem is a cold-blooded killer who'll stop at nothing to bloody us, this time in partnership with Iran and Russia. He's certainly looking to avenge carrying your slug in his left shoulder. You're the one who can put an end to him — but at the right time."

"Well, you've managed to stir my juices. I'm considering," Joshua lamented, "to return to what I was happy to leave behind. Anat, an even greater patriot than me, will be pissed. So I will give you my answer after I speak with her."

He rubbed his face with both hands, imagining the discussion with his wife.

"I need your approval to discuss the broad picture with her. I understand the need for secrecy. I trust Anat and ask that you do as well. I know you need my response quickly."

The PM, not responding to Joshua's request for spousal security clearance, held out his hand. The nonverbal cue for the meeting's end brought Joshua and Levi to their feet.

The PM said nothing as he looked into Joshua's eyes and held the handshake for a few seconds. As if making dinner arrangements, he said, "See you soon. I'd like to have you attend part of my Security Cabinet meeting on Sunday. My best to Anat." A nod to Levi brought the meeting to a close.

5
Leora and Mossad in Italy

Ari Kochav stepped out of his junior suite on the third floor of Pensione Lucchesi. Why this room, a meager one hundred square feet larger than the double-occupancy room two doors to his left, was a suite remained a mystery to him.

Mossad agents varied the hotels they booked on missions in Rome. Trastevere was a favored neighborhood because of its proximity to the city's Jewish District, not to mention the wide range of great restaurants. Ari had been a guest in the modest establishment just off Santa Cecilia Street for four nights, long enough to become acquainted with the day and night clerks at the front desk. Four nights provided more than enough time for Mossad's local team to visit his junior suite and sweep it for bugging devices. Mossad techies were thorough in their scanning.

Fluency in Italian made Ari's conversations with the clerks easier, although he was asked on several occasions about his Calabrian accent. Ari had been a new Mossad recruit stationed in a village in Catanzaro, the regional capital of Calabria. Mossad agents were trained to account for dialect inflections or nuances. They had to be prepared to answer any questions about a language anomaly.

Facility with languages may have been stamped into Ari's DNA. His Austrian-born grandfather spoke nine languages; both of his parents were fluent in five. When he was young, they'd spoken French when they wanted to keep their conversations from him. That stopped when he revealed at five years old that he was able to understand the essence of their private discussions.

While not dyed-in-the-wool Zionists, Ari's parents had decided to leave the U.S., immigrate to Israel and work toward developing the Jewish homeland, then a very young state. Two weeks after their arrival in Israel, they celebrated Ari's sixth birthday.

More often than not, his parents, despite the 6,000-mile separation, lamented the disturbing psychological state of his paternal grandmother. Together with her resourceful husband, she had evaded capture by the Nazis as they fled from one European capital to another. Their arrival at Ellis Island brought only ephemeral relief from the trauma of their harrowing escapes. For so many, the Holocaust left an indelible imprint.

The Holocaust was embedded into the psyche of Ari's Mossad colleagues. It lurked just beneath the surface in Israeli military and intelligence establishments. The country's commitment that Jews would never again be persecuted while an indifferent world stood by had been threaded into the national fiber.

Exactly twelve strides to the left of Ari's room was the staircase that he preferred using. Whenever possible, agents avoided elevators. He descended the three flights of well-worn wooden steps at 6:10 p.m. He'd waited for Paolo's shift at the reception desk and was happy that Katrina, whom he did not care for, had departed. He enjoyed the easy-flowing repartee with Paolo and was certain the clerk would understand the instructions he was about to receive.

"Good evening, Paolo," Ari began in impeccable Italian.

"How are you, Mr. Reyes?"

Ari's passport identified him as Francisco Reyes of Madrid.

"Hungry, but otherwise fine. Perhaps I'll have dinner at Mario's again. Your recommendation was perfect. If you don't mind, I'd appreciate a reservation — for two."

"Happy to be of service."

Paolo was about twenty-five, a student at the Rome Art Institute during the day, intelligent and hip. Ari admired his glossy mane of shoulder-length black curls that could have inspired a Bernini sculpture.

"In about one hour," Ari said, looking at Paolo with a studied sheepishness, "I'm expecting a friend who will join me at Mario's. She's attractive, so if there's a delay at the front desk, I will hold you responsible."

They both laughed.

"No problem, Mr. Reyes. Italy is very understanding when it comes to certain *friendships*."

"Thanks, Paolo. I knew I could count on your discretion."

They talked for a few minutes, and Ari headed for the staircase with a laugh and a wave when the banter became tinged with lasciviousness.

"Mr. Reyes," Paolo called out, "why do you always use the staircase? Claustrophobic?"

"Helps keep me fit after all the pasta I've been eating."

Ari returned to Room 320 to wait for Leora, his Mossad stable mate, whom he hadn't seen for three years.

At about 7, Leora rapped on his room's hollow door. She was every bit as attractive as when Ari last saw her. The low-cut crimson dress accentuated her athletic body.

Despite Leora's best efforts, she wasn't too steady on the four-inch heels that appeared overly tight. The cloyingly sweet imitation Carven cologne filled the room that may or may not have been a junior suite. Stepping across the threshold, she greeted Ari with a regional salutation in Italian, which she made sure was loud enough to be heard in the corridor.

"Hello," Leora offered in a muted voice once the door was closed behind her. She reached into her small evening bag, tore off a piece of adhesive tape from a new roll, and placed it over the door's peephole. Ari assured her that the room had been carefully scanned for surveillance devices.

For a moment Ari lost track of their mission and the importance of their meeting. Even dressed as an Italian call girl, Leora was classy. The agent emitted extraordinary sensuality.

"How are you? Those shoes look like they're mangling your

feet."

"Killing them," she responded in Hebrew. Once security was assured, muted Hebrew was preferred. "The young man at the front desk was a bit too friendly but polite. When I requested Mr. Reyes' room number and headed for the staircase, he asked if I was also claustrophobic.

" 'You know,' he said, 'Mr. Reyes never takes the elevator.' "

Leora kicked off her shoes, sighed in relief, and placed her evening bag, only slightly weighted down by her Beretta 9mm, a Mossad favorite, on the night table near the king-size bed. She sat on one of the two rickety chairs and massaged her aching feet. Ari pulled up a chair and sat six feet away. The past two years Leora had emerged as one of the brightest stars in the Mossad galaxy. She was highly respected by her colleagues and had proved herself to be resourceful, relentless, and brave. Her uncanny power of recall set her apart.

The room was attractive enough, with a two-star ambience. The bed's brown comforter blended nicely with the tan walls, which appeared freshly painted. The scented air spray used by housekeeping barely masked the odor of cigar smoke that irritated Leora's bronchials.

As she began speaking, she moved aside the two empty espresso cups on the bridge table between them. The air-conditioning unit, turned to its cacophonic loudest, drowned out the occasional exuberant hallway conversation.

"Let's get to it, as Paolo will expect that we'll go out to dinner after a while." What Ari really wanted her to say was: Let's renew the brief but torrid affair we had while in training in Jerusalem three years ago. But that was then; this was now.

"In a few days I'll be returning home," Leora began, speaking generally for safety's sake. "I'll meet with our boss at headquarters. He's preparing for a meeting with the big boss, and guess what? I've been invited to attend."

When Ari realized that Leora had been invited to a meeting with the prime minister, he grinned and offered her a thumbs-up.

"He also informed me that I'd be working with some recent retiree from the office. I'm pissed. The last thing I need is to work with some past-his-prime office geek who's returning because of some patronage deal."

Ari frowned as she complained about their boss's poor decision. "His name?" Ari mouthed.

"Joshua Canaan," Leora whispered back. "Have you heard of him?

Ari laughed. "Joshua Canaan is probably the most respected and feared operative that we've seen in years, maybe ever." Ari shook his head and then leaned closer, lowering his voice even more: "He's a brilliant strategist, a fearless fighter, and the only one of us who ever got close to Abu Yusalem — twice, no less. Yusalem carries a souvenir in his shoulder that Canaan left him in a firefight." Ari tapped his chest. "Canaan was the only shooter to consistently beat me at the firing range."

He pulled away and spoke at a normal volume when he added, "I'm not sure what levers they pulled to get him back, but I bet it was them begging him, not the other way around. For sure, the events on the horizon played a role in his return."

"I'm humiliated," Leora said, "not knowing anything about him. So that's between us, yes?"

Ari softened her discomfort by saying, "It isn't unusual for some colleagues to remain subterranean, even from us."

She was quick to return to the business at hand, saying, "Your messages as well as Aryeh's from America and Ze'ev's from Paris have caused uproars in the inner defense circles." She always referred to embedded spies by their code names. "My report to Levi will include your combined reports."

"There should be an uproar, Leora. Hopefully, clear thinking and decisive action will follow the reports. They've got our assessments. Jewish communities in Western Europe and parts of the U.S. are on the brink of atrocities. I know that you were sent here to ensure that my daily reports are in sync with my colleagues in America and Paris. Your visit bypasses my area handler and is a direct line to the Knesset."

Ari was a calm, understated pragmatist who never indulged in excessive dialogue or exaggerations. That was what made his accounts so threatening and ominous.

Leora sat separated from Ari by an unbalanced coffee table with cigarette burns in at least three places despite the "No Smoking" signs on the door. She'd always been impressed with his intelligence, calm demeanor, physical strength, and extraordinary marksmanship, especially with the MTAR-21 Variant, the IDF's semiautomatic mainstay.

He seemed to take his skills and accomplishments in stride, as if being so highly prized by Mossad was commonplace.

Leora trained her eyes on Ari and cleared all thoughts. Like all Mossad agents, she never used notes or cell phone recordings. Every nuance had to be committed to memory.

"I'll begin with the most surprising and most politically sensitive plot," Ari began. He knew that Leora received daily briefings from the three threatened communities. He wanted his report to be unambiguous, even if some of it was repetitive. Despite the gravity of his account, he fought off nonprofessional feelings, as he sat no more than a few feet from Leora's green eyes, her thick, wavy hair, and her overwhelming sensuality. He'd apparently been alone in the field too long.

"Aryeh, our man in the U.S. has a team member inside a violent white supremacist group — Stormfront. They've got hundreds of thousands of followers on their international website. There's an activist inner circle of about forty members who promote violence against Muslims, blacks, and Jews.

"About a year ago, members of Iran's Quds Force infiltrated them. Several of them had lived in America for extended periods. Their English was excellent, and their accents were attributed to overseas living while fighting for 'the cause.' They were acceptable to the racist group because of their hatred of Jews, Muslims, and blacks and their dedication to violence.

"Abdul Hazian heads the Iranian jihadists. He is articulate, has Caucasian features, and spews brutality. This is the same Hazian who in 1994 was indicted by Argentina as the leader of the terrorists who bombed our embassy and the Buenos Aires Jewish Community Center, killing over eighty people."

"The same guy," Leora interrupted, "who disappeared when the Argentinian prosecutor was found dead in his hotel room the evening before he was to present his case against the Iranians for their involvement in the bombings. Right?"

Ari nodded.

Leora sat riveted. Ari recognized the look; her computer like mind was transcribing his report to memory. "This bastard," she said, "has his fingers in so many plots. Can't wait to end his career."

"Stormfront's headquarters is located in Birmingham, Alabama," he continued. "Most of the twenty-five jihadi fighters are sleepers keeping a low profile. Hazian has focused attention mainly on anti-black and Muslim hatred, keeping his Jewish plot hidden from the group."

Ari shifted in his chair, once again feeling the anger that he'd been keeping under wraps for the last weeks of his assignment.

"Stormfront, with its goal of white supremacy, has been the camouflage Hazian and his crew have used to gather data on Birmingham's Jewish community. And the locals remained clueless. Every synagogue, Jewish agency, and NGO is on the Iranians' map. Their green light for widespread assassination will come from Tehran and will coincide with Rosh Hashana in a little over two weeks. Birmingham's four synagogues and other Jewish sites are to be targeted simultaneously.

"Ze'ev has reported a similar plot in Paris," Ari continued, his face taut and his eyes intense. "Twenty-four Iranian Quds Force agents have been part of a sleeper cell that has recruited a few French nationals. They lobby for the labeling of Israeli goods from settlements and advocate BDS activities. In truth ..."

"In truth," Leora interrupted, "they receive their orders from Tehran, yes?"

"Precisely," Ari answered. "In coordination with Hazian's attack using Stormfront as a cover, they have their assault planned in the Fourth and Sixth Arrondissements, Parisian districts with significant Jewish populations. Despite the increased French security expected, this group headed by Ibrahim Ashrawi will attack Jewish institutions on Rosh Hashana."

"Ashrawi, as I recall, is wanted for the murder of two Palestinian Authority politicians promoting dialogue with Israel, correct?" Leora asked.

"That's him. I'm not sure how he evaded us or how long he's been in Paris," Ari said. "He's dangerous and elusive. And, unfortunately, there's more. We have word that Abu Yusalem is in the Fourth and Eleventh Arrondissements. We believe that he's there to both coordinate the attacks and to launch an individual action of some kind. He doesn't like to be upstaged. Maybe that's the reason for Joshua Canaan's return."

"Keep going." Leora's smile gently arched her lip on the left side of her tanned face. "Your front desk guy will think we're screwing as an appetizer."

Something I'd much rather be doing now. Ari's mind wandered, but he repressed the amorous images and continued.

"Knowing you, I'm confident that you'll convey the scope of these attacks planned for Diaspora Jews. Not far from where we are now" — Ari returned to his emotionless military tone — "we're anticipating a suicide bombing attack on at least three of Rome's synagogues: the Great Synagogue, Di Castro Synagogue, and the Chabad Monteverde."

Leora's thoughts wandered. *Countering planned attacks thousands of miles from home was a challenge Mossad had never encountered. They were facing highly motivated terrorists in unfamiliar terrain. Small units of Mossad agents, no matter how well trained, would need help*. She regained focus quickly.

"Ishmael Al Fazzi — a graduate of the Hezbollah school of killers — coordinates the Rome command center. His group consists of twelve explosive experts. Al Fazzi spent six months in Iran, where he received additional training. This, like all of the operations that I described, has Quds Force stamped all over it.

"Months ago three Al Fazzi comrades infiltrated the Rome BDS office. Those operatives used information gathered for plans other than boycotting Israeli products. They compiled addresses and census material on the Jews of Rome in preparation for their Rosh Hashana attack.

"They had more planned for the Jews of Rome than the attack on the synagogues. They abandoned the BDS office after getting what they needed. It had become too risky to remain without arousing suspicion. Italian authorities are far less tolerant and more vigilant about anti-Israeli activities than their French counterparts."

Ari recounted how he, as Francisco Reyes, volunteered at the well-laid-out Rome BDS headquarters on Via Marmorata, a former American Express office that had been vacant for about three years. A tattooed young woman with pink and blue pigtails met him the entrance.

"Can I help you?" she said in colloquial Italian, showing she was local.

"My name is Francisco Reyes. I visit Rome frequently. I'm from Madrid and would like to learn more about BDS."

"How is it that your Italian is so good? You speak with a Southern accent."

"I thought that I would be asking all the questions, but I'm happy to have you get to know me better too. I lived and worked in Catanzaro in Calabria for years."

"What brings you to our office?"

"I've had many bad business experiences with Israel and Jewish-run companies. I oppose their illegal settlements and the oppression of the Palestinian workers there. I want to explore how I can help the movement."

"Are you involved in Madrid? That's where you are from, yes?"

"Madrid is too unorganized and torn apart with Basque separatist politics. My focus is on how to put pressure on the repressive government in Israel. I'd like to see what people are doing in your headquarters and how I can best help. Doesn't look like many workers are here."

She became defensive at that comment, Ari said, so he tried a softer approach. "I want to see how to best use my skills."

"Come tomorrow morning about 10; you'll see a full house of committed patriots. You'll also get to meet our three newest members here from the Middle East."

"Sounds great. See you tomorrow."

Leora was visualizing the BDS encounter as Ari told her about his return visit the next morning, when the young woman with the multicolored coiffure again greeted him. When Francisco Reyes asked her name, she said it wasn't important and instead asked for his passport, "just for the record." She made a note of something, then took him inside to meet the newest volunteers.

"We made our way through a maze of eight-foot folding tables where workers were drafting anti-Israel placards. Some signs displayed large swastikas and pictures of Hitler and Mussolini with slogans that need no repeating. Other posters highlighted emaciated Arab children living amid bombed-out rubble. Three photocopy machines were churning out equally condemning material. We headed toward a corner of the room where tables had been pushed together and three clearly Middle Eastern men were standing over maps of Rome. My pigtailed guide stopped at their workstation and introduced me."

" 'Gentlemen, apologies for the interruption. I'd like you to meet Franco, an interested volunteer. Visiting us from Madrid.'

" 'Francisco,' I corrected, with a nod to her. I wasn't sure if that was an accident or a test. I bowed politely and asked if I might join them for a while. No names were offered, but I was invited to pull up a stool. I did but stood alongside them and asked what they were looking for on the map. I noticed that they were keyed into the area around Rome's central synagogue.

" 'We are focusing on central Jewish locations,' one of the trio offered, 'so that we can organize handing out flyers and leaflets informing them of their countrymen's violations of international law.' His English was surprisingly good, just a moderate Arabic accent. The taller of the other two guys was surly, bearded and sporting a taqiyah. He hardly took his eyes off me for the half-hour I was with them. I had the feeling he was committing my face to memory to have me checked out through their security.

"What I learned was that they were plotting locations and routes to and from Rome's synagogues. They were also trying to compile home addresses of members of the Jewish community. They were all business, focused, and clearly had bad intentions. We never crossed paths again after that meeting."

Leora's thoughts again strayed. *What Ari was describing required months of logistical coordination, with many players on the ground. Where did the massive amount of arms Ari detailed come from? How did these major attack plans go unnoticed? How did this get by the counterterrorism agencies of three countries?*

"For weeks," Ari continued, noticing her distracted look, "this group of terrorists has been headquartered on a narrow strip of land, Isola Tiberina, on the Tiber River, only about two hundred yards from shore and very close to their main target. Their force is housed in an abandoned warehouse near the Fatebenefratelli Hospital. Only a short distance separates the two buildings, perfect cover for their operation. Two bridges make the island accessible from both shores."

"Do you really believe that Iran would be so out front with its Revolutionary Guard?"

"These plans have been in the works for months. It appears that Iran is doubling down on its intent to defeat Israel. It now aims to unleash anti-Semitic violence on a global scale. And they may have company. We're not sure how this will inspire other 'great friends' of the Jews of Europe, such as the Jobbik party or Golden Dawn or any of the sleeper cells that have penetrated England's or Sweden's BDS organizations."

Three sharp raps on the flimsy door of Junior Suite 320 found Leora's Beretta aimed at the taped-over peephole. Ari was impressed with Leora's instant response to the unknown.

A white slip of paper appeared through the generous space

under the closed door just as the knocking ended. It was a note from Paolo, who had ventured away from his front desk. Who knew how long his ears had been pinned to the door?

"Mr. Reyes," the note read, "I didn't want to disturb you, but I was unable to make a dinner reservation at Mario's. They're booked for the evening with a wedding reception. I took the liberty of reserving a table at La Tavola for 9:30. Let me know if this works for you. Paolo."

"Do you trust him?" Leora asked as she slid her weapon back into her bag.

"I don't trust anyone." Ari tried to stay focused, but it was hard when his eyes were riveted to her crossed legs and the cleavage exposed by her low-cut dress. The arched breasts that he'd caressed so often during their brief but torrid affair were tantalizingly close as they spoke. *How can I be thinking of this*, he wondered, *as I fill the room with the bad news she has to deliver to Jerusalem*?

An appropriate amount of time passed so that Paolo could assume whatever his undoubtedly fertile imagination had conjured up.

"Let's take Paolo up on his reservation at La Tavola," Ari said, "though I'm sure you aren't very hungry after my report. Even I'm feeling jumpy." He smoothed his hair back and checked to make sure his shirt was in place.

"I want you to convey to the Cabinet in Jerusalem," Ari added, resuming his dry reporting, "that we've infiltrated the contaminated BDS offices and have identified the Iranian leadership in each. We believe that we have an accurate timetable for their coordinated attacks on our communities."

Leora, still shoeless, stood and slowly walked to Ari and kissed him. The length and passion of their embrace flooded Ari with memories of an irretrievable but unforgettable past.

Despite his arousal, Ari reached for Leora's ill-fitting shoes and handed them to her. He moved toward the door, removed the tape from the peephole, reluctantly opened it as it creaked in protest and breathed in the stale corridor air.

6
Southern Hospitality?

The Best Western Carlton Suites was a clean, middle-of-the-road hotel just off Lakeshore Parkway in the Vestavia Hills neighborhood of Birmingham, Alabama. Yaacov Gilad, code-named Aryeh, with a passport that identified him as Simon Rothstein, enjoyed having his meals in the Arbor, the hotel's overrated restaurant.

His corner table in the tree-lined atrium was near four spotless floor-to-ceiling tinted windows that faced a landscaped garden. The view was nice, the food passable, but the coffee was barely tolerable.

Mr. Rothstein informed anyone close enough to listen that he was in Birmingham to market his company's software. He spent a good deal of time during his four-day stay sharing product information with several front desk clerks he'd singled out as the alphas. One never knew when a relationship with them would come in handy. He was certain he'd be back to this hotel at some point.

"Sir, sorry to disturb your lunch." Sandy, his favorite receptionist, a knockout redhead, approached the café table where he was just finishing his tuna salad, most notable for its abundant mounds of mayonnaise. "Your 3 o'clock appointment is here. Shall I escort her to your table?"

Mr. Rothstein, with calculated annoyance, answered, "Can you hold her off for five minutes while I finish my coffee and Danish?"

"Certainly, sir." Sandy sauntered off, aware that he was scanning her taut and glorious derriere.

It was 10 minutes past 3 when Yaacov watched Sandy usher a smartly dressed woman into the hotel's restaurant. She pointed to his table and returned to her position behind the reception desk.

Yaacov's appointment made her way toward him. She was dressed in a green business suit with a white collar made of fluffy material. She removed her brown horn-rimmed glasses as she approached. They exchanged overly loud formal pleasantries. Yaacov stood, shook hands with his guest, and slid back her chair as she joined him.

"The glasses look good on you," he told Leora.

"Good to see you, Mr. Rothstein. Shall we talk here?"

"I think it's best," Yaacov answered. "I've had a number of business meetings here. We've run a security scan of the area. I generally sit with my back to the public area. You should probably sit that way too. We're in a private section of the restaurant." Yaacov placed his laptop in front of him as they talked. "When did you arrive in Birmingham?"

"An overnight flight to Atlanta, a compact rental, and a two-and-a-half-hour drive. I just arrived and am exhausted. Can we get an espresso in this place?"

"It's better than the crappy coffee they serve." He ordered two doubles as the server reached their table.

"In a few days," Leora said, wasting no time, "there'll be a Security Cabinet meeting. Chaim Lavi of Aman will be there. His addition to the regular council members tells me that there's a major action to be considered. I've been asked to attend."

Yaacov whistled. "That's big. Congratulations."

Leora leaned forward. "There's more. Somehow Levi and the PM convinced Joshua Canaan to undo his retirement from the Office. We are partnering to eliminate Abu Yusalem as a threat."

"I can't believe that Canaan's back in," Yaacov said. "Must have been tremendous arm-twisting from the PM. He was almost done in by Yusalem in Budapest only weeks ago. He lost at least six family members in a bomb blast. I wonder if that was the motivation for him to return. What an amazing asset. A bit too quick on the draw if you ask me, but we're lucky he's on our side." He inclined his head. "The two of you should make a good team."

"Thanks."

"Unusual, isn't it," Yaacov said, "for this face-to-face dialogue, given our routine exchanges?"

"I suppose none of us thinks anything occurring now is routine or that our response will be typical." Leora, as direct as ever, got right to it. "Tell me about Stormfront and their capabilities. Then I want to hear about the Quds squad, your thoughts about neutralizing them, your assets at hand, and an exit route should there be a military action, which I fully anticipate."

Yaacov rubbed his hands together and leaned forward. "Abdul Hazian heads the Quds Force planted in Birmingham. He goes by the name Peter Baron, of Portuguese descent. His fair skin, fluent English, and short haircut gave him good cover as he climbed the Stormfront leadership ladder.

"He won over the group's leadership by publicly admiring Anders Breivik, the Norwegian terrorist who killed more than seventy people as his contribution to saving Europe from Islam."

Yaacov shook his head as he continued. "Hazian's cover is ingenious. He's a serious challenge."

He found it difficult to look at Leora without his thoughts wandering. With the discussion of attacks planned in Europe and the U.S., his mind strayed in another direction. He was reliving his mother's description of that September day in 1977. Many times he'd heard her lament about their walk from Leo Tolstoy Square in Kiev, Ukraine.

His parents and nine-year-old Peter, the brother he'd never met, were taking a leisurely stroll across the Dnipro Bridge. The walk was a pleasant kilometer over its arced span. At its high point, the bridge was no more than 40 meters above the Dnieper River.

They'd planned to catch a taxi to the Jewish food festival in Hidro Park. The family never reached the festival. A group of anti-Semitic thugs attacked them, stole his mother's bag, bludgeoned his father, and beat his brother to death.

His parents had been committed to rebuilding Kiev's Jewish community, decimated by the Nazis. After that attack, they no longer saw a Jewish future in Ukraine and immigrated to Israel not long after his father's recovery. The memories of his mother pervaded Yaacov's thoughts as he described the attack planned on the Jewish community of Birmingham.

"On the morning of Rosh Hashana, more than twenty Iranian terrorists will hit Birmingham's four principle synagogues with RPGs and automatic weapons. The coordinated attacks are planned for the middle of services, when attendance is at a peak.

"The synagogues — Knesseth Israel, Temple Beth-El, Temple Emanu-El, and Or Chadash-Chabad — will have some police presence during services. But they pose no threat to the trained and nihilistic Quds Force. They're on a mission to kill Jews and are prepared for martyrdom."

Yaacov nodded his thanks for the steaming espresso delivered to their table.

Leora's furrowed brow highlighted her emerald eyes. "America would interpret this as an act of war. The background of the killers would be uncovered quickly. Wouldn't they know that Iran was behind the attack on its citizens?"

"This unit has been scrubbed clean by Iran. Many of these terrorists have been in Birmingham for months. They have Chechnyan, Pakistani, Afghan, Turkish — you name it — passports and other legal documents identifying bogus points of origin. Anywhere but Iran. Abdul Hazian has passed himself off as an international educator on sabbatical. He claims to have arrived from Hyderabad, India, less than six months ago. He convinced his admiring Stormfront hosts that he had spent several months there as a volunteer educator."

Yaacov sipped his espresso, adding a lemon peel twist. "The Quds group is based under the radar in two rented homes in the

Vestavia Hills community, a suburb of Birmingham not far from where we are now. The day before their attack, they plan to assemble in the larger of the two houses, perhaps luckily for us.

"If we stage a preemptive military strike, the escape route for our force would require transportation southward toward Mobile, a trip of about 285 miles. Airports would be impossible points of exit as detection is too easy. Mobile is on the Gulf of Mexico."

Leora leaned forward, rested her left elbow on the white tablecloth, and nestled her chin into her palm. "So the entry and exit of an attack force would be by sea somewhere below Mobile?" She was committing it to memory.

"I leave to better military minds how to move a strike force in secret over 6,300 miles. But the answer to your question is affirmative."

"Yaacov, no one in the Office has forgotten how you extricated your tank squadron from the Hamas trap during our first Gaza war. It was sheer brilliance. You'll be called upon soon to best that performance.

"Now if you don't mind" — Leora smiled — "I'd like to order a late lunch before I take my dreaded rush-hour drive back to Atlanta. I leave late tonight for Paris, where I'll meet with another good friend. What's good on this menu?"

7
Leora and Quds Force in Paris

Delta's Flight 464 arrived at Charles de Gaulle Airport at 2:37 p.m., twelve minutes ahead of schedule. A matronly redhead with two tightly braided pigtails and thick tortoiseshell bifocals emerged as one of the last passengers deplaning. Leora toted a carry-on bag. Levi would be livid if she wasted Mossad's budget paying for checked luggage.

As usual, the airport was packed with frenzied passengers trying to negotiate the lengthy distances between gates, made more challenging by the confusing signage. Tension was heightened because most flights were well behind schedule. "At least there's no workers' strike today," Leora muttered as she made her way to the taxi stand outside Terminal 3.

She'd waited in line no longer than ten minutes when the yellow Peugeot taxi, next in the long line of airport cabs waiting for a fare, came to a jarring halt in front of her. Leora was fluent in several languages, none more than minimally related to French. She gave it a go anyway.

"Hotel Relais St. Etienne in the Sixth Arrondissement, please."

The driver's response was comforting as he recognized the hotel's name and entered it into his GPS. He courteously accepted her horrid French but began some touristy chatter in serviceable English.

Twenty-five minutes later the cab cut through the vast courtyard of the Louvre on its way to the Sixth Arrondissement. Leora's hotel abutted Saint-Sulpice Church, the famous seventeenth-century Roman Catholic masterpiece of French architecture. *I wish I were here as a tourist.*

The taxi pulled into Rue Garanciere, a street so narrow that the driver had to park with two tires on the slim sidewalk. Leora handed the driver a fifty-euro note, explaining that she was uncertain of the exchange rate in dollars. The driver, shaking his head, asked if she had a smaller denomination. She held out a wad of euros and allowed the driver to assist her in computing the fare and tip in dollars.

She stepped out of the cab, almost scraping its door against the brick façade of the building, and made her way to the modest entrance of the boutique hotel. She walked straight ahead after opening the heavy front door. No more than twenty feet down a pleasant entryway, an attractive twenty-something receptionist greeted her. The young woman confirmed that Leora would be staying one night in a third-floor double room and accepted one of her many passports.

Leora paid in euros in advance and without assistance. She had accidentally, she said, left her credit cards in a locker at the airport. She was prepared to leave a cash deposit, which would cover any additional expenses. Somewhat reluctantly, the receptionist agreed. Mossad agents generally paid for hotels with cash and used credit cards only as part of a plan.

Leora asked the receptionist to notify her when Mr. Nasir arrived. "I'll come downstairs to greet him."

"There's a lovely lounge with complimentary liquor just down the corridor. I'll ask your guest to meet you there, if that's alright with you."

"Perfect. Thanks. When you call me, I can be down about fifteen minutes later."

In less than five minutes Leora was in her room. Moments after arriving, the abrasive staccato of the room phone interrupted her fumbling with the coffee machine. *Why are European phones so annoyingly loud?*

"Mr. Nasir is waiting for you in the lounge." The receptionist's lilting French-accented English was charming.

Leora had met Avram Sadyah, code name Ze'ev, at a Tel Aviv

workshop conducted by Shin Bet. His eloquent Hebrew had the occasional guttural intonation of Arabic, attesting to his place of birth in Alexandria, Egypt.

He and his mother immigrated to Israel when he was fifteen. His father stayed behind for almost ten years, visiting Israel whenever possible. His position as the head of an international book collection campaign for the prestigious, state-of-the-art Bibliotheca Alexandrina, one of the world's premier libraries, afforded him significant governmental privileges, a generous salary, and protection from the Muslim Brotherhood, Alexandria's street bullies.

Leora had reviewed Avram's dossier before her flight to Alabama. By the time he was inducted into the IDF at eighteen, his Hebrew was barely distinguishable from that of a Sabra, a native Israeli. Eighteen months into his three-year tour of service, he was identified as a gifted tactician with unusual physical capabilities.

He successfully competed to join Israel's Delta Force equivalent, Shayetet 13. The elite and secretive unit had tracked down the Black September terrorists, killers of Israeli athletes at the Munich Olympics, on a daring operation into the heart of Beirut. They were among three or four of the world's deadliest counterterrorism forces.

Leora descended the three flights of thinly carpeted stairs. Just as Ari in Rome had an aversion to elevators, she believed that they were amenities she could do without. Too many bad accidents — natural and intentional — could happen on and near elevators.

She turned left toward the receptionist's desk to find Avram speaking to the pretty young woman in effortless French. Seated behind her narrow mahogany desk, the young woman seemed mesmerized by Mr. Nasir. He was striking with his olive skin and thick, wavy black hair.

Leora approached the desk and hugged Avram.

"It's so good to see you," Leora said. "Shall we have some coffee or a cocktail?"

"No, thanks, I had coffee on the way over here." His English was as flawless as his French. "Perhaps we could take a stroll before an evening chill sets in. It's a romantic time of day for a walk through the Luxembourg Gardens. We'll have that drink a bit later."

Leora thanked the receptionist and said she'd be back later for that cocktail.

As they headed toward the front lobby, Leora stopped to sit on an upholstered chair in the anteroom. She slipped off her shoes and placed them in her bag next to the fully loaded Beretta that had been waiting for her in a locker at the airport. She sighed in relief as she put on her New Balance walking shoes.

Outside, they turned south toward the Luxembourg Gardens. They walked slowly and casually as they headed east on Rue Gay-Lussac in the direction of the Sorbonne.

"Hello, Avram. I feel comfortable addressing you by your name while walking—yes?"

Avram nodded his approval.

"It's been a while. You look well."

Dressed in a black turtleneck shirt, beige cargo pants, and well-worn Clarks, he cut a trim, Parisian figure.

"Leora, good to see you. As we stroll, every so often I'll hold your hand. We should sit on a park bench in the center of the gardens. I believe it's important for us to remain in full view in a public place since I'm never certain if I'm being watched or followed. I'll fill you in as we walk."

He pointed across the street toward the gardens.

"You're my Brazilian girlfriend who speaks with a slight Portuguese accent. You're here for a day, passing through on business."

"Got it," Leora responded, smiling.

They turned into the gardens toward the Medici Fountain. Concrete benches offered little hope of a comfortable seat. The sculpted ivy hedges that surrounded the seventeenth century masterpiece mitigated the wind-blown spray. The noise of the gushing water muffled their conversation.

"Avram, I'm here to get as much information as I can carry in my head. I'm to report to the Security Cabinet in a few days. I met with Dov and Aryeh in Rome and Alabama. Sorry for the code names — habit."

Avram draped his arm around her shoulder, crossed his legs, and pulled out a pack of Gauloises. He lit a cigarette and casually offered Leora a puff, which she took despite her great aversion to smoking.

"I've reported to the Office that the Paris BDS operation provides a cover for Ibrahim Ashrawi," Avram said. "After assassinating two Palestinian Authority politicians, he escaped and made his way to Tehran, where he was welcomed." He dragged on his cigarette, turned his head and blew the smoke away from Leora's face.

"He spent a year and a half proving himself to Quds leadership. I'm not certain what civic duties he performed for them, but they earned him the honor of leading this group of assassins in Paris. There are twenty-four fighters prepared to become martyrs while killing as many Paris Jews as possible. They're heavily armed with RPGs, Kalashnikovs and TATP. This force has been here for several weeks, based in four apartments in the Eleventh Arrondissement, giving them easy access to their intended targets."

"What are those targets, and how many agents do you have on the ground in Paris?"

"It's quite a list that they intend to strike on Rosh Hashana. Their targets include Beth El Synagogue, Synagogue des Tournelles, and Synagogue Charles Liche." He grimaced, his jaw clenching and the tendons in his neck tightening. "There's more. Rue des Rosiers is home to many of Paris' Jewish businesses. Despite the holiday, many Jewish businesses will be open and busy with limited hours. A unit of this gang intends to spray them with automatic weapons. Their street targets include L'As du Falafel, the schwarma joint next to it, the Pitot Artisanale, nearby bakery shops, and an assortment of kosher restaurants."

"How did you penetrate that den of wolves?"

"There are three BDS locations in Paris. There's no shortage of hatred for us in this town. The second one that I visited was in the Nineteenth Arrondissement on Rue de Meaux within walking distance of Canal Saint Martin. I entered an abandoned warehouse. The welcome desk was more like an interrogation zone. Two young men greeted me and asked what I was looking for.

"I informed them that I was a small-business owner from Libya and had lived in Paris for months, looking to establish both a branch and supplier of my gift shop and toy store. They were impressed with my French, but more so that Arabic was my native language. They had several dedicated volunteers who had just joined them from somewhere in the Middle East.

"It took a few days until I met them. I returned every morning, prepared to spend the day exposed to negative information on Israel from outrageous sources on the Internet. Three days later I met Ashrawi himself. I had committed that face to memory at the Office months earlier. It was definitely he.

"A front door monitor introduced us. 'Mostafa Nasir, pleased to meet you.' I extended my hand, which he took eagerly, and he gave me some made-up Arabic name, Mohamed Abaza or something like that. The next few days were spent working side-by-side, identifying Jewish-owned businesses and institutions to disseminate BDS information. Over the next few weeks I was able to gradually share my rabid anti-Semitism and stories about Israeli atrocities to my brethren in Tulkarem and Qalqilya. Soon we were conversing in Arabic.

" 'Where is your shop in Libya?' The probe was on.

" 'Tripoli,' I said, casually giving him the address. I answered why my name was Mostafa and not Mustafa, the more common spelling in Libya. He and his partners were casual about the questioning, but it was serious. I gradually convinced them of my logistical capability and my dedication to harming Israel.

" 'Would you be OK if we checked out your background?' I was surprised at his polite request. 'Not at all,' I answered. 'Why would you do that? Not that it's a problem. Hopefully, your friends in Libya will purchase something when they visit my shop.'

"He was carefully gauging my response.

"About ten days later, after meetings at the BDS offices, I was invited to their apartment in the Eleventh Arrondissement. The Office made sure that all checked out in Libya. Within a few more weeks, I was talking strategy about their planned attacks. They trusted me and used my familiarity with Paris and my planning capability. They trusted me — but kept an eye on me."

Leora abruptly ran her fingers through Avram's hair and pulled him toward her to kiss him just below his left ear. She whispered, "A man across the fountain at 2 o'clock. He's been peering at us over his *Le Monde* for the past five minutes."

As they drew apart, Avram smiled, gently caressed her face, and said, "In my recent report, I sent the addresses of the group's apartments. I have three terrific agents here with me, though I've been the only one to penetrate the group. Even though I won their confidence, as the only outsider in the group, I'm watched. They're clever and don't trust anyone, so I'm not surprised that an agent of theirs is tracking us."

He brushed Leora's wind-blown hair away from her face and gently kissed her nose. He murmured, "I'm convinced that the Office and the Cabinet will opt for military intervention. I have several apartments and a warehouse that'll accommodate our personnel. We've put together an arsenal of automatic weapons, hand grenades, and protective gear."

Leora whispered a joke in his ear, and Avram laughed, his body leaning forward. They traded smiles.

"We've been waiting for this moment, watching Iran steadily add to its force. Should the Cabinet decide to do what must be done, I'll prepare an exit route for our force — probably to Le Havre, about 125 miles from here. I'll wait to hear from you on next steps. But why have Levi and the Cabinet sent an agent to personally gather information? Is there a need to verify my encrypted reports?"

"Avram, I'm not certain we've ever faced a similar situation.

We needed to have this face-to-face encounter to confirm all details. This threat will make us act in a way that we've never responded before. In essence, we would be invading three friendly countries."

Leora stroked Avram's hair and rested her head on his left shoulder. "We're also preparing a military response to the massive buildup of Iranian airpower to our north. We uncovered a Russian-Iranian plan to simultaneously attack us by air. So this year's Rosh Hashana brings many surprises."

Avram kissed Leora's forehead and said, "Let's go to a nearby café. We need to be seen in public as much as possible. I'm not sure how far my Quds friends will take this and how they'll act on any suspicions. What we should plan for is their having made you. I'm not sure whether I'm erring on the side of caution, but be on guard this evening in your hotel room. They're trained killers and will stop at nothing."

"I'll be ready — won't sleep a wink."

They walked hand-in-hand north, toward Café Adelaide on busy Boulevard St. Michel. Deliberately, they walked slowly and cheerfully past their tail.

Despite the evening chill, they sat at an outside table in full view of any interested party. Five tables to the north, they surmised, was that interested party. The street traffic, no more than thirteen feet from the patio tables, drowned out their muted conversation.

"Leora, I'm not sure where this is going, given our unwelcome company." Avram's tone had a sense of urgency despite his warm facial expression. "So let's assume the worst. Over the last months I formed a bond with Ashrawi. They had me checked out myriad times. I actually helped him plan the logistics of their plan. I'm a trusted member of his inner circle.

"Perhaps their suspicion was aroused because I haven't associated with anyone outside of the tight circle of contacts they're familiar with. They've snapped a number of shots of us, and they've spent too much time on their cellphones for my comfort. They are evidently checking you out with their central command. I have to assume that they're trying to identify you."

Avram spoke like a military officer mapping out an action. "At midnight I'll be in front of the hotel in a gray Renault, plate number FRA69JR. I'll be prepared to drive the 200 miles to Brussels to a Mossad safe house. Then I'll fly back to Israel with you, as I believe my work here may be compromised. I'll return with any of our guys I'm hoping will be sent to destroy what's brewing here. You must stay alert until then. I'm uncertain of their next steps."

"What about you? Won't they be suspicious if you suddenly disappear?"

"Tomorrow morning's *Le Monde* will feature a story on Page 3 that quotes witnesses who observed the attempted kidnapping of a man who was shot and killed and later identified as Mostafa Nasir — my name in Paris. It'll be suggested in the article that Arab terrorists attempted the abduction of Mr. Nasir for a ransom or for some as-yet-undetermined purpose. That'll account for my absence. The reporter has been on my payroll for some time. Just remember, you must be prepared for anything, and be downstairs at the hotel entrance at midnight."

"Two cappuccinos, please, and two of your excellent croissants." Avram made a point of calling the waiter over and ordering loudly and with hand gestures that marked him as a French bourgeoisie.

When no caffeinated foam was left to spoon out of their coffee cups, Avram requested the check from the harried waiter. They made their way through the maze of tables to the avenue.

Avram kissed her on both cheeks, whispered that he would see her at midnight, and made sure that anyone paying attention heard that they were to meet for dinner the following night at a popular restaurant near the Odeon Theater.

They parted, and Leora headed north for the short walk back to her hotel. She turned left on Rue St. Etienne and stopped to look into a shoe store window. She positioned herself to observe a reflection behind her while scanning the attractive displays of elegant shoes. She spotted the guy in the blue sweatshirt who sat near them at the café. As Avram had concluded, the Iranians were suspicious.

Leora took a step backward, bent to her left, and adjusted her hair while looking directly at the store's window. After a moment of coiffure rearrangement, she continued her leisurely pace toward Rue Garanciere, where she turned left down the narrow street to the hotel's entrance. The avenue was as far as her tail followed her.

She pushed open the outside door of the hotel; it seemed unnecessarily festooned with ornate, molded floral patterns. But then, this was Paris. The inside entry door was considerably lighter and easier to negotiate. The pretty, pert receptionist was as effervescent as ever.

"Good evening, Madame. Will you be having dinner in with us, or shall I make a restaurant reservation for you?"

"Thanks very much," Leora hesitated.

"Umm, Nicole." The receptionist anticipated Leora's question. "That's my name. Nicole."

"OK, Nicole. I'll go to the hotel's café and take a sandwich up to my room."

"May I have room service bring it up to you?"

"Thanks for the offer, but I'll do it myself." Mossad training had long ago taught Leora that bad things happened with room service deliveries.

About fifteen minutes later, close to 10 p.m., she entered her third-floor room with an impossible-to-pronounce mélange of cheeses on an aromatic baguette. The talk with Avram had her mind churning. Whether Avram's cover had been blown or not, she knew that much could happen before their midnight meeting.

Leora devoured the sandwich; she'd been unaware of how hungry she was. A bottle of Perrier, compliments of the hotel, helped wash down the crumbly meal. The unfashionable blue latex gloves covering fingerprints made eating cumbersome.

Acting with practiced caution, she wiped down everything

touched without gloves. She assumed that the Iranians would find a way to dust the room for fingerprints to identify her as an enemy agent. Leora carefully cleaned the coffee machine that she'd fumbled with earlier. The small travel bag that was her check-in luggage was empty and untraceable; it would be left behind.

She slid the upholstered chair to the far right of the door, which opened to the left inside the room, and sat, leaning her elbows on its uncomfortable varnished arms. Handbag on her lap, she removed the Beretta and screwed its silencer into place. The semiautomatic was favored because of its short recoil and fifteen-round magazine. Leora reached over to the wooden night table and flipped off the light with the remote control next to the clock radio.

A faint stream of light from an adjacent apartment building evaded the closed curtains. It took Leora a few moments to adjust to the darkened room. Beretta in lap, she glanced at the clock's digital face, which read 11:17, and waited, but for what?

At exactly 11:32, a faint thump startled her. Someone arriving late from a St. Germain café? Moments later she heard a creak outside her door, exactly where she'd noticed a slight irregularity in the flooring. Her heartbeat sounded like a bass drum.

Slowly and silently the door inched open. Had Nicole given them the key? Her positioning was perfect, blocked from the intruder's view.

The intruder entered the room with weapon in hand and was met by two rapid shots to the left temple. Mossad agents rarely shot to wound. He was lifeless before he slumped to the floor. Leora jumped up, prepared to exchange fire with accomplices, but the would-be assassin was alone.

Leora dragged his body into the room and closed the door. She picked up the two spent cartridges and dropped them into her pocket. Using the hotel phone, she sent Avram a message — three rings — to signify the rendezvous should commence sooner than midnight.

She left the room with the door slightly ajar and the assailant's body blocked from view. The cleaning crew would certainly be shocked in the morning. She placed her weapon in the bag but kept a finger on the trigger in case he had backup. She quickly descended the familiar staircase as she headed for the front entrance to see if Avram had acted on her coded call.

Nicole was slumped over the welcome desk, blood oozing from the bullet hole in her forehead. Such a shame, Leora thought. So lovely, and so innocent.

Avram was waiting. Pushing open the heavy front door was infinitely easier now; her adrenaline rush saw to that.

"Let's go," she said, sliding into the gray Renault. "Tomorrow's *Le Monde* article will need to include an attempted hotel robbery as well as your demise. It should also state that the assailant killed the desk clerk."

She forced a faint smile. "The article might add that the gendarmes arrived on the scene and prevented a worse catastrophe." Leora was composing the news article as they drove off. "It appears that the police shot and killed one of the intruders. A man later identified as Mostafa Nasir, who was visiting a woman in the hotel, was also shot and mortally wounded during the attempted robbery. The woman he was visiting is being sought for questioning."

8
Danger Spelled Out At A Cabinet Meeting

By 8 a.m. Sunday, the Jerusalem sun, unhindered by a single cloud, had ended wishful thinking of an early end to summer. Municipal workers, mostly East Jerusalem Arabs, had been busy for three hours watering the blossoming almond trees and islands of red corn poppies that migrated over decades to the Middle East from Europe.

Thickets of thirsty globe thistles, about to get their daily dousing, lined the center islands of Ruppin Avenue leading to the Knesset. Outdoor labor of any kind began before daybreak so workers could avoid the merciless midday orb that scorned all. This appeared to be a normal Jerusalem business day. But "normal" had few visitation rights in Jerusalem.

A black Mercedes sedan, sparkling from its recent waxing, came to a smooth stop in front of the Jerusalem Theatre. The burly driver welcomed the two passengers added to his routine of transporting and guarding Israel's defense minister.

"Good morning, gentlemen. I'm Menachem, Minister Yarkoni's driver." He extended his muscular, hairy arm for a cordial but excessively firm handshake. Levi and Joshua returned the greeting and pushed into the car, where Minister Yarkoni slid over.

"Good to see you, Zvi." The minister and Levi served in the military together and had been members of the Security Cabinet for several years. "And you are Joshua Canaan, yes?"

"Yes, sir. Zvi and I have worked together a good part of my

career." Without being asked, Joshua offered, "I've been asked to attend part of your meeting today. My cousins in Kiryat Shmuel, about five blocks from here, were kind enough to have me as a hastily invited overnight guest."

The car inched into Jerusalem's stifling traffic. Joshua was preoccupied with the discomfort of knowing more about the meeting than the respected defense minister. He was a stickler for the military chain of communication of Mossad.

His unease continued two days of soul searching with Anat, his deeply disappointed wife. She needed no private briefings to understand that once again Israel faced a serious threat.

She recognized that the ephemeral dreams of a retirement life of travel and togetherness were put on hold. Joshua was conflicted; his love for Anat superseded all else, despite flirtations and trysts. But this dangerous time required all hands on deck. He needed her understanding of his return to service. He received it.

Eliezer Kaplan Street, an extension of Ruppin Avenue, was a rush-hour nightmare six days a week. An astonishing array of new, old, American, and European cars crept for a mile and a half from Jerusalem's swanky Rehavia neighborhood to office buildings and government offices in Givat Ram.

"Look at this, gentlemen," Menachem pointed left and started playing tour guide. "How could any normal person just drive past the beautiful Monastery of the Valley of the Cross on our left and the redone Israel Museum just beyond it? How can we just take this for granted?"

"How do you know that we take it for granted? I think," Yarkoni said, "drivers in Jerusalem are resigned to suffer with too many cars on too few roads."

The Knesset loomed to the west a few hundred yards past and across from the museum. Menachem peppered the neighboring cars with futile staccato horn blasts strikingly similar to macaques marking their territory. Motorcycles weaved menacingly through spaces that left little margin for error, angering Menachem.

Near the apex of their slow ascent, he swung right on Eliezer Kaplan Street past Yaka Square, turned right again onto Rothschild Street, and entered the grounds of Israel's parliament building.

"Sir," Menachem addressed the minister formally when others were present, "this trip has turned what hair I have left white. Maybe I'll learn to fly a helicopter."

"With you flying a copter," Yarkoni quipped, "what hair I have left will turn white."

The entrance to the Knesset was opposite the Menorah Garden, a popular tourist spot. Well-trained guards in battle fatigues and red berets waved the familiar black Mercedes through the heavy metal portal.

Sunday morning meetings with the prime minister weren't unusual; the urgency of today's invitation was. Yarkoni was notified of the meeting of the ministerial committee on national security affairs on his encrypted phone. He was advised to prepare for a lengthy meeting. No agenda was attached.

The Security Cabinet included the minister of defense, the foreign minister, the finance minister, the Israel Defense Forces chief of staff, the head of Shabak — the internal security agency, also known as Shin Bet — the chief of Mossad, and the chief of the National Security Council. It was highly unusual for these meetings to include a representative from the powerful Directorate of Military Intelligence, Aman.

"With Lavi of Aman coming to this meeting, it will not be our usual coffee-and-bagel meeting that the PM loves so much," Yarkoni told Levi. That the prime minister was often referred to by his first name or as "PM" by Cabinet members reflected the informality of most meetings.

Israel was in a period of illusory calm. The southern front bordering Gaza was less tense. The antidote to tunnel incursions of military equipment and guerrillas from Gaza across Israel's border had been mostly successful. Hamas, Gaza's military ruling party, saw its crowning achievement ruined. Seismic and sonar detection pinpointed the maze of underpasses, enabling the IDF to destroy them.

To the east, construction of several hundred miles of sophisticated fencing was completed. Sensors and drone surveillance had virtually eliminated terrorist incursions from Jordan and Iraq. The volatile northern border was now bedecked with similar fencing and an array of missile defense capabilities that were the envy of many nations.

Hezbollah remained the ultimate power broker in Israel's northern neighbor, Lebanon, and a relentless foe. Forays into Syria on behalf of that country's dictator and resultant battle losses impaired Hezbollah's readiness for yet another war. They maintained, however, a mind-boggling 100,000 missiles aimed at Israel's population centers. Seismic exploration on the northern border aimed to uncover Hezbollah's tunnel networks. ISIS remained a remote threat, if only temporarily.

The cool but effective treaties with Egypt and Jordan were holding. Sunni Arab nations, most notably Saudi Arabia, increasingly communicated with Israel through an array of back channels. They looked to Israel as a powerful partner for holding ever-aggressive Iran at bay.

As the minister and his passengers made their way to the side entrance reserved for the prime minister's short list, Menachem stayed close despite the ever-alert Knesset guards. Menachem would be first into the private elevator descending two stories, first to exit the elevator, and at his side until the Cabinet meeting room door was shut.

As Yarkoni entered the conference room through the unmarked door, he repressed the previous hour, in which he'd foraged through his memory bank trying to recall an urgent Cabinet meeting with no advance agenda. His concerns dissolved as he marched toward the PM's espresso machine, recently imported from Italy.

It glistened on a Formica bar and sputtered out a rich and fragrant cappuccino. *This coffee,* Yarkoni thought, *makes even the most mundane meetings with the PM bearable.*

Levi, having stopped to chat with an acquaintance, entered

a few moments later. He instructed Joshua to make himself comfortable in an adjoining room until the PM invited him in.

Yitzhak Alon, the foreign minister, and Alex Meron, the finance minister, had preceded Yarkoni.

"Good morning," Yarkoni managed to suppress a yawn. "Has everyone brought their sleeping bags?"

Yarkoni was envious of Alon. He thought he had achieved that rarity in public service: fun. Alon traveled to many countries to be greeted by the façade of public rebuke and criticism while basking in the behind-the-scenes accolades of even Israel's most virulent public detractors.

The two ministers would often meet at The Aroma coffee shop in Jerusalem's German Colony neighborhood.

"How easy it is," Yarkoni would offer as a faux lament, "to bitch and moan about the state of our beloved Israel. Sometimes I wonder how we stay afloat."

Alon would laugh and describe experiences abroad. "Moshe, I know you know, but other countries are just as fucked up. They just hide it better. The greatest laughs I have are visiting our 'enemies.'"

"Which ones in particular?"

"All — almost. The great irony remains hidden. So many of these countries have billions of dollars' worth of business deals with us. That stays under the radar. In public they yell condemnations of the Jewish state — especially in the United Nations. What a joke."

Meron was likely the first to arrive and stake out his usual place at the conference table. The proverbial bean counter, his ministerial appointment suited him perfectly.

He traditionally and unabashedly supported positions that were to the right of even the most conservative government ministers. Meron was also an insufferable bore. The finance minister worried incessantly about the cost of social safety net programs while somehow securing funding for prohibitively expensive and internationally reviled quasi-legal settlements.

"Hello, Moshe," Alon, Yarkoni's longtime friend, greeted

him with a handshake. "Any idea what this meeting is about?"

Yarkoni and Alon had been IDF paratroopers seemingly centuries ago and had never relinquished the camaraderie of that select fraternity.

"No idea, Yitzhak. Alex, any thoughts?"

"None, Moshe," Meron answered in his signature laconic manner.

"Alex, have you ever answered a question with a full sentence?" Yarkoni prodded.

"Moshe, when you deal with our nation's economy on a daily basis, you're left depressed and speechless."

The air seemed to be vacuumed out of the chamber when the rear mahogany door opened and an unusually steely-eyed prime minister entered.

Eliezer Simcha had been prime minister for a year and a half. He had skillfully curtailed a third intifada, ordered a punishing but restrained response to showers of rockets from Gaza and carefully monitored and occasionally intercepted and destroyed nighttime convoys of sophisticated Iranian missiles addressed to Hezbollah. These were the day-to-day events of living in a volatile, hateful neighborhood. No cause for unusual alarm.

As if guided by a metronome, Igal Tzion, the Israel Defense Forces chief of staff; Ari Kahan, the head of Shin Bet; and Yosef Arnon, the national security chief, arrived within five minutes of one another.

The final arrival was General Chaim Lavi, director general of the powerful and generally subterranean Aman. Aman was the independent service charged with coordinating military intelligence among the three basic branches of the IDF.

It had been years since a Security Cabinet meeting included Lavi. With each new arrival, the tension mounted. The inevitable small talk and chatter of longtime friends and political adversaries allayed anxiety, but only minimally.

The PM sat straight-backed at the head of the twenty-foot-long teak table, one of the few extravagances other than the espresso machine in the otherwise sparsely furnished inner sanctum of Israel's power brokers.

Simcha was a svelte six-foot product of Israel's elite Sayeret Matkal, familiarly called the Unit. The commando unit was reputed to be among the most feared counterterrorism forces in the world. While impressive in an asymmetric battlefield, the characteristics of a hardened commando were often at odds with the political adroitness and finesse required to lead a volatile democracy. Small talk and compromise were not terms used to describe the hardline PM.

The walls of the conference room were lined with framed portraits of Israel's prime ministers — from the nation's founding father, David Ben-Gurion, to Benjamin Netanyahu, whom Simcha succeeded. At the center of the neatly arranged photographs was the nation's only female prime minister, Golda Meir. Most Israelis would say she had bigger balls than most of the nation's male political leaders.

The meeting room was devoid of high-tech distractions: no moving images on floor-to-ceiling screens, no satellite imagery pulsating incessantly, no complex algorithms marching across enlarged screens. This wasn't a venue for dry, academic PowerPoint presentations allowing participants to surreptitiously space out. All the state-of-the-art surveillance and military tracking gadgets were down the hall. This room was for looking one another in the eye and locking wits.

As coffee cups clinked around him, the PM slid his toward the center of the table and addressed his Cabinet. "We have a situation that will require courage and probably a suspension of rationality."

9
Laying Out the Challenge

Yarkoni bellowed, "Are we on the brink of war?" He stood and paced before returning to his seat. "Am I coming to a meeting to hear of a new threat? I haven't been on vacation — why the surprise meeting?" The minister rarely got annoyed in Cabinet debates. "What Arab nations are mobilizing their armies that I'm not aware of?"

ISIS was contained and had become a ragtag bunch of vicious nihilists. Terrorism was at a lull, albeit temporary. Hamas and Hezbollah were under surveillance, and Iran was — what was Iran planning?

Simcha stood, rested his right palm on the polished, dark-brown table, and locked eyes with each Cabinet member. In an emotional tone, a departure from his steely demeanor, he said, "We're faced with a series of unique challenges." He wasn't given to histrionics or political melodrama, so his direct comments produced unease. The others fidgeted in their seats.

"I've taken the unusual step of inviting a guest to join us, a man who isn't a member of our Cabinet. You will soon understand what's ahead of us. I'm determined to use our best to address the challenges. After coordinating with Zvi, I've asked Joshua Canaan, a recently retired senior Mossad agent, to attend our meeting. You'll soon understand how he can play an important role and why we have forced — coaxed — him out of retirement."

The Cabinet members were riveted to the PM's words, but his humor brought no smile to anyone's face.

On cue, Levi walked to the door behind the PM and ushered

Joshua into the room. He nodded a silent hello and took a chair near the end of the long table. After a moment, attention again turned to the PM.

"Diaspora Jews are threatened, as is Israel proper," Simcha said. "The danger exists in several Western countries. My words may sound foreboding. I assure you that I've thought long and hard about them. They've been on my mind for three days. Zvi and Yossi will outline our most recent intel."

The silence after the PM's comments seemed to last an eternity. He had the cut-and-dried approach, even in a crisis, of a veteran combat commander.

Levi didn't bother to stand as he started talking. In his late fifties, he'd been the director of Mossad for six years. His twenty-year post-army positions included cultural attaché at the Israeli embassy in South Africa, Germany, and France. His role had precious little to do with culture. He'd earned the reputation of a valuable and ruthless covert operative.

He was no longer the trim, charismatic diplomatic chameleon that flitted through Parisian nightclubs and upscale restaurants for four years. While he dined and drank, his unusual power of recall mapped points of entry and exit and gauged which well-dressed diners were potential enemy agents.

Levi had been instrumental in averting numerous plots against the Jewish community of Paris. Many of his covert actions also took him to Southeast Asia and East Africa. His assignments increasingly were carried out with a partner in whom he had unflinching confidence: Joshua Canaan.

The Mossad chief's oratorical finesse was a dismal second to that of the PM.

"I'll share information that we've been processing and analyzing for several weeks." Despite his collegial relationship with most of those present, his tone remained clipped and formal. "When I finish my piece, Yossi will give you the National Security Council's assessment. Then it's in your laps."

Slowly, Levi rose from his brown leather swivel chair and walked toward the dark mahogany door through which the PM had entered. He pushed a green button to the left of the door, and a four-by-four-yard map of the world slowly descended. The map and his laser pointer were the high-tech highlights of the meeting room.

"We believe there'll be a coordinated strike against us and Jewish communities in Europe and the U.S. We're convinced that Iran and Russia have been planning the attack for almost a year and a half.

"You'll understand why we worked hard to ensure that Joshua Canaan rejoined us. Abu Yusalem is involved in planning the Diaspora attacks. We don't believe that there is anyone more likely to kill or capture him than Joshua.

"Key operatives in Paris, Rome, and America have been feeding us intel regularly. As unusual as it is for Jews to agree on any subject, their data uniformly support our assessments."

Israel was birthed beside a petri dish of paranoia. But was it paranoia if the threats were real? Council members were repeatedly subjected to reports of danger in Israel proper, in the West Bank and throughout Europe. The information was sometimes verifiable. Too often, however, reports from usually reliable sources proved to be products of jittery imaginations.

Levi continued: "It's been clear to us for some time that there was a buildup of Russian aircraft at Khmeimim. The quality of their fighters and bombers goes way beyond the airpower required to harass ISIS or the assortment of rebel groups that they claim to be fighting.

"The 250 miles from Latakia to Tel Aviv, we know, can be covered supersonically in under half an hour. We've tracked thirty-two Sukhoi all-weather air-to-air fighters. Who are they fighting in aerial combat? There is no one." He slapped a hand against the map over Syria.

"Also, there's been a significant increase in the SU-25 for ground support; the SU-24M2, a tactical bomber; the SU-30SM, a heavy multirole craft designed for air-to-air combat and precision strikes; and, most alarming, the SU-34, the fighter we know as Fullback."

Levi turned to his colleagues. They were riveted, but they'd heard much of this before.

"They've also introduced their most advanced supersonic SU-35 into Syria." This produced a gasp. The 35 was a potent weapon. "We believe that Russia is behind a plan to expand its power base in the region at our expense. Let's hear from Yossi now. What I share with you is only part of the iceberg."

Taking his seat, Levi cleared his throat and made several notes on his pad.

Yosef Arnon, known to the council as Yossi, was the controversial chief of the National Security Council for more than a year. There was never a doubt about his strategic brilliance, only about his seemingly never-ending scandals, extramarital affairs, and sexual harassment cases. The PM resisted calls for his trusted chief's resignation because of how greatly he valued Arnon's clear and apolitical thinking.

He stood, took the electronic pointer from Levi, fumbled with it for a moment, and strode to the oversize map behind the PM's chair. At forty-five, Arnon was handsome, slim, and athletic. He brushed away the shock of unkempt salt-and-pepper hair from his forehead.

Hardly an advertisement for GQ-approved hair products, he rarely combed or even arranged the abundant locks that his female partners found attractive. His expression was serious, an anomaly for his perennially wise-ass approach to presentations — a quality that didn't endear him to the veteran military establishment.

"We've been tracking the unprecedented movement of Russian warships toward our Mediterranean basin," Arnon noted, pointing to the fleet's planned point of entry. "The Caspian Flotilla and Black Sea Fleet of their Southern District in the port city of Astrakhan are on the move and are on a Level 4 alert. Several of their cruisers have launched Kalibr-NK missiles as tests into Syria. They're accurate from about 900 miles."

Igal Tzion, the IDF chief of staff, raised his hand.

"Yossi, Zvi, are we receiving a briefing on Russia's military now? Are we preparing for war with Russia?" He turned angrily to the prime minister. "Eliezer, what's the point of your visits to Moscow and all the face-to-face talks with their president if this confrontation is on the horizon? How does what we're hearing today add up?"

"What's different, Igal," Arnon responded before the PM did, "is that Russia has been training Iranian pilots to fly their advanced aircraft only minutes from our northern border. We believe that the façade of warming relations and rapprochement with the Soviets has been them selling us a line of bullshit."

The unified murmur had a distinct note of *I told you so*.

"A step toward regional domination?" asked Yarkoni. As defense minister, he had often warned of the Big Bear's duplicity, only to be scoffed at as unusually paranoid. Yarkoni added, "We can handle Iranian pilots, no matter how well-trained. Russian pilots in limited quantity we can handle too. We need to know what level of force they'll bring to the table."

The barometric pressure in the windowless meeting room plummeted, yet only part of the oncoming storm had been identified.

Levi joined Arnon and, in an offhand way, added, "Mossad has more intel. We've been watching the growth of the international BDS movement. The Boycott, Divestment, and Sanctions debates on university campuses are split into two categories: activists who oppose our settlement policies and a much more sinister cabal using BDS as a cover. I'm waiting, Ari."

Levi turned and shot a glance at his colleague, who more often than not was his greatest adversary. Ari Kahan never missed an opportunity to lobby for his lonely liberal viewpoints and policies. He saw himself as a beacon of liberalism in a dark right-wing abyss.

"You're fucking right to wait, Zvi," Kahan said. "No harm intended." Kahan virtually jumped out of his chair. His antics often trivialized his political views. "Our settlement policy is a scourge on our national conscience and causes us endless internal and international bleeding. No wonder the BDS movement has gained influence internationally. I often wonder if I were a college administrator in America with billions of dollars in my foundation, would I invest in Israel?"

Alon shouted his response: "Ari, the time will come for this review, just not now."

Kahan had somehow navigated the thin ice a liberal political appointee must negotiate in what he termed a "reactionary political arena." He remained in the position because he was an effective head of Israel's internal security ministry, the Shin Bet. Security trumped politics — most of the time.

Kahan spouted views held by many Israelis. He persevered despite being a minority of one in the Security Cabinet. He argued at every council meeting that how Israel was viewed internationally was intertwined with "misdirected policies."

"Ari, we'll debate settlements at a later time," Levi said, nodding thanks to Alon for interceding earlier. "You may find more sympathy for your position than you believe. Let's put that aside for now, OK? As you all know, we've been tracking the activities of Ibrahim Ashrawi from his stay in Isfahan, Iran. He left Beirut more than two years ago, gave up his position as public information director with Hezbollah, and has managed the disinformation platforms that Iran uses to feed the flames of BDS.

"Ashrawi's operation, based in Paris, provides fake news on social media sites. It quotes anonymous or fictional sources on an attractive website and posts phony Israeli policies that advocate persecuting our Arab minority. In short, using BDS, he's pushing to hurt us while publishing anti-Semitic smut. That's only part of his strategy."

Levi marched halfway around the table and returned to the map.

"I repeat this," Levi continued, "because it's part of Iran's plan. They camouflage their actions while encouraging world leaders to label us a pariah state.

"With us beaten up on the international stage and on the short end of the blame game of the Palestinian conflict, an attack on us and the Jews of the world might find a biased international community looking away."

Igal Tzion extended his right arm, palm facing Levi, and rose slowly. He had been slouching in his chair, unusual given his military demeanor. Now he stood erect.

Tzion was Israel's first chief of staff of North African descent. All his Moroccan family shared his olive complexion. He walked left and stood just in front of a portrait of Theodor Herzl, founding father of modern Zionism, whose steely gaze seemed to be directed at the chief's left shoulder. Tzion's rise through the military began in earnest when he commanded Israel's Seventh Armored Brigade at age thirty-one.

"Zvi," he began, "sorry to stop you, but I want to know more about your warnings on the attacks on the Jewish communities in Europe and the States. I know this isn't my immediate area of responsibility, but I'm deeply concerned.

"As chief of staff of the IDF" — Tzion was animated and angry — "my job is to coordinate military deployment of our armed forces to protect our homeland. How can our tiny country take on the responsibility of protecting millions of Diaspora Jews? We're spread thin with enemy forces at our borders. It's unrealistic to believe that we can protect Jewish communities thousands of miles away."

Alon stood, pushed his swivel chair back with his right thigh, and extended his left hand, palm out, toward Tzion and his right hand in the direction of Levi. The palm-out gesture was ingrained in Cabinet gesticulations as a means of interrupting a colleague to gain the floor. It wasn't easy to counter Tzion, especially when he generated an angry head of steam.

Alon momentarily lowered his gaze to some object in the middle of the glistening table. The nonverbal gestures were pure Alon, theatrical but a clear request for the floor.

"Sorry, Zvi and Igal, for interrupting," the foreign minister said. "My mind is churning faster than I can find words. I'll try to make sense. Igal, your thoughts about Diaspora Jews and our role as their protectors have been our dilemma since 1948. The world's Jews see the benefits of our relationship as west heading east; that is, donations flowing to us from the USA and Western European Jewish communities. Israel's strength and viability are, thankfully for us, an emotional and intellectual necessity for them.

"The Jews of New Jersey," Alon continued, hands flying "don't have a tank force. The Jews of Connecticut have no nuclear-armed submarines at their docks in Mystic Seaport, and the Jews of Paris seem to be missing an air force. These are real-life facts. Thanks to you, Igal and Aman" — Alon nodded at them — "and all of us protecting our homeland, we do possess these. Diaspora Jews are more vulnerable than they know and are now in danger from a vicious enemy.

"I need to add one other thought — at least one. In mid-April we observed Holocaust Memorial Day. Which of our families wasn't deeply affected? Who of us isn't moved to tears when our country comes to a standstill every year as the siren's blare reminds us to honor those we've lost? Who of us hasn't been affected?

"Sorry to rant," Alon said, not meaning it. "For all of us Jews, memory and history are central. With our military capability, how can we not protect Jews who will again be defenseless? Are we willing to have future generations remember us as standing by while Jews, no matter where they are in the world, are slaughtered?"

Alon knew when it was time to quit the floor. Although given to histrionics and a need to hammer his positions home long after an audience was beaten into submission, he stopped. He looked around the conference table, pausing at each of his colleagues, and slowly sat down.

Silence was generally an element left at the entryway of Jewish gatherings. Israel's Security Cabinet was no exception. The accepted norm was at least three members speaking simultaneously. Alon's impassioned pitch, however, left the boisterous bunch in contemplative quiet.

The PM sat back and thanked Alon. "I suppose you were

pre-empting the ongoing question of our role as police force for Diaspora Jews." Simcha nodded at Alon, then locked eyes with the men around the table. "We're faced with military challenges. We have, through Mossad and other means, worked to prevent violence to Jewish communities throughout the world. We've used covert operations and targeted eliminations. I believe that what we're about to hear is in unmapped territory — even for us."

Levi stepped toward the table. He rocked his head slowly — left to right and back — and stroked the back of his neck. "Yitzhak, you and the PM bring up a key challenge for Mossad. What I'm sharing with you now is based on the most extensive intel that I've overseen." He took a deep breath. "I'll briefly recap what we know at this point.

"Iran has funded, trained, and armed assassins working out of European BDS offices. In the States" — Levi gestured for Yossi to hand him the pointer and aimed it at Birmingham — "the Iranians have penetrated the neo-Confederate group the League of the South, also known as Stormfront. That group has established links with the anti-Semitic Jobbik party in Hungary and the fascist Golden Dawn in Greece. What is clear to us at Mossad and at the National Security Council is that on Rosh Hashana, Iran plans to strike from our northern border and is coordinating attacks on Jewish institutions abroad."

"I want to make something very clear," Tzion said, scanning the table and pointing toward the ceiling. "Should we decide to protect Jews outside our borders, despite my concerns, we'll use all of our resources to face this threat. I fully understand and agree — we have no choice. We're stretched to the breaking point militarily and" — he shot a glance at Meron, the tight-fisted finance minister — "budgetarily as well. But my full support will go with our decision in here."

The PM nodded in acknowledgment at Tzion and stood to call a recess.

10
Russian Chemistry

Rue Lacharriere 23, in a quiet section of Paris's Eleventh Arrondissement, featured a well-manicured garden. A front company for the Iranian government had rented the furnished luxury apartment a year earlier. The lead-time was necessary to allay neighborhood suspicions with the appearance of Middle Easterners entering and leaving the apartment.

Paris had been hit by terrorist attacks with alarming frequency. The government called for increased vigilance to assist authorities in preventing further attacks.

With the customary Parisian joie de vivre tempered by civic unease, Abu Yusalem took great care to remain above the fray. He was always meticulously groomed and nattily dressed. He enjoyed the tailored Armani suits, silk ties, and alligator shoes made possible by his generous Iranian budget.

Yusalem carefully hung his trousers over an armchair when he rolled out his prayer carpet, faced Mecca, and prayed as close to five times daily as his unpredictable schedule allowed. He was a devout Muslim. He had no trouble coupling his adherence to the teachings of Islam with his life's dedication to defeating Israel and ensuring that an Arab government ruled the land that he believed rightfully belonged to Arabs.

His cover was elaborate and expertly choreographed. Rue Lacharriere 23 housed one of the most dangerous terrorists in the world. His clean-shaven face, Caucasian features and excellent French were a perfect cover.

The traditional Parisian corner crowd, a mix of seniors and

the unemployed, seemed proud to have such distinguished residents in the neighborhood. Flanked by three of his ubiquitous "business" associates wearing store-bought blazers and business suits off the rack, Yusalem headed to a meeting in a small warehouse on Rue Beccaria, near St. Antoine Hospital.

His obsessive adherence to punctuality found him leaving for engagements at 1:30 every afternoon, just after midday prayers. His compulsion to be on time overtook his commonsense need not to be predictable and therefore trackable. Nonetheless, he remained uncanny in his elusiveness.

The black Peugeot DS 19 luxury sedan that ferried Yusalem around Paris pulled off the narrow street into the tight parking lot of a warehouse. With some maneuvering, they made room for the two cars they were expecting within fifteen minutes.

Yusalem's associates exited the car first, each carrying an attaché case. An assortment of automatic pistols weighed the cases down. None of the leather satchels was ever latched.

A burly aide pulled the warehouse's creaking, rusted front door open. They left the padlocked entrance ajar for a few moments so that the stale, chemical-laden air could escape.

A ten-by-ten-foot table took up a good deal of the space in the center of the small warehouse. Four stainless-steel canisters sat on the workspace, each labeled with multisyllabic formulas that meant little to the early arrivals. Overhead spotlights were turned on, and the powerful ventilation system was activated.

Abu Yusalem was getting antsy. He was eager to prepare the sarin-laced bomb to kill as many Jews as possible, but he had limited time. His dizzying travel schedule was necessary as he coordinated the attacks in Paris and Rome. He was busy, as well, sending and receiving encrypted messages from his team in Birmingham.

His expertise and skill in military planning were also called on in Lebanon. He would link the tri-city attacks with Hezbollah's unleashing of barrages of rockets at Israel's population centers. There was just over a week remaining before Iran, Russia, and their surrogates launched a mortal blow against a despised enemy. Three simultaneous goals would be achieved: Israel would be defeated, Jews would be slaughtered in at least four locations, and he would become an adored Arab-world hero. All three objectives were of immense importance to him.

Yusalem had received word that his bombing of the Dohány Street Synagogue in Budapest failed to eliminate his greatest antagonist, Joshua Canaan. At times, Yusalem's information sources rivaled those of Israel's famed Unit 8200. He was certain that Canaan would be reactivated, and he looked forward to another face-to-face with him.

Twenty minutes after their arrival, a jarring five-second alarm announced that the expected guests had reached the parking lot. Yusalem instructed one of his colleagues to lower the alarm, as it was grating. Despite his propensity to violence and extensive battlefield experience, Yusalem had a neurotic aversion to sudden loud and abrasive sounds.

Both cars arrived at about the same time. One of Yusalem's guards, attaché case at his side, pushed open the front door and welcomed the three visitors. This was their third meeting in the past month.

Yusalem greeted them with a nod, no handshake. For years he'd been suspicious of the vulnerability of entrusting a hand to anyone other than a family member. Close aides knew to avoid even inadvertent physical contact with their killer boss.

Most assumed he had a fear of bacterial infection. It seemed ironic to his closest confidants that a man who killed with impunity could suffer such foibles.

The visitors — three *chemists* — virtually in unison removed their jackets and donned white laboratory garments. Dr. Vasiliev, one of Russia's most prominent chemistry professors, took the lead.

"I hope that you are well, Mr. Yusalem. We are close to getting our little toy in order." Vasiliev's heavily accented English and his weak attempt at a lighthearted icebreaker brought only a glare.

"We have obtained the thirty-five percent hydrogen peroxide that we had trouble locating. That's a step in the right direction. Dr. Popov, my Belarusian colleague, has secured the necessary amount of beryllium and boron. We're well on our way."

"To be perfectly clear," Yusalem snarled, "I don't give a damn about your ingredients and in which supermarket you buy your products. We have little more than a week to go, and I need to see the results of your assignment, not a progress report on the stages of your work."

Dr. Kazemi, Iran's leading chemist, a man who had befriended Yusalem when he spent four months in Tehran, interjected in Farsi.

"We're almost there. The missing elements are oxide and magnesium, and they are relatively easy to obtain. Dr. Vasiliev is a day or two away from receiving a shipment from a local contact. Once we have those missing ingredients, we'll assemble the bomb and show you how to arm and safely handle it. Trust us. Your mission is vital to us as well."

Kazemi's comments calmed Yusalem. The Farsi he'd learned in Tehran was rudimentary, so only part of the message of assurance got through to him. Still, he understood what he needed to.

Assembling the bomb was in their hands; he just wanted them to go faster. He would need to see more progress before he left for Beirut in two days.

11
Plans Are Developed

The three-hour break in the Cabinet meeting, while unusual, allowed the espresso to take its toll. Simcha called it extended pee time. Yarkoni offered a quiet "Thank God. My bladder was bursting."

The welcome recess also sparked a hushed murmur as taut faces spoke of drama that was yet to come.

The Cabinet members returned to the windowless room within ten minutes of one another, a rarity for Israel's boisterous and contentious leaders. Somehow, every temporal or organizational limit seemed to be a personal affront to an Israeli. Today was different. The ominous news required behavioral shifts, even for intractable leaders.

During the pause, two elderly women sporting pressed white aprons placed china plates and cutlery atop straw placemats before each seat. No choices were available; each plate had a portion of baked fish filet — probably bream — salad with a handful of olives, and a scoop of baba ganoush. Aromatic warmed Arabic pita, from Ali's Bakery just inside the Old City's Jaffa Gate, was stacked on three platters.

As the group reassembled, Alon, the foreign minister who had been mostly silent for the first part of the meeting, said, "Eliezer, I guess this meal means we'll be here a while."

The PM didn't respond.

After ten minutes of uneasy banter and a surprising lack of complaints about the cuisine, the PM gently slid his plate a foot or two toward the edge of the conference table, rolled back a few feet in his swivel chair, and stood quietly. He girded himself for the discussion.

"There's no shortage of political opinions in this room. Our standard joke is that for every three Jews we have at least five opinions. What we face today allows us no room for divisiveness, no options for vacillation, and no tolerance for political turf issues." Despite the side comment, the PM was clear and to the point. "There's a threat to us that is greater than the 1973 Yom Kippur War. For the first time, a military attack on our homeland and coordinated actions against Diaspora Jews are planned by Iran — with the assistance of a global superpower.

"The intel that Mossad and 8200 have compiled over the past two weeks is comprehensive. Much of the data have been reviewed with Igal and several of his IDF generals. I haven't reached out to any of you, all of whom I respect deeply, because much of the information was not vetted and so remained inconclusive — until now."

The PM's informal style rarely had him standing at the head of the table while addressing his Cabinet. This was different. One by one, he established steely eye contact with the most powerful leaders in Israel.

"I hold all of you to a pledge of absolute secrecy," the PM said, clenching his jaw. "More importantly, I will look to you — Moshe and Igal, together with Chaim — to guide our discussion on Israel's response, here and globally. Each of us has a role to play. I expect that we'll need at least another day or two to prepare a unified course of action."

Simcha pointed down the table. "Zvi, the floor is yours." The PM sat down stiffly, crossed his legs, and drew his cup of chilled espresso closer.

Levi stood, fumbling with the laser pointer for a moment as he approached the extended world map in four strides. Pointing the red beam to Rome, Paris, and Alabama, he began in his usual military cadence.

"The intelligence reports we've received over the last two weeks led me to send a top agent to operatives in these three sites. I received summary encrypted reports a few days ago but wanted the intel to be verified face-to-face before presenting it. I've invited that agent to report to you personally. Yes, this type of personal Mossad report is highly unusual. The challenge ahead of us requires that we're crystal clear. No room for misinterpretation. This will allow for direct questioning."

Levi's inclination to gesticulate wildly during impassioned talks produced a lighthearted moment. As he waved his left hand, he accidentally swept the PM's empty lunch plate to the floor. It had been placed precariously close to the table's edge. It crashed on the unforgiving stone tiles. "You see, Alex," he said, aiming his remark at the tight-fisted finance minister, "why we need budget approval for carpeting?" Undeterred, he continued.

"We're fortunate that our most senior officer has agreed to come out of his two-month retirement to help on our European front. When the prime minister and I met with him, we hadn't yet formally concluded that he would return to service. We didn't get a chance to hear from him at our earlier meeting this morning." There was a murmur of approval.

Levi stepped to the right of the lowered map and opened the mahogany door that no longer squeaked after an aide oiled the hinges. He signaled to Joshua in the corridor.

He entered, sporting black slacks and a light-gray, short-sleeve shirt. No jacket. No tie. He nodded to the Cabinet members as he made his way toward the rear of the room, to the same seat he sat in earlier. Cabinet members had only just met him. They were keenly aware of his reputation, but his identity had been withheld from all written reports.

Less than a minute later, Leora entered, dressed in a smart but modest green pantsuit. She stood next to Levi with her back to the lowered world map. Levi said, "We'll dispense with the introductions. This senior agent met onsite with our key operatives in the targeted cities. She briefed me extensively and is now prepared to address you and respond to your questions." He nodded to Leora.

"We've been receiving encrypted messages from Rome,

Paris, and Alabama for about one month." Leora got right into it, no small talk. "Our operatives have managed to infiltrate two BDS offices and a violent, racist group in the States." She stood straight-backed and unmoving, hands clasped in front of her. She spoke emphatically and clearly so that she reached the far end of the room.

"These offices are being used as a cover for Quds units. They're trained fighters who are in those locations for one reason only: to kill Jews and create international mayhem. They're loaded with automatic assault weapons, suicide vests, and high explosives. You've been informed of the force size in each venue and the names of the leaders of these bands. No need to repeat that now. Their commanders are no strangers to any of us here. They are terrorists we've pursued for years."

Leora maintained eye contact with her breathless audience. She spoke confidently, without notes and with a familiar military clarity and brevity.

"My director" — she shot a quick glance at Levi — "sent me on an assignment to meet with our field agents. Each of them has operatives who have penetrated a local BDS office. They report that Quds agents use these headquarters to gather data on Jews. We have no reason to believe that the local BDS organizers in Rome and Paris or Stormfront racists have any knowledge of foreign infiltration."

Leora nodded when Levi poured a glass of water and pushed it toward the end of the table, but she didn't move from where she'd entered the room.

"The Iranians are involved, alongside local residents, in planning boycotts of Israeli goods from the West Bank. They help produce anti-Zionist placards and leaflets. These are their front activities. At the same time they've been compiling information on Jewish locations in their target communities. They've been skilled in using these offices as information sources.

"It is now clear to us," Leora said, taking the pointer from Levi and aiming the beam at the map, "that the Iranians are preparing a coordinated attack on Jewish institutions in these locations. The morning of Rosh Hashana, less than two weeks from today, is their target date."

She turned back to her audience.

Levi stood and waved his hand, palm out, toward Leora, signaling for her to pause before concluding. He reached her in three short strides.

"You have heard that our agent" — he looked left at Leora — "visited our operatives in three target locations. Her visits helped us understand that Birmingham, Alabama, will present us with complex logistics. Whatever we decide, the white supremacist, anti-Semitic organization Stormfront adds to our challenge because it's in the States. But Paris remains the thorniest undertaking.

"This officer," he again looked at Leora, "met with our operative in Paris and had a violent encounter with an Iranian assassin. Well, she is here, and the terrorist's family is in mourning." Leora stood next to Levi and stared impassively at a distant wall. There was a murmur of approval from the Cabinet.

"Our intel shows no deviation in Quds activity levels and no changes in their daily surveillance. We're reasonably sure that our assets covered their tracks. No elaboration now, but I'll meet with any of you when we adjourn to give you a full accounting."

Leora glanced at Levi, whose nod said *continue*.

"There may be copycat attacks, but these are beyond a doubt the Iranians' three primary targets. We have veteran operatives embedded in those sites. Our agents," she concluded in a measured tone, "have penetrated the three locations. They're experienced but vastly outnumbered. Rogue operators and lone-wolf assassins are not running these Iranian hit squads. They're trained troops, and this looks like war."

Leora closed on that ominous note, looked at Levi, and braced for a flood of questions.

"Zvi and Madam Agent — how shall I address you?" Yarkoni asked as a prelude to his real question.

"Agent is fine. I don't mean to be rude."

"If you had to put a percentage on the reliability of this information," Yarkoni asked, "what would it be? Think long and hard, as what you've outlined for us is potentially apocalyptic."

Virtually in unison, Levi and Leora answered, "One hundred percent." Levi added, "Barring no change in orders from Tehran or Moscow."

"Judging by your report, we're looking at over sixty assassins in three separate locations; am I correct?"

"Yes, Defense Minister, that's our assessment." Leora recognized Yarkoni because his picture appeared in Israel's daily newspapers with regularity.

Joshua stood and took two steps toward the group. His left knee still tightened when he sat for a while, but he ignored it.

"I suppose you need to know why I am again taking up a chair at this meeting. Levi and the prime minister shared some information with me regarding the challenge we face. Your Cabinet meeting is sobering." He gestured at Leora. "I learned a great deal from the agent's report; no way could I make a presentation like that without notes. Her reports gave us exact addresses of the bases of these terror groups, the number of fighters in each Quds unit, the names of the leaders of the terror squads, the weapons to be used, and the planned time of attack. All committed to memory.

"I'm also not here to complain that Zvi will try to withhold my salary, claiming that I retired." Light laughter; they were all well acquainted with Levi's reputation. Only Finance Minister Meron admired it.

"Not two months ago I was once again a target of Abu Yusalem. I've spent a good part of my career tracking and chasing him; I almost succeeded twice. He is, as we know too well, a cunning and highly skilled killer. I'm informed that Yusalem is coordinating the terror attacks on the three Diaspora communities. He's Russia and Iran's golden boy and looks forward to dealing Israel a devastating blow."

Joshua shifted his weight to relieve the soreness in his left leg.

"Yusalem," he continued, "is also working with Hezbollah. He's delivering Iran's orders to launch a simultaneous attack on our north. We can anticipate that they'll fire barrages of rockets toward our populated areas. He's also in the final stages of assembling a dirty bomb laced with sarin gas to be detonated in Paris' Fourth Arrondissement. Russian and Iranian scientists are working with him and plan to time their bombing with their Rosh Hashana offensive. Abu Yusalem is the centerpiece of asymmetric attacks."

Joshua stared at the PM.

"I plan to kill him before Rosh Hashana."

A stream of questions regarding logistics of the assassin groups went on for the next ten minutes: How convinced was Mossad that they had the correct locations for the Quds forces? How often did they assemble in the BDS and Stormfront offices? How many Mossad agents were on location? How firm was the attack date? How could additional forces be integrated with Mossad agents on site? How would Joshua accomplish what he hadn't succeeded in doing over the last few years? Why not take them all out now?

At the first lull in the questions, Levi thanked Leora and Joshua. Leora headed toward the exit. Within six feet of the door, she stopped and told the Cabinet members that it was an honor to present to them. With a slight tremor in her voice, she added, "Know that the agents in these cities — as well as others throughout Europe — won't fail Israel."

Levi turned to Joshua and thanked him for allowing the short-circuiting of his retirement. Now more than ever, the country needed him.

Levi left the meeting room with Leora and Joshua. He returned after escorting them to the adjoining conference room.

The prime minister stood and, with a calm that belied his internal churning, said, "Part 1 of our situation is now in front of us. Perhaps Part 2 is even more ominous." The PM looked to Arnon, the chief of the National Security Council. "Yossi, outline the threat that's even closer to home."

Tzion, still seated, slammed his right hand against the table, causing the plate and cup in front of him to bounce off the placemat. "Have we ever faced such complex such challenges, both here and abroad?"

Arnon took a moment to down his espresso. Clearing his throat, he nodded to Tzion and answered, "None of us has, Igal."

Arnon seemed edgy. He'd been back to the shiny coffee novelty three times in the last hour and a half.

"The Russians," he began, "have introduced their sophisticated S-300 and S-400 air defense systems into Syria. Why? Have the remnants of ISIS and the Syrian rebel forces now developed a clandestine air force? Besides that, they've moved their aircraft carrier, *Admiral Kuznetsov,* just off the naval base they built in Tartus. The carrier is a mobile platform for MIG-19s, SU-33s, and an assortment of attack helicopters. They've just deployed their much more deadly MIG-29K/KUB fighters on that floating tub. Perhaps the ragtag remains of ISIS have also formed a naval force that threatens mighty Russia."

Arnon's sarcasm drew begrudging laughs. Yarkoni, the master of cynicism, helped defuse the spiraling tension.

"How did they manage to keep the *Kuznetsov* out of the repair docks for so long?" He referred to the long and troubled operating history of Russia's lone aircraft carrier. His comments brought a subdued murmur of approval.

Arnon took a few steps toward the conference table and got back on point.

"The Russians have been training Iranian pilots on their advanced strike aircraft the SU-34. Some of the better Iranian pilots have been selected to train on the Sukhoi-35s, which pose a bigger problem. The 35s, as we've discussed, are a challenge for us, even with Iranian pilots.

"Pilot training at Iran's Hamadan Air Base has gone on for months. The Kremlin has the world believing that they use that base as a staging ground for missions into Syria aimed at ISIS. The truth is that they're preparing Iran for an attack in our backyard."

"How could we have been so naïve, so stupid? How could we have fallen for Russia's sweet talk?" Tzion couldn't contain himself as he almost leapt out of his chair and again slammed his hand against the table.

Yarkoni, in complete agreement, nodded toward Tzion. Arnon knew better than to ignore Tzion's outburst.

"Igal, I couldn't agree with you more," Arnon said. "I think most of us were so focused on regional peace that we lost sight of reality. I've got to continue with the second part of our challenge." Arnon took a deep breath and continued: "8200's assessment is that Iran has planned an air attack against us on Rosh Hashana. There's been no detected enemy ground troop deployment; they'll want to ensure surprise. Their targets are sure to include our offshore oil and gas rigs, our power plants around Haifa, and the nuclear reactors at Dimona.

"Our intel points to attacks on our bases at Nevatim, Ramat David, Tel Nof, Hatzor, and Hatzerim. Ramat David and Neva-tim are home to our new squadrons of F-35s."

Arnon looked to Brigadier General Chaim Lavi: "Chaim, help us put the pieces together."

Lavi had led the clandestine Aman for seven years. His reputation as a fearless, if somewhat cavalier, warrior was legendary. Since the 1950s, Aman had functioned as an independent military intelligence service equal in stature to the regular army, air force, and navy.

With about 8,000 personnel, Aman's director had a formidable fighting force of naval intelligence units and some of Israel's elite commando detachments under his command. He produced many of the intelligence estimates on the risk of war and the strength of opposing forces.

His most daring mission came just after his promotion to assistant director of Aman. He served as the commander of one of Israel's finest counterterrorism commando units, Sayeret Matkal. He personally led the Hammer Squadron, Aman's F-16 and F-15 fighter group, on its most important mission.

With Mossad's partnership, Sayeret Matkal had identified the nuclear plant that North Korea was covertly building in a remote region of Syria's eastern desert. The reactors were to go online within weeks. Once operational, they would be environmentally risky to attack.

The Al Kibar plant, built in secrecy, was destroyed in secrecy and left as a heap of rubble. Lavi's squadron headed home with no losses.

Chaim Lavi was respected. When he spoke, people listened.

Levi stood and waved his hand apologetically. "Chaim, can we break for ten minutes? Even the head of Mossad has to occasionally take a leak."

In unison, the foreign and defense ministers sighed aloud. "Thank God." Overdue pee breaks generally evoked deity-related appreciation.

Levi left for the adjoining room to give Leora her next assignment. Leora and Joshua were in deep conversation about eliminating Abu Yusalem.

After scoping out their next few days' work, Levi paused at the door. "Should you be interested, Menachem, Alon's driver, is available. I'll send him in."

Less than twenty minutes later, the shiny black Mercedes pulled into the small settlement of Ma'ale HaZeitim on the Mount of Olives, just inside the Arab neighborhood of Ras-al Amud.

The IDF operated an indoor firing range nearby. Joshua and Leora made their way to the control desk inside the entrance, presented IDs, and received permission to use their personal Berettas.

Uncharacteristically, Joshua activated the conveyor system first and halted it when the target was at the fifty-yard marker. He took careful aim, braced his bronzed right arm with his left hand just below the elbow, and fired five rapid shots. The sound was deafening in the low-ceilinged range. The retrieval found that all five shots hit their target, albeit in a random pattern — two in the chest and three in the head.

"Impressive." Leora stood at the conveyer button and replaced Joshua's target with a new one. Barely pausing after its fifty-yard slide, Leora fired seven shots in rapid succession. No braced elbow. Suppressing a grin, she retrieved the target, which showed six hits to the head, no more than four inches apart. The seventh shot hit the figure's throat area.

Joshua said nothing, just raised both eyebrows. Menachem smirked and said, "I promise not to say a thing to anyone."

12
Security Cabinet Meeting, Day 2: The Plan Emerges

"Good to see you all back this morning." Prime Minister Simcha looked drained, with dark circles under both eyes. "Even Moshe made it on time today."

The defense minister wasn't amused.

"Zvi, brief the Cabinet in greater detail on our Mossad agents' actions in Paris," the PM said. "Should we worry?"

Levi described the events that Leora and Avram encountered in Paris and again assured his colleagues that he believed that they'd covered their tracks. He was hopeful that the Iranians wouldn't be spooked and disappear into the shadows, to emerge at another time and place. "Whatever we decide, it'll be aimed at taking out all the Iranians. We've got to let them think that their plans are a go. Time will tell," he concluded.

"Thanks, Zvi," the PM said. "Moshe and Yossi, what do the Defense Ministry and National Security think is down the road for us?" He looked to his right and nodded toward Yarkoni to begin. "What's your assessment of the military situation we're facing?"

"We'll get a shitload of the usual at the U.N., whatever actions we take," he answered, "and maybe some unpleasant repercussions from our friends. They all like to beat on us about preemptive actions."

"Igal," the PM looked left at his tight-assed chief of staff, "after Moshe, give us your take on operational options." The PM sat back in his leather chair with a deep sigh.

Yarkoni skipped an opening joke and his usual irrelevant free association. "A quick summary of our assessment, based on yesterday's Cabinet session.

"We face about forty-five advanced aircraft to our north. The SU-34s and -35s, we know, present the greatest challenge. We don't see any mobilization of ground troops or armored forces; they know we monitor all deployments."

Yarkoni continued, "The *Kuznetsov*, if it's still afloat, is not far out to sea, off Tartus. It's got eighteen to twenty fighter planes. The Russians, as we discussed, have SA-300 and -400 anti-aircraft batteries all around their bases at Tartus and Latakia."

Alon interrupted, "Moshe, don't tell us the Iranian pilots are going to fly Russia's trophy fighters."

Yarkoni nodded. "They've been training Iranian pilots for over a year; I wouldn't doubt that an occasional Russian pilot will join them. The Kremlin also tested long-range ballistic missiles — they say to better target ISIS.

"We all know that their radar has been tracking our fighter flight paths for months. They can follow most of our aircraft all the way to our Nevatim base in the Negev."

Yarkoni paused, exhaled loudly, and made his way to the front of the rectangular room, where he drew down the world map. Pointer in hand, he continued, raising his voice an octave with a passion often missing from his presentations. "The Diaspora community, as we've discussed, is facing a threat. I know we've expressed differing views on our role, but I'm satisfied we're all on the same wavelength." He glanced at Tzion, who nodded in agreement.

Aiming the laser beam at Alabama, Rome, and Paris, he reviewed the threat of Iranian Quds units poised to attack Jewish institutions in less than nine days.

Joining Yarkoni, Arnon said, "Moshe and I have assessed this situation. I'm not sure what I can add except that it's complicated immeasurably by Russia's complicity — politically, financially, and militarily."

Alon was already at their side in front of the map. The room was quiet. A rare occurrence in Israel's history was transpiring: Its Cabinet was focused and of one mind. No coffee cups clinking. No fidgety member shifting in a squeaky chair. Arnon and Yarkoni passed the pointer to Alon. He hadn't intended to use it, but holding it gave him something to do with his hands.

The foreign minister was a dapper dresser, the only Cabinet member to attend the open-collar meetings wearing a necktie and sport jacket. His colleagues often joked that he had more suits than all the rest of the Cabinet combined. His retort was often biting and condescending: "That would amount to, what, three suits?" His slim, five-foot-eleven frame belied his appetite for European desserts as a coda to sumptuous meals in Europe's capitals.

Alon held a Ph.D. in political science from Hebrew University's Department of International Politics. He was an accomplished student of European history and international relations. He knew he'd need to draw on every atom of creativity to help Israel avoid a political, if not a military, nightmare.

"OK, here goes." Alon took a deep breath and pointed toward Simcha. "You, our PM, your predecessor, and all of us have been played by the Russians. Perhaps I am the greatest offender. Having been invited to Moscow several times to bask in dreams of a rapprochement with the arms supplier of our enemies, I was intrigued by the possibilities. We have been too focused on thumbing our noses at the previous American administration and cozying up to the Big Bear."

He slapped the pointer against his palm.

"Yitzhak," Tzion called out with a rare smile on his face, "how many times do we have to remind our prime minister of our political blunders?"

"I don't have an answer Igal — maybe until we all get it? Russia," Alon continued, eager to repeat the obvious, "is positioning itself to be the major power in the Middle East, and we stand in the way. We" — Alon raised his voice — "are the link to potential U.S. intervention, which may block the Kremlin's adventurism. America's hands-off policies in our neighborhood opened the doors for them."

Alon again slapped the pointer against his hand. "Can I go on, or do we need a pee break?" he asked facetiously. Not a smirk or murmur. "If we preemptively attack their planes on the ground in Syria, Moscow will be outraged at our 'one-sided' belligerence and will declare it an act of war. If we attack the Iranian assassins as they are set to launch their attacks in Alabama, Paris, and Rome, we will be accused of territorial aggression. Three of our best friends may condemn us for having landed an invasion force across their borders."

Tzion stood, beside himself in frustration: "That's a big part of the dilemma that I was talking about."

"Igal, I couldn't agree with you more about this lose-lose situation. If we contact those friends in advance" — his caustic tone conveyed the catch-22 confronting Israel — "they'll insist that their law enforcement handle the 'allegations,' and no doubt they'll screw it up."

He rolled his chair close to the table and leaned forward. "The Iranian bastards," he said brusquely, as he slapped the table, "need to be dealt with in a way that they'll understand for years to come. How to do this effectively is left to better military minds than mine."

"Is this my cue?" The sinewy chief of staff slowly rose, rolled back his chair, took a sip of his cool coffee, and addressed the PM directly. Tzion's iron gaze matched Herzl's as he spoke. "Mr. Prime Minister, you may not like what I'm about to say. I express my opinion as a military man. You'll have my military assessment and the options open to us."

Igal Tzion, a national hero, spoke with his usual bluntness. His rise through the Israel Defense Forces became part of the country's contemporary lore.

His parents immigrated to Israel in the '50s, joining many other persecuted Jewish families forced from their homes. Many Jews set up domiciles in the frigid caves of Morocco's Atlas

Mountains.

Tzion was born on Kibbutz Hatzor in the Negev. His meteoric ascent in the military earned him the respect of virtually all of the country's fractious political parties. The young prodigy's military exploits became legendary. Tzion also was an ardent student of major battles of the last century. He often lectured on military strategies at the military academy. His charisma was a close second to that of the fabled Moshe Dayan.

"We're threatened on a multifront arena. However, because" — Tzion nodded at Levi — "Mossad does what it does best, we also stand at the doorstep of an opportunity in our history: to deal our enemies a blow."

"Igal, not like you to compliment," Levi took a chance interrupting the volatile chief of staff.

Paying little attention to Levi's comment, Tzion continued, "You know I have doubts about the political and military advisability of our offshore actions. We'll see what decisions we make as a Cabinet. It won't be long until you get my assessment of our northern and European situations and what I recommend we do.

"Russia and us? No intelligent being can trust the Big Bear. You should pardon me, Eliezer." Tzion softened his criticism by addressing the PM by his first name. "It's clear that they've been preparing their surrogates for a long time: training, equipment, and political cover."

Simcha interjected, "Igal, we're all guilty of wishful thinking."

"America has been weak in the Middle East, so the initiative has gone to the Kremlin. The Americans are far more powerful than Russia and remain our biggest supporter. The Russians don't want a confrontation with them. We are a non-NATO ally. They have to think many times before moving against us militarily. That's where Iran comes in — the Kremlin's perfect cover."

Tzion slowly scanned the room. "We've been worried about their response to a preemptive strike on their aircraft in Syria.

In my opinion, we have no choice."

Ari Kahan almost leapt out of his chair. "Igal, what do you mean no choice? Before America responds, with all of the congressional bullshit they have to go through, Russia could wipe us off the map."

"If we allow them to take off, Ari," Tzion was restrained, "we'll have dogfights over Tel Aviv's hotels. We should take them out when the bulk of them have rolled off the elevators that bring them to ground level from their underground bunkers. Obviously, Ari, we need America behind us.

"We know that the Russians have installed advanced surface-to-air missiles. They've also introduced their most sophisticated rocket launchers. We've taken this into account and have prepared squadrons of our 35s and our electronic-jamming 16s. I'm certain we can temporarily blind them.

"We've got to talk to the U.S. in advance to prep them on our findings and our plans. We hope," Tzion continued lifting his right hand heavenward, "that we can persuade the Americans to move elements of their Sixth Fleet into our Mediterranean basin. Repositioning their battle group is critical to keeping the Russians from a military response. They'll think many times before tangling with the Sixth Fleet's aircraft carriers."

Meron didn't say much, but his die-hard skepticism was always on display. "Igal, what makes you think the Americans will respond positively? What's different? Isn't it just a few new faces over there?"

Tzion took a sip of water and cleared his throat. He disliked speaking in front of others; he was more comfortable barking military commands. "Advance notice to the U.S. is critical. Then it's up to us to make a convincing case to them. So, Alex, Ari, I hope I've answered your questions. It's a big gamble.

"There's a second part to my thinking." Tzion was itching to sit down. Extended dialogue was really tough for him. "We have the most effective counterterrorism force in the world. The Americans will argue with me, but I'll settle for a tie.

"I propose that we covertly enter the three countries — the

sovereign boundaries of three of our friends — with a small force of commandos.

"Zvi, Yossi, Chaim, and I met throughout the night to work through scenarios. We'll present you with a plan to covertly enter each country, take out the terrorists, and safely get our troops out in secrecy. We're prepared to act on Sayeret Matkal's credo: Who dares wins. I know that you've heard my reservations, but this is our chance to act decisively."

Responding to the murmurs and discomfort of the other Cabinet members, the PM stood and assured them that the plans being shared with them were just that: plans and proposals. "We'll leave this meeting — whenever we do — with a unanimous agreement. There should be no dissenting opinions. We'll have plenty of time to debate and revise. Plenty of time, that is, within the next forty-eight hours."

As soon as the prime minister concluded, Levi and Tzion asked members to follow them down the corridor to the communications center. In stark contrast to the conference room, it was ablaze with technological gadgetry. Twelve-by-twelve screens covered the four-hundred-square-yard wall space. Each screen displayed sites of interest for the military. Techies were busy doing what techies do: sitting at monitors and multiple keyboards that had more controls than any Cabinet member could comprehend.

Levi asked that four locations be brought up on the screens. Meron, the laconic minister of finance, murmured half to himself and half to Alon, "My grandchildren would love this room." The straight-backed operators produced real-time satellite imagery of Birmingham, the Trastevere district in Rome, and Paris' Fourth and Eleventh Arrondissements, the main nexus of the city's Jewish businesses and the location of the terrorist base.

"With no problem," Levi said with an element of pride, "we can access the synagogues and other locations of the three cities we're discussing. We have the capacity to read Moshe's bad handwriting on a postage stamp from a height of over 30,000 feet."

The chief of staff took five long strides, joined Levi, and stood in front of the massive screens showing the challenging scenarios for commandos.

"Birmingham, Alabama," Tzion began after talking more in the past half-hour than in the previous two weeks, "is about 460 kilometers or 285 miles north of the Gulf of Mexico. I believe that for our American plan, we should use miles rather than kilometers. Our submarines will play a major role for us. We'll add ten commandos to each crew. Landing is planned for two nights before Iran's attack. Vans will be waiting for our force. We land at Orange Beach at Gulf Shores and drive up Interstate 65 to our site in Birmingham.

"We team up with Levi's local agents and put an end to Abdul Hazian and his crew. Speed and efficiency are the keys here; we'll need at least four hours to make our way back to our waiting ride home — a submarine."

The PM asked, "Is there no other way for us to enter and exit the U.S.? Detection by our best friend could be catastrophic. I'm deeply concerned about any action on American soil."

Lavi didn't say much publicly; low profile was his credo. "We're hopeful that this will be the most secure and undetectable way of entering the States. Airports are too easily monitored and closed off.

"We have six Dolphin 2-class diesel-electric submarines. They're technological wonders. The sub is capable of thirty-five knots above water and can leave our port in Ashkelon or Haifa and reach the Gulf of Mexico in less than nine days. The sub has an almost undetectable underwater signature, which will be needed to enter and exit the Gulf. It has a range of over 9,000 miles without refueling."

Forever inappropriate, Alon smirked and broke the tension, "Moshe, your signature is undetectable above water."

Tzion had little regard for Alon's wise-guy stuff but often participated in criticizing Yarkoni's unreadable handwriting. He avoided commenting and thanked Lavi. He guided the group about ten steps to the right and gestured toward a number of office chairs on casters. Pointing to a screen just to their right, he continued. “Here we have real-time coverage of the Trastevere district in Rome. The Tiber River, you’ll see, is just to its east, and there is Rome’s major synagogue only meters from the river.” The techie followed Tzion’s talk with his cursor.

“Tiberina Island is where the Fatebenefratelli Hospital is located,” Tzion said. “There is also an abandoned warehouse that’s been home base for ten terrorists. It’s a convenient location for an attack on the synagogue. On Rosh Hashana much of Rome’s Jewish community will be there. Questions?”

“Just like those animals,” Yarkoni was shaking his head, not in disbelief, but in anger, “to set up their headquarters within pissing distance of a working hospital.”

Tzion responded, “Are any of us really surprised?”

He continued: “A second sub will take our commandos on a 1,300-mile trip to Fiumicino, in the Tyrrhenian Sea. Our guys will have vans waiting for them for the twenty-mile trip to Rome on Highway A-91.

“I share these details,” Tzion said, his voice trailing off at times, “to give you a better understanding of both the possibilities of success and the complexity of the missions. We’ll team up with Zvi’s Mossad agents on this site too.”

Tzion pointed to two screens about fifteen feet to their right and asked the techie controlling those monitors to zoom in. “Our next challenge,” Tzion found some inner resolve, he hated public speaking, it was wearing him down, “Paris presents a greater operational challenge as the terrorists’ targets are widespread.

“Iran has twenty-four killers in place; some have been there for weeks. Their targets are the Synagogue des Tournelles and the Synagogue Charles Liche, both in the Fourth Arrondissement. They also plan to attack Jewish-owned businesses in the same district.”

He pointed to both oversized screens. “The screen on the left is the Fourth Arrondissement; to the right is the Eleventh, where our targets live in four rented apartments. The yellow rectangle identifies their building."

Arnon called out, "These are really challenging operations. Taking out over twenty terrorists in the middle of a major city. I'm going to ask later to see a detailed plan."

"Yossi, I couldn't agree more. Paris is our toughest operation. I go back and forth in my mind about having the Paris authorities take care of it. But you know and I know that these bastards would be back in circulation in a month or two.

"With your and my concern in mind, we plan to move our guys by sub about 3,000 miles to Le Havre. Vans will bring the team on a 120-mile trip on the A13 to Paris. This is, Yossi points out, a risky and very complex undertaking. I welcome thoughts and recommendations."

Without waiting for either, he moved on. "There is one more significant element to our plan." Tzion thankfully deferred to Lavi, who took a few steps forward and pointed to a satellite transmission of the Gulf of Oman, due south of the Persian Gulf. "We'll need a week to position our fourth sub in the Gulf of Oman."

Lavi's voice was barely audible. The whirring of the computers and a corner generator made it even harder to hear him. "We anticipate," he began, "that Iran's hardliners will demand military revenge after we complete our missions. We'll let the Americans know that this sub carries nuclear-armed supersonic and hypersonic cruise missiles targeting Tehran, Isfahan, and other sites in Iran. Of course, America and Russia will recognize these nuclear-armed missiles with their satellites. We anticipate and need their detection."

The general paid little attention to the gasps that filled the room. "We'll remind our apocalyptic friends in Iran that their dedication to eradicate Israel could turn their country into a radioactive wasteland. In addition, I'm asking our PM to open the nuclear missile silos in the Negev."

"Chaim," Yarkoni warned as he stood and paced nervously, "this hasn't been done since the '73 war."

"Moshe, I'm not sure what our alternative is," Lavi sounded almost pained. "Our military will immediately notify the Americans that we've trained our nuclear-armed Jericho 3 missiles at Tehran and at major nuclear reactors throughout the country. They'll have spotted that in seconds. We're able to deliver multiple payloads to targets 4,000 miles away with good accuracy." Lavi stopped speaking, took a loud and deep breath, and looked to the PM.

Eliezer Simcha scanned the Cabinet members' faces and, with disarming finesse and calm, said, "Gentlemen, we've got much to put into some reasonable perspective. Let's take this info back with us to the Cabinet meeting room." He thanked the technicians for their work in securing the necessary satellite imagery. Cabinet members filed out of the center silently and headed back to the drab conference room.

13
Preparing an Attack

Calm, rational analysis was often missing in action in Cabinet debates. It was a true Jewish miracle that the portraits of the state's founders and legends that dotted the room didn't wear perennial scowls. Today was different; external threats distilled disparate viewpoints into unified policies and actions.

A short line formed at the espresso machine. "Thank you, Alex," Kahan said with feigned deference, "for approving the expense."

The brief diversion produced a few chuckles.

Meron answered, "Costs will be distributed over the next two years." He patted himself on his left shoulder and added, "Finally, my generosity and vision are appreciated."

Simcha stood, and, as all returned to their seats, he said with surprising pathos, "For a few moments yesterday, I wondered if I was the leader Israel needed at this time." His face was expressionless, but he spoke with sincerity while maintaining eye contact with his Cabinet. This was unusual candor for a hardened commando officer. "My answer to myself is that I believe unequivocally that *we* are the right team to answer the challenge *we* face."

Unused to emotional discourse, the PM switched gears quickly. "What are we telling our wives and families about our extended meetings?"

Yarkoni pointed a mock accusatory finger at Meron and said, "My wife understands that Alex discovered a serious budgetary deficit that we must address."

There was a murmur of approval, some snickering, and a brief discussion about similar scenarios in the other families.

"We're less than nine days from Rosh Hashana," Simcha said, getting back on track. "How and when do we inform our citizens? How do we get them to shelters? At what point do we mobilize our reserves? How do we prepare our country for the prospect of war without tipping our hand?"

Kahan, the Cabinet's liberal burr under the saddle, offered an approach.

"Shin Bet can call for a national preventive drill," Kahan said, using his usual hand gestures but dropping his patented cynicism. "Tomorrow's papers and the 8 p.m. TV news can feature a headline story about the nationwide public drill requiring all bomb shelters to be prepared to accommodate our citizens two days before Rosh Hashana. We'll also hit every social media platform that Israelis are glued to."

"Why specifically so close to Rosh Hashana?" asked a wary Alon. "Can you imagine the outcry of the rabbinic cabal?"

"Precisely because it was Yom Kippur 1973 when we were caught with our pants down," Kahan answered. "A reflection on the past will justify our timing to the public. A limited call-up of reserve units, ostensibly to help in cleaning out the shelters, as part of a national exercise should not seem out of the ordinary. If we announce it publicly and limit the call-up, it shouldn't cause alarm, even under the ever-watchful eyes of our Russian friends."

Kahan's plan seemed reasonable to the Cabinet.

That left the thorny issue of American notification. How much — and when?

Alon and Yarkoni spoke at the same time, with Yarkoni nodding for Alon to begin. "If we were dealing with the last administration, I would have greater reservations than I feel now. Your relationship with their defense establishment, Moshe, and mine with their secretary of state lead me to believe that we can trust them or at least get a fair hearing. Except for Birmingham, I would bring them into our plan."

Brushing his thinning hair back, Yarkoni said, "I agree, and I disagree, Yitzhak. I agree about the American notification of our plans. The Russians, as we speak, are moving their Black Sea armada through the Bosporus and heading toward Syria. It should take them about five days to be in position. We have no real answer to that naval power.

"Where I disagree is about Alabama. America is the only friend that will either help us to eradicate the Quds units or assist in capturing them in the act. I can't say the same about Italy or France. Who knows what would happen if the terror forces were jailed in those countries?"

Alon interrupted, "We all know damn well what would happen. An international botch-up."

Yarkoni nodded and went on, "We can't undermine our relationship with this new administration in Washington, and we need their power. With us, Russia is a lion; with America, after all the macho bluster, they're a paper tiger. I'd like to convince them, together with you, Igal, that we could pull this off successfully."

The PM looked to Lavi for Aman's views. "We have proof of the Russians training Iranian pilots *in our backyard.* We've long known of the positioning of their advanced fighter planes, bombers, the Kremlin's sole aircraft carrier off Latakia, and destroyers capable of launching Kalibr missiles."

He interrupted the general, waving both hands, "Let's stay focused on notifying America."

Levi stood and interrupted: "We also can't minimize the threat of the Quds units that have infiltrated a number of BDS headquarters."

Again, the PM signaled a halt to the comments, extending both arms palms out. "I'm pushing you to stay focused on the merits and liabilities of informing our American ally. The timing and scope of what actions are needed are critical." Simcha wasn't ready to back-burner this most important issue.

Peering at his political nemesis, Kahan of Shin Bet, the PM asked facetiously, "Can we go on, Ari?"

Five minutes later, all agreed they would come clean to their greatest friend. They hoped that the current American administration would be more assertive and supportive than the previous one, which they saw as feckless and ambivalent about support of the Jewish state.

"So we've agreed that we'll inform the U.S. of our proposed actions," the PM said. "I say *proposed* because we've got to agree on actions we'll take. Only then will I request an urgent meeting with their ambassador."

He pointed to three of the men. "Moshe, Yitzhak, Igal, I ask that you join me. I hope the ambassador can meet us tomorrow. Yitzhak, you'll need to set this up after I call the American president to tell him of the urgency of our visit."

The military plans would be debated. Israel had fought multifront battles, but never in such far-flung regions with a global power openly supporting its adversaries. Tzion stood and addressed the Cabinet with Herzl's portrait glaring over his left shoulder.

"It's less than nine days to the eve of Rosh Hashana," the chief of staff began, looking at the PM. "What we decide here will be put into the military pipeline within minutes after a green light. Eliezer, I'll need your prime ministerial blessing."

Tzion was revved up; this was what he enjoyed reporting. "OK, here goes. I'll put our air force on full but silent alert. Our squadrons of F-35s will be on standby. Without calling up reserves, I can put a number of our elite brigades on battle-ready alert. I'll ensure that Tel Nof and Hatzerim air bases retain forces large enough to repel any trouble that may come from Gaza."

Yarkoni asked, "Igal, I know we've talked about our military action plans. But how sure are you that putting our air force on full alert, even silent alert, can go undetected?"

"Moshe, I agree that it's risky. The alert must be low profile. I'll try to coordinate it with the air force's war games. I'm open to suggestions after the meeting." Tzion moved on. "I've begun assembling teams of commandos drawn from Sayeret Matkal and Shayetet 13. Unit commanders will be informed of the European and American targets only when they're at sea on the submarines. I'll meet with our naval commanders before the day is over.

"Our second sub will leave for the Gulf of Oman tomorrow evening. It'll be armed with eight nuclear-tipped MIRV cruise missiles — God forbid they should be needed. Remember, we'll inform the Americans of this in advance and understand that Russian satellites will detect the warheads when our sub surfaces in the Gulf."

"What do you mean the *second* sub will leave?" Meron asked. "What happened to the first?"

It would be the finance minister who caught Tzion's omission.

Tzion smiled wryly, a rarity for him. "The first sub left two days ago with ten commandos on board. They're headed for America but don't know why yet. If America says absolutely no Israeli action on their soil, we'll turn back." He held out both hands in faux apology. "They needed almost nine days to get there."

There was a collective gulp. It didn't go unnoticed that this action came before the Cabinet's first meeting and debate. No one commented on this unilateral decision.

Tzion continued, speaking with characteristic calm, almost as if he were describing Monopoly moves, "We'll also prepare our land-based missiles once the PM gives us the go-ahead."

Tzion abruptly stopped talking — as if prompted by a silent cue. With an air of theatrics, not generally his style, he took four long strides to his left, paused, and then slowly sat back in his swivel chair, eyes directed at his colleagues.

Yarkoni, taking the initiative, picked up on the Security Council chief's look of consternation. "Yes, Yossi?"

"What are the consequences of Italy and France exposing our actions?"

"In my opinion, disastrous," Yarkoni shot back.

"And the consequences of inaction?" Tzion asked as nonconfrontationally as he could.

"Even more disastrous," Yarkoni responded with even greater conviction.

"Why does the Masada scenario come to mind?" Kahan moaned. "I guess I support our developing plan. Apocalyptic leadership heads Iran. Let's present them with an apocalyptic vision of *our* design."

The PM stood, "Ari, no guessing here — you agree or you don't? No cute stuff."

He was prepared to conclude the meeting when the door behind him opened and an aide entered and whispered, cupping his hand over the PM's ear.

"Ambassador William Sundblad has responded to my text message," Simcha announced, "and will meet with us at 8:30 tomorrow morning. He's cleared his morning calendar for us. We'll reconvene tomorrow at 3 p.m." The PM rapped his knuckles against the table and said, "I need to hear from each of you before I attend that meeting. Do you endorse the plans we heard from Igal, Chaim, and Moshe?"

Each member voiced approval with no apparent reservations.

"I support our military plan," the PM affirmed, "and will hold back implementation until our meeting with the ambassador. Our resolution should remind us of our commitment that Jews will not be persecuted or slaughtered with impunity. We've been down that road too many times in our history." He inhaled a long, deep breath. "Until tomorrow afternoon, gentlemen."

14
America, Israel Needs Help

Menachem weaved the black Mercedes through a maze of concrete bollards into the American Embassy's diplomatic parking area. They now faced the eastern side of the embassy just in front of the guard booth.

Two Marines approached the car, one on each side. The vehicle was swept for explosives despite its government plates and the scheduled meeting. The sentries saluted the prime minister after the brief inspection and ordered the protective metal arm raised.

Yarkoni had arranged to pick up Tzion, Lavi, and Simcha at the prime minister's residence. The ride to the embassy was infinitely more pleasant because of its controversial move to Jerusalem. It was temporarily housed in the former Prima Prince Hotel on King George Street in the heart of West Jerusalem.

The modest-size hotel had been under financial duress for some time as new and glitzy accommodations attracted tourists. Its bankruptcy afforded the new American administration a convenient option as it engineered the diplomatic migration from Tel Aviv to Jerusalem. A permanent embassy was to be completed within eighteen months; the interim site had undergone several months of reconfiguration, giving it an appearance of permanency.

An attaché greeted them as they got out of Menachem's shiny black chariot. "Mr. Prime Minister, gentlemen, how are you this morning?"

"Jared, very good to see you," the PM responded. "Thanks for making this visit possible on such short notice."

"Not a problem, sir. I caught the urgency of the request."

They made their way to the entrance as a gentle westerly breeze redolent with the scent of Jerusalem's pines caressed them. The sun was brilliant despite the early hour, with no clouds in sight. For a millisecond the PM thought, *what could be bad on a morning like this*?

Jared ushered them toward the ambassador's conference room. It was no coincidence that his office and the adjacent meeting rooms were windowless and located at the center of the building. American voters weren't the only people bitterly divided over the embassy relocation.

Palestinian leadership felt that the Americans' decision was a betrayal of their claim to Jerusalem as the capital of their future Palestinian state. Many left-of-center Israelis felt that the move complicated potential peace talks with the Palestinians.

The ambassador's offices and meeting area had been reinforced. The odors of curing cement and wet paint hung heavily in the narrow, bare-walled corridor. Ornately framed portraits of presidents and the U.S. Constitution would fill that space once the pale-gray paint dried.

Security rather than aesthetics was the prevailing concern. Despite an Israeli police detail and the Marines guards, caution was the Middle East's perennial prescription.

As they neared the ambassador's private rooms, a door swung open.

"Hello, Eliezer. Moshe, good to see you," William Sundblad greeted them warmly. "Welcome, General Tzion and General Lavi."

"The prime minister you call by his first name, and me," Tzion joked, "you formally refer to as General Tzion."

"On your next visit my greeting will be 'Hello, Igal.' Please come on in."

Tzion focused on the "come on in." Why both *on* and *in*?

Sundblad had been the ambassador to Israel for almost eighteen months, about as long as Simcha had been prime minister. He was born in Kansas City, Missouri, fifty-some years earlier. In his early thirties, he moved to New York after graduating from Columbia Law School. He remained in New York for twenty years, founding the successful international law firm Sundblad and McPherson.

At the time of his appointment as ambassador, his firm had 130 affiliated attorneys and countless associates, law interns, and support staff. Sundblad was proud of the firm's history of international corporate representation specializing in mergers and acquisitions.

Significant financial achievements of the eminently successful often are accompanied by physiological or psychological infirmities. Sundblad, an immensely successful attorney, had severe gastritis and a right hand that trembled bearing the weight of a glass of water. His skin was sallow, and his receding hairline made him look older than his years. He retained his piercing gaze, his sharp mind, and his inexplicably strong love of Israel.

The PM often wondered from where Sundblad's passion for Israel sprang. Conversations with Sundblad, more often than not, were steeped in professional objectivity and a demand for viewing all sides equally. He grasped the essence of complex political situations that flourished in the Middle East like an algae bloom in an untended swimming pool.

"Gentlemen, are you OK with Jared remaining with us while we discuss what brings you here?"

"William, if you're OK with Jared," the PM said, "we certainly are."

"Before we start, coffee or a cold drink? Jared, will you ask Alan to come in, please?"

It took only moments for Alan, a well-scrubbed twenty-something, to return with their drinks. Yarkoni thought it a nice touch having a man take the drink requests.

"Gentlemen, we have all morning or longer if we need; Jared, make sure the door is shut." Sundblad rolled his chair from behind his polished, cluttered desk and brought it near his visitors.

"Mr. Ambassador, our country is facing a very serious threat." The prime minister's formal salutation confirmed the gravity of the visit. "We're here to share our intel and our plans. You represent our closest friend and ally, and we'll describe in detail what we need from you."

The ambassador leaned toward Simcha and focused on the PM's face. Sundblad's furrowed brow accentuated the wrinkles on his forehead. He was concentrating and totally tuned in. Jared was pecking away at his iPad. His and Sundblad's were the only such devices allowed in the embassy.

"Please understand that we're informing you in advance of our actions. We're not asking for direct military assistance. That is, no American boots on the ground. We're now eight days from a major attack on our country."

The PM, then the chief of staff, then Lavi detailed the Rosh Hashana threat.

Halfway through the briefing, the ambassador waved both hands toward the PM, turned, and said, "Jared, please get the communication center to patch in the secretary of state. Tell them to green-line it."

Simcha assumed the ambassador was speaking about an encryption band.

"Sir," Jared said, "it's 1:45 a.m. in Washington."

The look on Sundblad's face conveyed that no further comments were necessary.

"I'll be right back, Mr. Ambassador. Gentlemen."

Within minutes, the sixty-inch computer screen on the conference table to the left was filled with a surprisingly clear-eyed career politico. Bryce Emerson had been a lukewarm supporter of Israel since becoming secretary of state.

He brushed back his full head of graying hair with both hands and grumbled, "Not much we can hide on a large-screen transmission. Thank you, William, for making me part of what must be an issue of great importance." The comment conveyed no trace of sarcasm.

The Israeli government welcomed many of the secretary's

political positions. The right-wingers, however, were deeply concerned when he continually questioned the value of Israel's settlements — music to the ears of Shin Bet's Ari Kahan. Emerson bridled at the seemingly inviolable Israeli contentions that settlements held religious and strategic importance.

"Hello, Mr. Secretary," Sundblad greeted Emerson. "Apologies for the hour." He acknowledged those sitting at his conference table. The PM and in turn Tzion, Lavi, and Yarkoni shared the Iranian-Russian plan of attack and the military actions Israel would take to thwart them.

Emerson was a thoughtful, if disagreeable, international personage. His raspy smoker's voice contributed to his reputation as a cantankerous politician, which, while it was well deserved, obscured his incisive, analytical mind. The American president valued his opinions and regarded his reports on foreign affairs as indispensable.

Simcha allowed the silence after their report to hang over their collective heads. He knew that Emerson never shot from the hip; silence wasn't disengagement but intelligent absorption.

"Mr. Prime Minister and gentlemen, you may attribute this part of my response to the early hour here and the certainty that my guard is down somewhat. But your attack force on American soil? No fucking way. Other than that, let's talk."

None of them reacted outwardly to Emerson's declaration. Simcha knew they had room to negotiate. Emerson's opening gambits were often intentionally provocative.

"Your analyses and action plans put us on the brink of a major international military conflict, possibly a nuclear confrontation. Help me to better understand your sources of information and your degree of confidence."

"Mr. Secretary, we have not met. I'm Chaim Lavi, brigadier general in charge of Aman."

"I know who you are, sir, and I have a great deal of respect for your accomplishments. I know all about Aman. Forgive me for sounding like what in truth I am, a grumpy secretary of state."

"Then you know, Mr. Secretary, that Aman is an independent military intelligence body coordinating the efforts of our military branches. Our Inner Cabinet has met over the last several days to analyze the data from our Mossad agents in Syria, Belarus, France, Italy, and, you should pardon the indiscretion, America.

"We're certain that the Russians have helped plan, train, and fund the Iranian Quds Force for attacks on Jewish communities in Europe and America. Russia has trained Iranian pilots to fly their most advanced aircraft based in Syria.

"Their aircraft carrier is stationed off the coast of Syria, and their powerful Black Sea Fleet is, as we speak, moving through the Bosporus — supposedly on a training exercise. They've been using Syria as a testing ground for their most advanced hardware. Our satellites have picked up the stationing of Russia's most advanced Iskander missiles in Latakia. These missiles, as you no doubt know, have a range of 400 miles. We're in easy range.

"Our assessment is that the Russians have played us all; they're using the Iranians as their proxies and see this as a major step toward achieving Middle East dominance. They're betting on the indecisiveness of a new American administration and the prior eight years of American disinclination to stand up to Russian aggression."

"Igal Tzion here — we've met on several occasions, Mr. Secretary."

"General Tzion, it may be an ungodly hour here, but the time of day hasn't affected my memory," Emerson said caustically. "Go on."

Tzion hesitated, swallowed twice, took a sip of tepid American filtered coffee, and looked straight at the monitor and into the reddened eyes of the grouchy secretary of state.

"Mr. Secretary, we have about eight days to deliver a major blow to Iran's global terrorism and Russia's support of their efforts. We want to inform you, our greatest friend, what we intend to do." He didn't wait for a response.

"The Russians have been prepping Iranian pilots to fly their most advanced aircraft. The training has been ongoing both in Latakia and Iran. We knew of the collaboration, but our agents only uncovered the real intent a short while ago. We intend to take those aircraft out before they leave the ground on the morning of Rosh Hashana, which falls on September 7.

"We intend to use, among other aircraft, the F-35s which we purchased from you. Should we fail to launch a preemptive strike, we'll face Russia's SU-34s and SU-35s in dogfights over your embassy and our Tel Aviv hotels. Of course, a preemptive strike opens us up to Russian and international condemnation, as they'll deny the real intent of their proxies. They will no doubt declare this an act of war.

"Teams of our commandos and Mossad agents will eliminate the attackers who plan mass murders of our Jewish communities in Rome and Paris — also to be carried out on Rosh Hashana. We have plans to transport our teams by submarines to and from locations off the Italian and French coasts."

The secretary's brow became more deeply creased with each revelation.

"Tell me again," he said, lighting a cigarette, "how reputable and vetted this information is." He seemed satisfied that the confirmation was identical to that of the start of the transmission. He slowly exhaled a plume of gray-blue smoke. "Go on."

"Mr. Secretary," Yarkoni began.

"Hello, Moshe," the secretary grumbled. "Good to hear from you too."

Yarkoni thought that Bryce Emerson did his best to sound like a gruff Winston Churchill impersonator. "Mr. Secretary, this brings us to the next step. As a clear message to Iran, should they consider a retaliatory assault with their ballistic missiles, Israel will send two forms of warning. Within the next hours, we'll dispatch a submarine to the Gulf of Oman, a sub equipped with cruise missiles that will be armed with the nuclear warheads that we have publicly maintained we do not have.

"These missiles will be locked in to key targets in Iran."

Yarkoni paused to let the point sink in. “Our submarine will surface in the Gulf and will be detected by Russian satellites, which will identify our weaponry and the plotted trajectory with no difficulty. This is what we want.

“Further, Mr. Secretary, our land-based missiles will also be mounted with the same ‘nonexistent’ warheads targeting Tehran and their nuclear reactors throughout the country. We expect the same satellite detection.

“Finally, sir, we would like to confer with you on the elimination of the twenty-four Quds fighters heavily armed and currently plotting attacks in Birmingham, Alabama. They are poised to join their comrades in a coordinated attack on Jewish institutions.”

“And for this you wake me in the middle of the night?”

Emerson’s ill-timed humor brought no response.

“What are you asking of us? I’ve just texted my assistant and asked that an emergency meeting be set up with the president tomorrow. That is, later this morning.”

“Several things, Mr. Secretary,” the PM answered. “Your understanding of our imminent danger here and abroad is paramount. Russia’s Black Sea Fleet and their Caspian Flotilla are on their way here and present a challenge to us that we cannot meet. Their publicly announced training maneuvers are a paper-thin cover.”

“Our request,” Yarkoni concluded, his throat parched, “is that you consider moving battle groups of your Sixth Fleet into our Mediterranean basin. The Russians will think many times over before risking any confrontation with that force. No boots on the ground on your end. No direct military assistance.”

“Well, I can already hear the answers of the secretary of defense and the chairman of the Joint Chiefs.” Emerson feigned a moan. “My undersecretary just texted me that the president has asked them to attend the meeting. While they’ll offer total support, they’ll question whether you’ve vetted the data 100 percent and if you’re acting rashly and disproportionately. And they’ll bitch and yell: ‘Moving a battle group of aircraft carriers and their escorts isn't military assistance?'

"But we're behind you. We'll give serious consideration to an Israeli action on American soil despite my earlier response. Bill, we'll be back to you shortly; keep the line open. Gentlemen, will you reconvene in Bill's office at 10 p.m. your time?"

"We'll be here," Simcha answered. "For our teams to be in place off Italy and France and in the Gulf of Oman, we'll need to dispatch them within twenty-four to thirty-six hours. And, of course, we need to hear from you about Birmingham. Good night, Mr. Secretary. And thank you."

The Israeli entourage stood moments after the transmission ended.

"Thank you, Mr. Ambassador," Simcha said as they shook hands warmly.

"I know that you've heard that we're 100 percent behind you. As you no doubt understand, we'll need to play this cautiously to avoid a superpower nuclear confrontation."

"We never doubted it, William. This is an unprecedented attack on Israel and the world's Jewish community. We're prepared to take the battle to our enemy. We do, however, need you to keep the Russians at bay."

Jared and William ushered the four Israelis to the door. "We'll see you at 10 p.m."

Sundblad waved goodbye with his left hand. His right hand trembled as he raised a fresh bottle of Evian to his lips.

15

Preparing for the President

Early arrival at an Israeli Inner Cabinet meeting occurred as frequently as the appearance of Halley's Comet. Today was different. The PM and his embassy team arrived at 2:15 that Tuesday afternoon.

Half-empty sandwich platters were arranged in random patterns in front of Alon and Alex Meron. "Good to see that you sustained yourselves in our absence," Simcha quipped.

Cabinet members had varying levels of interaction with the astute but abrasive American secretary of state, so when Simcha reviewed their discussion, commentary was unnecessary.

"We've been asked to return to the embassy at 10 tonight. The secretary will meet with their president, the chairman of the Joint Chiefs of Staff, and who knows whom else. I believe that he understood and maybe endorsed our actions — except for Alabama. No surprise. We made it clear that we needed the Sixth Fleet to move quickly to drive some sense into our Russian friends."

The PM munched on a triangular egg salad sandwich and sipped the double espresso that Alon, without being asked, had placed in front of him.

He leaned forward, peering down the length of the table. "Ari, what's your thinking about timing for the announcement of public air raid drills?"

"I've convened a meeting of the editors of four major papers and the director-general of the Israel TV Network," Kahan responded. "We meet tomorrow morning. Unless there's a suggestion to the contrary, I'll call the drill two days before Rosh Hashana. Shelters will be ready for any eventuality, and the rabbis won't be too upset."

There were no dissenting comments.

"I know that we need America's blessing on our major actions," Tzion said. "We're asking for an enormous act of support: the immediate movement of a battle group of the Sixth Fleet and their approval of an Israeli military action on their soil. These decisions must be made now." He was his usual emphatic self as he slapped his knee.

"We're meeting with the Americans, if only electronically, in a few hours; can't plans wait until then?" Yarkoni's question had an irritated tone that Tzion found provocative.

Tzion extended both hands onto the table. "We're on a very short fuse. In order to position our submarine off America's coast, we need about one more week; we took a risk with that early departure. The Gulf of Oman mission will also take over a week. Positions off France and Italy, while closer, will take four to five days.

"I've had commanders assemble and equip our commando teams for a voyage in the open sea. We're not sure how the dialogue with America's president and military men will go, but we need to act."

"What does 'act' mean, Igal?" Alon asked.

"We need to dispatch our sub to the Gulf," Tzion said. He was at ease giving military directives. "We've already released our first commando unit headed for America. That trip will take the better part of a week. If the Americans object, we'll listen to their plan. If it's better than ours, we can always turn back.

"As we speak, we're preparing our missiles that will target sites in Iran. When the PM says go, we arm the nukes." Tzion turned to Simcha with a nod. "We'll need two days to complete this. All fighter pilot and technician leaves are canceled, and all are in a state of readiness. They're not sure why, but they'll know soon enough.

"Two additional points, Mr. PM." Whenever Tzion addressed Simcha by his title, it had a touch of cynicism. "First, we meet as early as convenient tomorrow morning, as we are only eight days out now.

"Second is that you, Zvi," Tzion looked to his left, "bring your agent, the one that made the presentations to us, back to review our strike plans in the three foreign locations. And since you coaxed Joshua Canaan out of retirement, his opinion will be invaluable."

Levi rose and slowly smoothed his salt-and-pepper hair on both sides, where it was a little thicker. "Just last night I received a call from our agent requesting that she accompany the force headed to Italy. She'd prefer France but feels uncertain how her blown cover will affect plans. Under different conditions, I would have agreed to put her on a team. But she and Joshua Canaan will track down Yusalem before he attacks. I'll ask her and Joshua to come immediately. If you're OK with it," he turned to the PM with his right palm extended, "both of them could be here within the hour."

Leora and Joshua stayed for dinner. She was impressive in her two-hour detailed analysis of each attack plan. She assessed the points of arrival, the transportation to the target areas, the means of addressing the terror groups, and the route, time frame, and destination of the exits. Joshua agreed, added some strategic points, but reminded all that he hadn't scouted any of the locations.

Mossad agents rarely advanced rapidly. Mossad had spotted Leora in her first year at Israel's premier technical university, the Technion.

Leora and her parents had emigrated from Rio de Janeiro nineteen years earlier when she was twelve years old. Her parents, Louisa and Roberto Benafull, had anticipated that Brazil's economy would deteriorate and that Jews would become the scapegoats. They planned a rapid immigration to Israel. The Benafulls, descendants of a line of Portuguese Jews, were reluctant to consider name changes in their new country.

Her parents arrived in Israel with daughter Livia in tow and settled in Tel Aviv's northern suburbs. They soon selected an Israeli surname, Bargal, to help in their assimilation.

"No one's heard of the name Livia. The kids in my class keep pushing me to sound more Israeli," Livia lamented to her parents. Her father was reluctant to change both her given name and surname.

Her mother was more understanding of the preteen's need to be part of their new culture. "What name sounds right to you?"

"Leora is the name I want to be called," she told her parents over dinner.

With her father's reluctant consent, she soon assumed her new name. What she didn't shed were her almond-shaped emerald eyes and her striking features.

Leora had a photographic memory in addition to a mind that was continually searching for scientific cause and effect. Her second-year physics professor at the Technion moonlighted as a consultant for a military hardware startup linked to Mossad.

At a meeting with a Mossad contact, he described Leora. "I'd like you to meet this young woman who is exceptionally intelligent, has an unusually retentive memory, and an inclination to challenge conventionality."

"She's already been identified as a prospect," the Mossad agent answered. "We spotted her during her mandatory military service before the Technion."

Leora's marksmanship turned many heads during her military stint. Her skill with handguns and semiautomatic weapons seemed to come naturally. She brought a unique ability to remain calm and focused on a task in the face of almost any challenge.

Her career with Mossad began shortly after she graduated from the rigorous four-year program with honors — in three years. When she accepted an offer to join the Office, she informed the panel of three male interviewers that she would refuse any assignments requiring her to entrap targets using sex. "I would like to be clear that, as honored as I am to be considered to join Mossad, I look forward to working as an equal, side by side, with the men of Mossad." An uncomfortable silence, some whispers exchanged by the panel, was followed with "We're pleased to have you join us at Mossad."

Now, as a respected member of the Office, Leora reviewed the three plans of action on foreign soil as outlined by the chief of staff. The finance minister refrained from asking about travel expenditures.

Leora confirmed that the plans were just as she and the embedded agents had envisioned them. New to the mix? The plan for her and Joshua Canaan to eliminate Abu Yusalem. Both Leora and Joshua shared their dedication to help Yusalem achieve his goal of martyrdom in Paris. In three days they would set out to eliminate Yusalem as a global threat and as the linchpin of the coordinated attacks on Diaspora Jews.

16
Meeting the President

The black Mercedes idled in the reserved parking area. At 9 p.m., the prime minister, the defense minister, the chief of staff, and Aman's General Lavi met in the dimly lit corridor outside the PM's office. Menachem greeted them by his shiny chariot and held the door open for his passengers.

They pulled into the American Embassy about forty minutes later. Once again, the car was rigorously inspected.

Jared was waiting at the entrance. The PM wondered: *When will I find an attaché willing to attend a late-night meeting?*

"The ambassador is waiting," Jared said, greeting the visitors. "We've set up in our new communications room. The large screen should help with lots of participants."

Simcha thought, *how could Jared be so bouncy at this hour*?

The narrow corridor leading to the ambassador's office and the media center once again irritated their nostrils. The vapors of curing concrete and new carpeting were more intense in this area than near his private office. Jared, with an apparent sense of pride, ushered them into a surprisingly large open area.

Tzion, whose family had often stayed at the Prima Prince Hotel, thought he recognized the space as its former dining room.

William Sundblad, in a short-sleeved shirt and no tie, a rarity for him, was waiting with the usual array of bottled water, orange drinks, and cloverleaf-shaped butter biscuits. He guided them to a row of vinyl office chairs. "I set these up here," Sundblad explained, "so that we can view the large screen better and have a good exchange of thoughts."

Yarkoni braced himself. "Exchange of thoughts" implied divergent viewpoints.

Despite the imposing floor-to-ceiling screen, Tzion could think only of his family visiting the former hotel. He recalled with mortification his two-year-old nephew tossing a glass to the floor of the dining room. With a floor of stone tiles, there was no hope of avoiding breakage.

How can I dredge up such trivial memories when war is on the horizon? Tzion thought perhaps breakage was a metaphor for something more sinister, as breaking a glass at some Moroccan festive events might augur bad luck.

"Jared will arrange for our secure transmission from Washington. I know, I know what you're thinking," Sundblad feigned a scowl. "We learned a lot a year and a half ago about vulnerable elements in what we thought were secure communications. The Russians are good at finding chinks in the armor."

"Well," Lavi said, "thankfully, we found a — what is that word? — In *their* communications armor."

Sundblad defined *chink*.

Jared manipulated a few dials, sparking a fifteen-second interference crackle. Despite the lack of the familiar swooping sound that signaled the start of a remote electronic connection, the screen lit up. A clear picture appeared — easily recognizable men sitting around a polished brown conference desk.

Sundblad, setting down his bottle of water and steadying his trembling right hand, began.

"Good afternoon, Mr. President. Thank you, Secretary Emerson, for your counsel during our earlier review. While I believe we're all acquainted with one another, allow me to introduce General Al Peterson, chairman of the Joint Chiefs of Staff."

The general nodded.

"To the right is the director of the CIA, Alex Pratley, Secretary Emerson, and Mr. Jack Blaine, White House chief counsel."

"Hello, Mr. President," Simcha began without getting the sign from Sundblad to proceed. "To my left is Moshe Yarkoni, Israel's defense minister; General Igal Tzion, IDF's chief of staff;

and finally Brigadier General Chaim Lavi, the director-general of Aman."

While most participants were acquainted with one another, the formal intro lent seriousness to the meeting.

"Mr. Prime Minister, great to see you again, if only from afar," said President Richard Trainor. "It may be afternoon here, but I realize it's quite late in your neck of the woods."

Simcha had been invited to Washington to meet with Trainor twice in the eighteen months of his presidency. They had formed a strong bond.

The acrimony that was the hallmark of the relationship between their predecessors was thankfully a thing of the past. President Trainor had privately shared with the Israeli prime minister that he regarded his country as among the staunchest and most powerful of American allies worldwide.

"Gentlemen, I want you to know that we understand from Secretary Emerson's report that you face a serious threat. We're also aware of the risk to members of the Jewish communities in Rome, Paris, on our territory, and to your own homeland. Your country is an important ally. We're prepared to back your efforts — short of committing our troops at this point."

The President continued, "We have, however, mobilized elements of our Sixth Fleet: the aircraft carriers *Dwight D. Eisenhower*, *Harry S. Truman*, and *Ronald Reagan*, with a number of guided missile cruisers and destroyers as their escorts. Al Peterson will convey my formal order to move our forces toward the Mediterranean. Now, gentlemen, we're ready to listen."

"Thank you, Mr. President," Simcha said. "First and perhaps foremost, Russia has deceived the world. They claim to be withdrawing from Syria while they're building their military capacity throughout the country. They're field-testing their most advanced armaments on Syrian populations — all in the name of fighting terrorism. They've trained Iranian pilots to attack Israel on the morning of Rosh Hashana, September 7."

General Peterson snapped, "Hold on, sir. I would ask that you speak only for your country. It won't do any of us any good to have you speak for the world." Peterson was used to looking straight at a screen or someone across the table and speaking his mind. He may have been a supporter, but he spoke for the most powerful country on Earth and wasn't shy about it.

"Thank you, General. You're correct. Apologies for getting carried away."

Undeterred and not really apologetic, Simcha continued: "Iran plans to attack Jewish communities in three cities outside Israel. They are determined to hit Jews anywhere they can. They've infiltrated Quds Force commandos into BDS offices in those cities mentioned.

"They're well-armed and constitute enough troops to be considered an invasion force."

Pratley rattled off a quick response: "Isn't that what you guys intend to do, invade other countries?"

"General Pratley, I believe that we are all able to make a sharp distinction between terrorist acts and self-protection — even on foreign soil."

Knowing how confrontational Pratley could be, he continued, "We've tracked Abdul Hazian, Ibrahim Ashrawi, and Ishmael Al Fazzi, terrorist leaders familiar to you, for months. Each one heads a terror squad. The combined Quds forces in the three locations discussed are sixty-one terrorists. The deadliest of them, Abu Yusalem, the coordinator of these and other attacks, has been in our crosshairs for weeks."

"Sorry to interrupt, Mr. Prime Minister," Peterson interjected more calmly. "I know that y'all will share the details of these operations, but how reliable are the data? A number is gonna suffice for now."

"General Peterson, Chaim Lavi here. I can tell you with the greatest assurance that we are 100 percent confident in these reports. We have had some of our most trusted Mossad agents embedded in these terrorist groups.

Making no attempt to hide his annoyance about Pratley's comparisons, Lavi continued: "We've had weeks of drone surveillance of our northern borders. Aman's intelligence unit has cracked the encrypted communication system used by Russian and Iranian pilots training at Khmeimim in Syria and Iran's air base at Hamadan. And last but not least, our Unit 8200—which needs no introduction to you—has exhaustively vetted all our data."

"Thank you, General," Peterson answered.

"Thank you, General Lavi and General Peterson." Simcha took the reins again. "As you can imagine, we've been monitoring the Russian buildup in our backyard with alarm. They, as you know, are constructing a massive air base near Latakia, with the longer runways required by the SU-34s and SU-35s.

"They are, as we speak, expanding ports off Tartus with deep-water berths able to accommodate Russian warships. A long stay is planned." He paused for comments — he could only imagine what Blaine, a certain anti-Semite, was thinking. "Their proxy, Iran, is using vast amounts of the billions of dollars released through their nuclear deal to develop and purchase advanced weaponry, including intercontinental ballistic missiles."

Blaine couldn't resist. "Those purchases are the direct result of our previous administration's wishful thinking."

"Thankfully, Mr. Blaine, I was not on that planning committee." The PM felt that parrying Blaine's comments with some vanilla humor would hide his antipathy. Staying on point about what Israel faced, he went on: "The Russian aircraft we're most concerned with are the forty 34s and 35s. Russia has helped plan the attack from our north. Our intel reveals that they aim to strike our chemical plants in Haifa, our nuclear facility in Dimona, and a number of air bases in the north and in the Negev region.

"We believe that we can jam or take out their S-400s, S-300s, and SA-23s in a preemptive strike." Simcha, with a puzzled look, held out both hands. "What? Did they install surface-to-air missiles to ward off the powerful ISIS air force?"

The PM took a long breath and a swig of bottled water before continuing. "Here is where we run the greatest risk of a confrontation we cannot win. If we take out their fighter planes on the ground, Russia will claim that we declared war on them. After all, the planes were only *innocently* parked on the tarmac.

"Further, a successful attack can come only if we fly the stealth fighters purchased from you. We hope this won't roil the international political waters. Russia monitors all of our air movements down to the Negev. Only the stealth fighters evade their satellites and radar."

"The plot thickens for us, Mr. President," Emerson said, emphasizing what his American counterparts understood clearly: This was yet another way the U.S. could get entangled in a war not of its making.

"Sir, you are absolutely correct," Simcha responded. "However, if we don't launch a preemptive strike on those Russian planes and Iranian pilots, we'll be in dogfights over our heavily populated cities of Haifa and Tel Aviv."

"Gentlemen, how long have you known of this plot?" Pratley asked. He had been through the mill, approved as the CIA chief only after long and laborious Senate hearings. He was an outspoken tough guy pushing for expanded covert operations worldwide.

He didn't speak the duplicitous language of self-serving politicians, which made him unpopular in Washington's political circles. But he admired Mossad and had a deepening friendship with Levi.

"Mr. Pratley, this is Igal Tzion, IDF chief of staff."

"Good evening, General," Pratley said. "I'm familiar with your résumé as a military commander and armored-warfare strategist. Shit, we could learn something from a guy like you."

"Thank you, sir." Tzion loved the praise but pretended to take it in stride. "We assessed and analyzed all the data before concluding seventy-two hours ago that it was, unfortunately, accurate. We took the unusual step of sending a top Mossad agent to each of the three foreign sites where attacks are planned to get full assessments from lead agents.

"As for the northern attack plan, we've had several locals

embedded in work crews in the air bases. They've fed us invaluable intel at great personal risk."

Simcha interjected, "The Russians, as you are no doubt monitoring, are moving significant elements of their Caspian Flotilla, supposedly heading for the Mediterranean on a training exercise." Simcha wasn't at all sure that the Americans had been carefully tracking the Russians. "Finally, sir, our satellites and drones have detected Russian Iskander SS-26 missiles in Latakia. We believe that we can disable their tracking systems."

Peterson leaned forward, chin on his clenched fist. "Mr. Prime Minister, what do y'all want of us? What are your plans to counter these threats? What actions do y'all need from our president?"

The chairman of the Joint Chiefs was a hard-nosed pragmatist with a sharper military mind than anyone in the president's Cabinet. No need for small talk, just clear action plans, an understanding of the political implications, and a backup should Plan A fail. He was no friend of the Israeli government's policies regarding settlements; he saw them as tinder for conflagration. But he understood that Israel had become a military and technological powerhouse and was the bedrock of stability for 1,000 miles in any direction. Protecting it against Russia was in America's interest.

"Mr. Prime Minister, may I respond?" Yarkoni asked in a faux deferential voice.

The PM nodded.

"Moshe Yarkoni here, defense minister. I introduce myself only because I haven't had the pleasure of meeting your counsel, Mr. Blaine. What we need of you, Mr. President, is vital to our success. Perhaps most important is an understanding that Russia is orchestrating this threat. They have trained Iranian pilots and overseas Quds Force terror squads to achieve regional domination. They've parked their *Kuznetsov* aircraft carrier within swimming distance of our shore. We've asked you to position your powerful Sixth Fleet near us to make the Russian navy less adventurous.

"We must preemptively strike," Yarkoni involuntarily smacked his lap, "the Russian planes and Iranian pilots before their attack from the north. As you are aware, supersonic fighters can reach us from Syria in under a half-hour."

"Kinda like attacking us in Washington from Philadelphia," Pratley sounded like his typical confrontational self.

Not sure whether Pratley was being Pratley or offering a helpful comparison, Yarkoni acknowledged the comment, "Yes sir. That is about the distance we are dealing with."

He moved on, "We have counterterrorism commando units ready to board our subs to head to Paris, Rome, and Alabama. We have ingress and egress plans, which we will share with you. Two sensitive issues — at least two — are connected to these plans.

"First," Yarkoni gulped, "is your permission and cooperation for an Israeli force to operate on American soil. Second is your diplomatic cover when the United Nations condemns us for military actions on foreign territory. Proof is generally irrelevant in that theater. We'll take every precaution to avoid detection, but we'll automatically be guilty in the world court.

"Mr. President and gentlemen," Yarkoni was winding down, "you may wonder why we wouldn't simply inform the French and Italian governments about the attacks. We could give them the exact addresses where these forces are located. We could let them know what the terrorists had for breakfast. Then, of course, is the issue of the twenty-four terrorists living in the Vestavia Hills suburb of Birmingham. Involving French and Italian authorities will lead to dubious police actions — maybe international prisoner swapping or extradition of those apprehended."

Yarkoni was overstaying his welcome in the spotlight. Others were itching to respond. He got it and concluded, "We want to ensure that they won't live for another day and another attempt at our people.

"I apologize for the heated rhetoric and for running on like that, but this is what we believe. And now it looks like the prime minister wants to discuss a point with you."

Simcha sighed, brushed his hair back with his right hand, and said, "I am certain that this is an earful, but you are the only ones on Earth we can share this with." He paused, waiting for affirmation that was not forthcoming. *Would they say, "Go it alone and keep us posted?" Would they discourage our actions? Wait until they hear what I'm about to share.*

"We need to hear from you, Mr. President, whether a mission is feasible on your soil. We believe that our forces can execute an effective action that will eliminate all of the terrorists and withdraw without being discovered."

"Let's hear it," Pratley challenged. "Maybe the CIA and FBI can learn something. Actually," he continued with none of his patented sarcasm, "I think we can. You've got those Matkal guys, who are damned good!"

Relieved to delay his final point, the PM turned to Tzion to run through the Birmingham operation.

Afterward, Peterson sounded pained, "Youch! A foreign action, and on my home state of Alabama, no less. Bill, keep the lines of communication clear after we go dark."

Sundblad nodded and gave a short wave of acknowledgment.

The PM could put off the blockbuster point no longer. "Gentlemen, we anticipate a response from Iran urged on by Russia. They've been testing ballistic missiles over the past year, allowed by their nuclear agreement."

"Yeah," Pratley responded, "we've been monitoring those guys real close. They've been busy developing their weapons systems."

The PM was relieved to hear Pratley's confirmation. *We'll see how long that lasts*. "We believe they'll launch missiles able to hit us from Tehran. Their southern bases pose even greater threats."

Simcha spoke calmly. The more critical the situation, the more placid his tone became. "Within hours after the conclusion of this transmission, a Dolphin 2-class submarine will head for the Gulf of Oman. Most of the journey will be subsurface, and it will take about a week to reach a strategic location at the mouth of the Gulf.

"The sub will surface, and Russian, American, even Iranian satellites will detect that eight MIRV hypersonic missiles carried by that sub are armed with nuclear warheads and are aimed at Tehran, Isfahan, and other major Iranian cities."

The PM paused as the White House counsel blurted, "Holy shit. Excuse me, Mr. President." The room went silent.

Simcha continued undeterred: "Our land-based cruise missiles will be armed with thermonuclear warheads aimed at Iran's nuclear sites: Fordow, Isfahan, and other major reactors."

He wound down by reminding the Americans that Israel was somewhat smaller than New Jersey and that a preemptive attack on the country could cause enormous civilian casualties.

"Russia and the Iranians took that into account when they planned a blitzkrieg on Israel using forty of their most modern fighter aircraft. Are they aiming only at Israel's offshore natural gas rigs or chemical plants? Clearly not." He paused and slowly scanned the faces on the screen.

"Those chemical plants in your north are really right on top of heavily populated areas, aren't they?" Emerson had visited Israel many times.

"Absolutely correct, Mr. Secretary. They plan an all-out assault on Israel and its heavily populated regions. If their plans succeed, Russia will sit back and cynically criticize Iran in the U.N. With Israel's defeat, they'll achieve regional domination."

"Mr. Prime Minister," Trainor began, a sober expression replacing his generally placid demeanor, "this could put us on the brink of a nuclear holocaust. ... You should pardon the association with that malevolence.

"It's clear that Russia will go crazy. Destruction of their most advanced aircraft deployed in Syria and three separate assaults on their ally Iran will be intolerable. Nuclear weapons aimed at their allies would be too much to bear and might cause a declaration of war."

"President Trainor, we have little choice," the prime minister said. "We have no affinity for Armageddon. Nuclear weapons have been developed by Israel as a life insurance policy that we look forward to paying the premium on forever with no collection on its benefits."

"You, sir," Emerson interjected, "will be the first country, maybe since the Cuban missile crisis of the '60s, to threaten a nuclear strike."

"Sir," Simcha responded, calmly and coolly, "Iran possesses hundreds of missiles capable of carrying massive payloads that can hit our population centers. You know it. We know it. No one can say with certainty that they haven't developed chemical or even nuclear weapons. We believe that they have."

"So you know what the inspectors of the International Atomic Energy Agency, the global nuclear watchdog, don't know?" Pratley asked with a heavy dose of cynicism.

The PM answered only with "Yes." He paused, waiting for a reaction that didn't come. "The reason that we'll expose our warheads to satellite detection is to avoid being backed into a doomsday scenario forcing us to use them. The Russians will easily detect them."

"Can you be absolutely certain that they will identify your nukes?" Peterson asked.

"Sir, nothing is guaranteed. We'll look to you to warn them if they miss it, and to hold them back from overreacting. We'll follow the policy of mutually assured destruction. With your support via the deployment of your fleet and your cooperation in our Birmingham action, Russian military retaliation is unlikely."

"A lot of *ifs* in this picture, Mr. PM," Blaine's voice dripped with sarcasm.

Disregarding the counsel's tone and comment, Simcha concluded, "Russia is up to its neck in this. They've provided scientific backup to Abu Yusalem for his Paris dirty bomb. They support the Quds Force attacks to be coordinated with Iran's air assault on us."

Simcha sat back, opened another bottle of water, and let the silence wash over both locations. The quiet was punctuated by loud sighs on two sides of the globe. The world seemed smaller, alarmingly fragile, and infinitely more combustible.

"Mr. Prime Minister and gentlemen, give us an hour or so, and we'll get back to you." President Trainor was the only one to speak. "I know that it's late in Israel, so I hope that you brought your sleeping gear. Bill, we'll reconvene in about an hour. Jared, thanks for hanging in there. Will that be OK for all of you?"

"We'll be here waiting," Simcha said. "Thank you, Mr. President."

As the giant screen went gray, the PM thought: *Maybe I'm thanking our best friends prematurely. I'm not sure how all of this was received.*

The screen went dark in the communication center adjoining the Oval Office. President Trainor sat back in his swivel chair and scanned the four key advisers. Peterson's comments broke the silence: "What we've just heard could put us on the brink of a nuclear confrontation with the reds. We need to understand that."

"Al," Bryce Emerson said, "what's even more volatile is how trigger-happy Israel might get if the Iranians or Russians get spooked and launch an attack on their cities earlier than Israel anticipates. All of us in this room know they've got a nuclear arsenal and can deliver it."

"This whole mess is made so much more complicated with the attacks planned on the Jewish communities in three cities. From my point of view, CIA is capable of supporting or clearing the way for their commandos. We would then need to hand it off to the FBI. If you, Mr. President, give us your blessing."

Trainor said, "The issue, Alex, is not my personal approval, but whether we are willing to go all out for a key ally. Push has come to shove. A foreign power acting on our soil — how to sell this?"

The president didn't wait for a response. "This could be just what we needed to tame the ayatollahs without dirtying our hands — too much."

"That arrogant little speck on the globe," Blaine blurted, "has given us more grief than any country other than maybe Pakistan. I know it isn't a popular sentiment, but why risk all-out war for them? What have they done for us?"

"Jack, this isn't the time for personal grievances," Peterson said, locking eyes with Blaine. "You've had a hard-on for them for years." Although friends with the counsel, Peterson didn't play the grievances game. "Country first" was his credo.

"So, Mr. President, as the head of your Joint Chiefs of Staff, I tell you that we need to stand behind an ally who is threatened. And to answer your point, Jack," he faced Blaine directly, "what they've done for us is to keep the Soviets in line until now, remained a democracy in a sea of despots, been a key support for Egypt and Saudi Arabia's effort to keep Iran in check, and, goddammit, they are about our most powerful ally — small as they are."

Blaine knew better than to go one on one with Al Peterson.

"So," Trainor asked, "do we have a consensus? Bryce, Alex, and you too, Jack. What is our decision? I want to get back to them."

17
We're With You?

Sundblad wiped beads of perspiration from his brow and receding hairline using his steadier left hand. He sighed. "Well, that was fun."

The Israelis were taken aback until they realized that Sundblad was being sarcastic. He gently rocked his head back and forth in disbelief at the complexity and danger of the past half-hour's discussion.

"So, Mr. Ambassador," Tzion said, "how do you think it went, and what do you think comes next?"

Sundblad wasn't Jewish; he didn't answer a question with a question. Rather, he gave a direct response.

"President Trainor is confronted with his first political and military crisis. And it's a big one. Pratley and Peterson have been warning the president about Russia's duplicity and yearning to reestablish the Soviet Union." He paced to the screen and back. "Their actions in Crimea and Ukraine" — he shook his head slowly, emphasizing his point — "have helped expose Russia's true ambitions. We understand they'll stop at nothing to subvert Western governments. Nothing, that is, short of confrontation with America.

"They understand that our military is more advanced and more powerful than theirs. They're trying to catch up but still have a way to go. That is in our favor."

The word *our* wasn't lost on the Israelis.

"There's across-the-board belief in our Cabinet," Sundblad said, "that Iran is the greatest threat to world peace and a breeding ground for global terrorism. Our government may look at your actions as a contribution.

"Conversely, Blaine isn't a big supporter of your country. He continues to be locked into the policies of your predecessor as prime minister and to what was seen as his resistance to the peace process. And, as you know, Secretary Emerson has a keen understanding of Israel's political, strategic, and military importance. That view is tempered by his opposition to your country's settlements in contested areas."

Sundblad tapped at the blank notepad in front of him. "I believe that the president will decide on full support for your plans. But the Alabama incursion, on American soil? The jury is out on that one." He pursed his lips and focused on the wall across the room.

Ninety minutes flew by. With no notice, the floor-to-ceiling screen came alive with a series of crackles and whines. Jared fiddled with some knobs and a cursor. The American contingent appeared, with the president now seated closer to the screen.

"Thank you, gentlemen, for waiting. I trust the ambassador has been a good host."

His relaxed opening, with some harmless humor about Sundblad, might presage a positive outcome, Simcha thought. The Israelis hung on every word.

"We have," Trainor began, "spent the last hour and a half reviewing the many issues raised. Director Pratley has received input from agency analysts. Under less compelling circumstances, our discussion would get greater scrutiny. However, we don't have the luxury of time." He glanced down at his notepad. "And like you, we've made plans for catastrophic scenarios."

Yarkoni was sitting on the edge of his chair. "Get to it," he whispered under his breath.

Trainor leaned forward and cleared his throat; "I'll start from the end and work backward. We will support you."

Simcha felt the hair on the nape of his neck tingle.

"We think your plans in France and Italy are doable. We'll cover for you when the usual crap occurs in the U.N.'s kangaroo court.

"We understand and agree that the French and the Italians, though continuing to improve security, wouldn't handle what you described to our satisfaction. I believe you've been on target with your concerns."

The president paused for a sip of water and continued, "Our CIA has confirmed unusual Internet and scrambled telephonic chatter from familiar enemy sources. They interpreted the data as imminent terrorist actions but were unclear until now who the intended target was."

The Israelis exhaled in unison.

The president faced Peterson on his right and nodded toward him.

"With the president's approval," Peterson began, "I've given the secretary of the Navy and our chief of naval operations a directive to prepare to move significant elements of our Sixth Fleet into the Mediterranean basin."

The general's thick Southern drawl made him hard to understand, but his message was clear. He spoke with the universal military cadence; the Israeli commanders appreciated the no-bullshit straight talk.

"Additionally, I've *awdered* our Seventh Fleet in the South Pacific to be on *hi* alert. *Ah* believe that I speak for us *round* this table, *havin'* conferred with our president" — the general waved his right hand at each colleague — "when I say that we're deeply concerned with your submarine bristling with nukes surfacing in the Gulf of Oman. We need to be reassured that a provocation or misreading won't set off a nuclear disaster."

Pratley interrupted, "Can you forward the reports to the CIA of Mossad's breaking of the encrypted Russian-Iranian pilot communication?"

Simcha was surprised that Peterson wasn't upset about Pratley's deflection from his worry about the nukes. That subject, Simcha surmised, would be brought up many times before this day ended. "You'll have our decoding report within twenty-four hours," he answered.

"Are you certain *y'all* can jam the Russians' anti-aircraft missiles?" It was as if the nuke issue was too hot to handle. Peterson's question betrayed his skepticism. "We'd be interested in getting those reports as well."

Tzion responded to the second point, leaving the nuke issue to the prime minister.

"General, we're as certain as one can be before battle testing. In our simulations, we have an almost 100 percent success rate. I'm hoping that we'll forward our results after" — he let his sentence trail off.

In his raspy, cigarette smoker's voice, Emerson, who had remained unusually quiet, offered: "We'll back you with FBI forces in Birmingham. Are you convinced that your plan to return your force to the submarine will be flawless?"

"Sir," Tzion said, "the same answer that I gave to General Peterson's question regarding the jamming of the 300s and 400s applies. If our action is carried out as planned, the answer is positive. We believe that we'll neutralize the terrorists and return in secrecy. We're also confident that we can successfully jam the enemy's missile radar. Be assured, sir, that we will share all that we learn from these battles — positive results or other."

"We have a demand of you," Trainor said, coming upright from his slouch. "You must guarantee a major push toward a peace initiative with your hostile neighbors. Shortly after these military actions, we look to you to begin dismantling other settlements that are not of strategic import.

"We want credit for developing a peace plan and need your guarantee that you'll disengage from several other additional settlements not long after that. You choose which; we won't get hung up on a timetable — yet. We also want your assurance that the commanders of the sub in the Gulf of Oman are on a tight leash and that should Iran launch missiles, your air defense system and conventional weapons will deal with them. No knee-jerk nuke response.

"Finally, we have no guarantee how the Russians will respond to your preemptive attack on their planes. We do know that they'll think many times before ordering a military response with our fleet in your backyard, but that doesn't mean they won't respond at all." He leaned forward, looming larger on the screen with his face getting distorted. "We believe that U.S. military confrontation with the Russians is long overdue and that it will be just that, a confrontation with no actions required. I repeat, no nuclear response from you. We need your guarantees on these issues."

"Mr. President," Simcha responded with relief he was trying not to show, "you have our government's guarantee that the nuclear option will not be our primary deterrent. We are prepared to turn Iran radioactive if our country is on the brink of disaster. As we don't foresee that scenario, largely because of your support, we can give you the commitment that you request."

"The guarantee that we demand of you, Eliezer. This is not a request." The president allowed a moment of silence to emphasize his point.

"Understood and agreed, Mr. President. It is also our understanding that Zvi Levi and Mossad will coordinate the Birmingham action with Mr. Pratley. Is that your understanding as well?"

"It is," the president said. "Godspeed. I believe that we have decided that General Peterson, General Tzion, and Defense Minister Yarkoni will be coordinating progress on all of your actions. Our Sixth Fleet will be on the move within hours. Thank you, gentlemen.

"Good evening. Stay strong. Eliezer, we're with you."

The giant screen went dark.

18
Leora's Other Side

Israel's arid weather was outdoing itself as afternoon temperatures baked the coastal region. Optimistic reports forecast more moderate temperatures that evening.

Late August was generally hot and humid during the day, with relief at sunset compliments of the cooling breezes off the Mediterranean. This year's *chamsin*, the dry, relentlessly hot winds that blew in off the desert to the east, was unusually intense.

Leora's apartment in the gentrified area of Nahariya, a quaint seaside town north of Haifa, generally benefited from the cooler evenings. She and Shimon rarely used their central air conditioning and noted that they had more modest electric bills than their friends in Tel Aviv.

Leora had convinced Levi that she needed a brief break. She knew this was a 24/7 period. The barren field no more than two miles north of her apartment had served as a helicopter-landing site ferrying her to Jerusalem in the past. She could be ready at a moment's notice.

Shimon Almani, her devoted husband of six years, was due home at any moment. The progeny of Israelis of Iraqi descent, he had three brothers and two sisters dispersed across the tiny country. He was eager to begin a family but accepted — reluctantly — the current demands of Leora's profession. He was less accommodating when Leora insisted on keeping her maiden name — albeit assumed — of Bargal. Their mailbox read "Bargal-Almani."

More often than not, the last year found Leora and Shimon

moving in opposite directions. Leora's assignment as Mossad's senior liaison to European field operatives called for extensive travel; close communication was required with agents throughout Europe during this crisis period.

Levi early on identified Leora as a fearless, intuitive, and highly reliable officer, able to handle complex assignments. She was now dedicated, with Joshua Canaan, to tracking down Abu Yusalem.

Shimon was no stranger to Israel's defense challenges. He'd earned a Ph.D. in astrophysics from the Technion at twenty-eight. He met Leora at a university faculty party. He would tell her at intimate moments, "I was struck not only by your looks, but also by the composure and ease with which you exchanged ideas with Smilovitz and Epstein," two biggies at the Technion.

Leora would laugh and answer, "Shimon, your athletic body and olive complexion turned me on immediately. I fought off the impulse to stroke your smooth face. Somehow I restrained myself at that first meeting."

He'd been recruited by the Defense Ministry to help solve ballistic missile reentry challenges and was intimately involved in Israel's worst kept secret—the nuclear arms industry. The clandestine nature of both careers and their connection to the country's security allowed for discussion in classified and restricted areas.

Leora relished her free afternoons. She generally used public transportation, as Shimon took their car to his remotely situated lab. The No. 14 bus stopped with its patented jolt about a block from the Nahariya open-air market. She stopped at the usual stalls for carrots, tomatoes, and other fresh vegetables. She headed for the stand that sold her favorite yogurts and Israeli wines. She favored the early-harvest merlot and bought three bottles. Many of the veteran vendors greeted her warmly but complained about her sporadic appearances. It was hard not to notice the green-eyed Brazilian.

The past year hadn't allowed for many dinners at home, and Leora was eager to discuss pressing issues with Shimon. She'd received clearance from Levi and the internal security team of Mossad to speak openly with him. One member of the team said, "After all, if we can't trust the lead scientist of our thermonuclear projects, whom can we trust?" Such thinking was a radical departure from the vaunted secrecy of anything and anyone associated with Mossad or the Defense Ministry.

Leora jogged up the two flights to their modest apartment. She opened the double-locked door and paused upon entering to breathe in the familiar odors she'd missed: Shimon's after-shave lotion and the lavender hair gel he began using about a year earlier.

She made a beeline for the chaise she'd purchased at a local market. There was barely enough room for the extended chair; it leaned against the wrought-iron railing of her terrace. Sitting on her second-floor perch always brightened her spirits. She had carefully selected its inlaid Italian stone tiles with the colorful floral designs. The twenty-foot-long, six-foot-deep balcony overlooked a nicely maintained garden with magenta and vermillion bougainvillea at its borders.

She sipped the merlot, picking out the cork particles that always found their way into wine bottles she opened. The fresh breeze that caressed her town seemingly marked the end of the stifling *chamsin*. The floral-scented evening air compensated for the oppressive heat of a typical summer day.

She heard the front door creak open and was greeted by an over-the-shoulder kiss on both cheeks. Shimon was home earlier than usual. He was determined to take advantage of every moment with the woman he adored.

"Grab the glass that I left for you on the kitchen counter and come here immediately," Leora said. "I need more hugs." Shimon was happy to oblige both requests.

They sat side-by-side, sipping wine that was probably pressed too early. The Golan Heights vineyard they visited several times generally produced fine wines; the Nahariya open-air market carried only its mid quality label. They paid it little mind.

Never certain which of their endlessly curious neighbors might be sipping a glass of post-work wine beneath them or on either of the two stories above their apartment, they were accustomed to sharing only small talk on the terrace. They discussed the highlights of their supposed routine workdays — Shimon as a computer parts salesman and Leora as a human services consultant, a job that kept her traveling.

Once inside their living room with the double-paned terrace doors shut, they shared more about the real issues they encountered.

"Shimon, I'm so happy to see you. It's hell being away from you for so long." She pointed to the cut-up vegetables and fresh yogurt on a small platter as they pulled their chairs closer to their modest dining table.

"You know just about everything that's in the works, right?" she asked. Leora assumed that lead scientists of the country's nuclear weapons program would be called on for their guidance in warhead preparations. "The Americans agreed to move major elements of their Sixth Fleet near us. They've given us the green light to act on their soil in Alabama. One of our Dolphins has been en route for four days and will soon be at the Strait of Gibraltar before heading across the North Atlantic toward the Gulf of Mexico."

"When did we get America's approval for an action on their soil?" Shimon was incredulous.

"A few hours ago," Leora said, grinning. "If the American answer had been 'no way,' the sub would have turned back. I *think*. They needed to get started early in order to reach America two days before Rosh Hashana. Another sub is heading west through the Mediterranean for Rome. Too many details?" she asked when his eyes widened.

"Keep going," Shimon answered. Her ability to retain detail often amazed him.

"Another Dolphin will pass through Gibraltar in a few days, head north to the Bay of Biscay to a position off Le Havre. One detail that I haven't yet shared with you has been the destination of the final sub." She hesitated and said, "Only because it was just finalized, and I thought it might make you worry excessively, as it did me."

Leora swallowed hard. "In two days another sub will travel through the Suez Canal. Egypt has been cooperative but insisted on escorting us all the way to the end of the canal. It then heads through the Red Sea into the Gulf of Aden and swings north through the Arabian Sea to a position in the Gulf of Oman. That sub will be loaded with nuclear-tipped Popeye missiles. It'll surface in the Gulf, where Russian and maybe Iranian satellites will track it. Should be easy for them to determine the trajectory of our missiles — aimed at Iran."

Shimon reached for her hand. "God willing," he said, "calm, rational heads will prevail."

"There's always a first time," Leora sighed. "About the northern front in Syria — you're up to date? Also on the missiles aimed at Iran's nuclear facilities with the warheads that you helped design?"

He nodded. "I hoped that we'd never be called upon to use them," he said. "Enough." He waved his hands in surrender. "Pour me some wine."

"One more thing." She stopped to fill his glass. "I asked Zvi for permission to join the Matkal boys and pay a little visit to the Quds Force in Rome. I know Rome well and thought I could be helpful."

"And Zvi's answer?"

"Surprisingly, he said no. He had another assignment for me, a critical one. They're pairing me with an agent named Joshua Canaan. I'm not sure if you've heard anything about him." She paused, staring into Shimon's clear brown eyes. "One of the teams at 8200 has been tracking Abu Yusalem. They have conclusive evidence that a sarin-laced bomb will be detonated in Paris' Jewish neighborhood on Rosh Hashana. Our assignment is to take him out and keep the bomb from further development. Yusalem is working with Russian scientists who seem very close to completion."

"Well," Shimon whispered, "I'm not surprised about your request to go to Italy. But working with Joshua Canaan will be an eye-opener. Some of us at the ministry have had contact with him. He was key in the assassination of two Iranian nuclear scientists. Every assignment he's ever had has been dangerous and violent. He's as clever as Yusalem and has spent years tracking him, several times just missing ridding us of that scourge. I've got mixed feelings about your volunteering to go on a mission that he's assigned to. I know that you're superb at your shitty and dangerous profession, and I'm proud of you, but I can't bear the thought of your getting hurt or worse. Sometimes I wish that we both had the careers that our neighbors believe we have."

The rest of the evening was spent enjoying the modest Israeli dinner of organic yogurt, vegetables, and a heavy dose of Israeli wine, followed by passionate and wildly creative sex.

Shimon's words of fear for her safety echoed through Leora's mind during their long-overdue lovemaking. She knew that an assignment with Canaan put her on the front line of a confrontation with Abu Yusalem.

19
Mossad Visits The City of Lights

Richard and Marla Tyler entered their top-floor apartment on 16 Rue Pasteur, a four-story building on a quiet residential street in Paris' Eleventh Arrondissement. The international management-consulting firm Bradbury and Associates had recently taken out a one-year lease for the two-bedroom apartment. The arrangement was unusual because many Parisian neighborhoods frowned on rentals.

A Bradbury representative had met with a committee of residents who oversaw the landscaping and maintenance of the well-preserved building. It didn't hurt that the corporation's representative was nattily dressed, spoke French fluently, offered a 25 percent premium over the astronomical rental price, and deposited ten thousand American dollars into an escrow account to cover any damage caused by the company's executives.

Bradbury and Associates was, in truth, a Mossad shell company. The elaborate company website featured portraits of the Tylers, who, according to their online bios, were a highly acclaimed husband-and-wife management-consulting team. Their pictures would be deleted from the faux website the evening of their arrival for fear of being made by Ibrahim Ashrawi or Abu Yusalem. Otherwise, the website remained intact.

Once inside the nicely appointed — and, for Paris, rather spacious — apartment, Joshua Canaan and Leora Bargal, no longer Mr. and Mrs. Tyler, could end their intentionally emphatic American-accented hallway conversation.

Unit 8200 had some time ago located the bomb-making

laboratory on Rue Beccaria and the Iranian-rented apartment on nearby Rue Lacharriere. They decided to keep the Iranians under surveillance rather than intervene. It was politically risky not notifying the French authorities about the Iranian workshop.

Abu Yusalem's appearance at the laboratory signaled that some large-scale action was in the works. The agents of 8200 had decided to play a dangerous waiting game. They only recently learned that a sarin bomb was being assembled.

It was six days to Rosh Hashana, and Leora and Joshua had intensified their focus on trapping and killing their target. Yusalem played an important role in the attacks in the three Diaspora locations. He had to be eliminated — but at the right time. He'd recently visited with Hezbollah leadership and was planning to return to Lebanon one more time.

Mossad agents inside Hezbollah's secondary tier of command in Lebanon signaled Levi that the terror group's plans had come together. They would unleash barrages of rockets the morning of Rosh Hashana.

Yusalem's fingers were in so many terrorist pies that Mossad didn't fear that killing him would spook his accomplices and cause them to change the timetable of their attacks. They'd assume that an old enemy — rivals in Hezbollah, Islamic Jihad leaders, an endless list of terrorists he had double-crossed — finally caught up with him.

"You choose," Joshua said, dropping his carry-on bag on the small dining room table near the living room. "Actually," he added, not waiting for Leora's response, "take this bedroom if it's OK with you." He pointed to the larger, airier room.

Leora threw her bag on the bed in her designated room. "Nicer room, yes, but I don't care for privileged choices, OK?"

"Got it," Joshua answered. It was going to take some time to get used to his partner's direct manner.

The next ten minutes were spent unpacking the few items they'd brought with them. Joshua's disassembled MTAR-21 Variant and its silencer were oiled and waiting for them in the apartment, thanks to local Israeli operatives. Beside his weapon were two of Leora's favored 9mm Berettas and a small straw basket brimming with fifteen-round clips.

Joshua laid the automatic aside and smiled at Leora as she examined the barrels of the Berettas. "Let's check out the roof. We should make sure that we've got good visuals," he said.

Joshua was antsy and already moving toward the door. They had to determine the line of sight to Yusalem's apartment. A clear shot was a must; it had to pass over a small street.

Complaining about the narrow staircase and dusty banister, they reached the roof two steps at a time while involuntarily recording mental notes. The creaking door opened with ease, and they stepped onto the warm tar surface. Had inquisitive tenants asked what they were doing, they would have waxed eloquent about the eastern view of the city on an unusually clear day.

They stood silently, elbows on the four-foot-high, ochre-tiled guard wall. Joshua breathed in the intoxicating Parisian afternoon breeze, made all the more captivating because it intermingled with Leora's scent, a subtle but unfamiliar perfume. The afternoon sun played on her coarse, wavy hair and brought out reddish highlights, something he hadn't noticed.

Joshua could inhale the ambrosia of sensuous women while resisting the impulse to act. *Mostly.* Over his twenty-year career, he had two spontaneous sexual encounters. He felt they had no significance beyond the immediate pleasure of generating enough body heat to work up a good sweat.

Casual sex was nowhere to be found in the manual of a covert operative's missions. Attractive undercover agents, male and female, employed sexual come-ons to lure enemy targets into dead-end bedroom encounters. At times, the intimacy of working in spy teams produced friendly-fire liaisons.

Mossad forbade them publicly and mostly looked the other way when they happened. Joshua enjoyed women, the Russian beauty Natasha at his swimming pool meeting with Levi being the latest to stir his imagination. Abu Yusalem, however, was a far more intoxicating obsession.

Leora was aware that they were standing quite close together and virtually rubbing arms as they looked eastward to Rue Lacharriere. Her imagination was every bit as vivid and colorful as Joshua's. She, like Joshua, remained riveted to the task at hand.

"Looks like Levi was right in his description of our apartment's vantage point," she offered. "Our building is several degrees higher than Yusalem's apartment. From here I estimate 850 meters over Rue St. Ambroise. I hope that your legendary skills as a marksman haven't been diminished by your retirement."

Trying not to take a reference to his retirement as a slur on his age, Joshua said, "Tomorrow will tell. We'll be five days to Rosh Hashana. I can't afford to screw up. With normal weather conditions, I should be able to hit a one-shekel coin from here — which, of course, is illegal."

Leora laughed.

"How did you compute the distance so quickly?" Joshua was impressed.

"Computed days before we got here," Leora answered with a touch of self-deprecation. "Homework." In truth, Leora had a mathematical gift and could tally numbers and measure distances without electronic devices; these were some of the attributes that had made her such a high-profile asset in Mossad. Joshua didn't tell her that he had completed the same homework and had computed the distance and trajectory to his target as well.

"Yusalem's schedule was well documented by 8200," Joshua noted. "I'm surprised that he's kept to a predictable routine. Maybe he feels overly secure or so riveted on creating a successful bomb that he's let his guard down."

"From what I've learned about him," Leora observed, "he is obsessive and crazy about being punctual."

"Well, if 8200 is accurate," Joshua smirked, because its reports were generally accurate, "we should be waiting for his exit to the limo at 1:30 tomorrow afternoon. I'm looking forward to dirtying his designer suit."

"When we succeed, Joshua," Leora said, avoiding the "if" word, "might our action not spook the Iranians? From my understanding, the PM and the Cabinet see this as an opportunity to deal them a big-time preemptive blow. So we must not miss."

His glare was easy to interpret: She need not state the obvious.

The nine steps to the roof could be covered in seconds, minimizing the risk of being spotted by a neighbor. Joshua was performing some silent computations as they made their way down the staircase, careful not to leave prints on the banister.

The late-afternoon sun and early-evening breeze ruffled the curtains of the modest living room. The apartment had surprising cross-ventilation; no need for an air conditioner. The décor and ambience seemed paradoxically placid, given the actions that were ahead of them.

Parquet floor panels were arranged in geometric patterns. White, billowy drapes framed the three living room windows. Gray fleece throw rugs neatly covered areas of the living room and small foyer. The room's armchairs, with their floral-patterned slipcovers, brought back Joshua's fateful meeting in the conference room at the PM's residence only days earlier. He envisioned the apartment's owner as a late-in-life widow.

They simultaneously realized that they hadn't eaten all day and were starving.

Joshua offered to bring in a light dinner. They agreed that it might be too great a risk for Leora to walk or drive to the nearby mini-market. After her close call with the Iranians in Paris, her change of hairstyle and addition of horn-rimmed glasses might not be enough of a disguise should she be spotted by Ashrawi's cell.

Only Abu Yusalem himself could identify Joshua despite his donned glasses and altered hairstyle. Mossad agents had learned never to underestimate Yusalem's cunning and intelligence.

The likelihood, however, of the terrorist shopping for cheese, yogurt, and wine at a shop a mile or so from his apartment was remote.

Joshua, with excessive politeness, asked, "May I borrow one of your Berettas?"

"Let me think about it," Leora joked. "Depends on what you plan to bring back for dinner and how quickly. I'm ravenous."

He hurried down the four flights, prepared for any of the tenants who might appear and strike up a conversation. He was ready to make the Bradbury and Associates pitch. Thankfully, no door opened, and he exited the building and turned left about fifty yards to his rented dark-blue Ford Escort. He'd parked with both passenger-side tires on the sidewalk. He wasn't alone: These gymnastics were the parking method on Paris' narrow side streets.

The rental's GPS would guide him to the closest mini-market. He was aware that he'd have to account to Levi for what was sure to be a disputed amenity. He could hear Levi ask him what was so bad about using his smartphone GPS.

His Parisian shopping adventure was productive and uneventful. He jogged up the four flights, two plastic bags in hand, feeling only a tinge of soreness in his rapidly healing left leg.

"Honey, I'm home," he quipped, "and I return your Beretta in pristine condition."

"Thank you for doing the shopping," Leora said, paying little attention to Joshua's humor.

He laid out several packages of cheese, yogurts, three types of salami, and an unwrapped baguette that the bakery owner had thrust into his hands. Two bottles of Perrier and a bottle of red table wine were the last items he unpacked.

"I hope that our local colleagues who rented this apartment thought of silverware and, most importantly, a corkscrew," Joshua said, beginning the search.

The drawer near the sink contained both.

He washed the day's sweat away and joined Leora at the dark-stained breakfast table, made roomier with one of its two leafs extended. She'd set out their light dinner and succeeded in opening the wine. She poured herself and Joshua half-full paper cups of the Bordeaux.

"The wine is surprisingly good. Israel's wines are getting better too, though."

"Don't make me compare our wines to classic French vintages. It's not fair. Besides, there are cork particles in mine."

Leora frowned.

They downed half of their first glasses, and Joshua opened a bottle of Perrier. They both broke off chunks of the aromatic baguette, crunchy and freshly baked. They cut off slices of the cheeses that Joshua couldn't name if his life depended on it. Their distraction was short-lived.

"Let's talk about tomorrow," Joshua began.

Leora squinted and scowled as if to say, *so soon*? It usually was Leora playing the "let's get to business" professional.

"Can we put off our planning for a few more minutes?" Her question left little room for a negative response.

Joshua smirked. "Sure, what do you have in mind?"

"Two issues are on my mind," Leora answered. Her laser-beam directness began with a disarming eye-to-eye engagement. "First, an apology. I'm certain you have no idea for what, but that isn't important — yet.

"When I heard that I was to go on this assignment with you, I had no idea who you were. To me, you were some old retired guy that Levi pulled out of his golden-years pension. I was puzzled, at least until Levi filled me in.

"You're a legend in Mossad, and I admit I knew nothing about you. You seem to be a modest guy, so I imagine this isn't a subject that you're comfortable with. So I want no answer from you, as I asked no questions. Just accept my apology."

Joshua laughed. "Your no-bullshit approach was brought to my attention prior to our arrival in Paris, but it's fun to see it in action. But my forty-eighth birthday is still a few months away, and you already have me on humanity's dustbin. My feelings are hurt."

Joshua asked that they move on, as he would need time, he joked, to recover from her disparaging perceptions.

"I'd like to know," Leora said, this time with more deference in her voice, "about your encounters with Abu Yusalem. How did he get away from Superman?"

They both laughed.

"I normally don't dwell on my failures, but if I refuse to tell you about them, I'll be accused of age-related memory impairment." Joshua shifted in his chair. "Yusalem has a driving need to kill as many Jews as he can before resigning himself to a comfortable and eternal martyrdom. He makes no distinction between Diaspora Jews and Israelis.

"He grew up in Ramallah under our occupation. I call it what it is, occupation, though you can think of Ramallah and the West Bank in any way you like. Makes no difference to me. I fight for the state of Israel, whether I agree with the politics or not.

"His seventeen-year-old brother, two years his junior, stalked and then stabbed two teenage Israeli girls hiking near their settlement. One girl was badly wounded; the second suffered only superficial lacerations. Shin Bet tracked him down, arrested him, and demolished his parents' four-bedroom home." He waved one hand. "Reduced it to a pile of rubble.

"The government's policy was to make such attacks on Israeli citizens as costly as possible to the extended family. Abu spent months consoling grieving parents whose remaining years were spent living in tents in a Ramallah suburb. And so, Abu Yusalem, terrorist extraordinaire, was born. The killing of Jews became his life goal, a perpetual retribution.

"I was on assignment in the Czech Republic about three years ago when I planned to visit the Krnov Synagogue, built in the late nineteenth century. The twin towers at its entrance and the round, arched windows with ornate carvings framing them were exquisite. I took a Shabbat morning off to attend a service.

"I'm not sure if Yusalem was tailing me or if it was a coincidence, but he planted an explosive device near the ark — in a prayer bag, no less. It detonated, leveling the ark and sparking a serious blaze. Many injuries but, thankfully, no deaths."

Joshua looked away before catching Leora's eye. "My family wasn't as fortunate in the redux in Budapest a few months ago."

He drank some of his wine. "After the explosion, as the smoke cleared, I raced out of the sanctuary, convinced that he was still in the building, admiring his handiwork. I had my Beretta drawn. I ran toward the staircase leading to the gallery when I saw him racing up the steps. He stopped and fired, grazing my right thigh. Take my word for it, there is a scar just here." He pointed to his leg.

"I emptied my eight-round magazine at him. There was a good deal of blood on the staircase, but he disappeared. Like some phantom. It was several weeks later that I heard he carried my .32 ACP slug in his shoulder in an area too risky to remove. That was my souvenir to him."

Leora helped herself to more wine and crossed her legs under her, getting comfortable.

"About one year after the Krnov Synagogue encounter, I almost had him." He frowned. "Am I boring you, Leora?" Receiving no response other than a slight scowl and Leora's patented stare, Joshua, feigning sincerity, said, "How does anyone work with you? You're very hard to look at without one's mind wandering."

"I suppose," Leora said, one brow raised, "that when you reach a certain age, your mind starts to wander. Go on."

Joshua tried ignoring the age-related sarcasm that was fast becoming a leitmotif in their relationship. He'd told Anat, back in his Tel Aviv apartment, that he felt he was too old for this battle. Maybe Leora was reminding him of that truth.

"I was on a three-day vacation visiting a friend in Kfar Saba. I got a text message that Abu Yusalem was reported to be in a café in Tulkarem. I could reach the West Bank coffee shop in ten minutes while authorities would take about ten minutes longer.

"The proprietor of the café was already under surveillance, as he was a known Hamas sympathizer. I entered the café, and there was Yusalem. Despite being deep in conversation with Ibrahim, the owner, he spotted me. I drew my pistol just as Yusalem fired three rapid shots at the ceiling, causing pandemonium among the forty or so patrons.

"Ibrahim pushed against me. I kind of bounced off his stomach; he must have weighed close to 300 pounds. He raised his arms, blocking my view of Yusalem. When I pushed him aside, Abu the magician was gone. Not a trace of him anywhere. No other Mossad operative has even seen him in person, yet I blew it twice."

"Do you wonder why Yusalem's three shots were aimed into the café ceiling and not at you? He's also an expert marksman." Leora looked genuinely puzzled.

"Might have been too easy. We've been engaged in a multi-year cat-and-mouse game, with him trying to kill me, but apparently only with an element of originality. He could have hit me in the café but chose not to. I offer him no such slack. When the opportunity arises, I'll take him out."

"Hardly a failure. He carries your slug as a reminder of how close he came to martyrdom. Thanks, Joshua, for filling in the gaps. I appreciate it. And despite your advanced age" — she uncharacteristically laughed, a wine-induced response — "it really is great to work with you. I'll have tales to tell my grandchildren one day."

Joshua filled the two paper cups halfway, putting a dent in the eleven-euro bottle of Bordeaux. "Very classy," he began, pointing to the cups. "Let's get to our review before I forget who we're after."

He leaned forward after checking his phone for the weather outlook. "Looks like the forecast is for showers tomorrow. That's probably good for us — not many spectators."

Joshua laid out the action plan to begin just past noon the next day. Leora reviewed her role; they agreed that the plan was good and set to go.

The next hour was spent trying to examine any shortcomings of the plan. Every Mossad covert action had a second and third backup. If something went wrong, the adversary's expected response would be anticipated, which would lead to a range of options. If those failed, improvise!

Joshua was impressed with Leora's analytical approach. Her insights and questions were probing, and she never forgot any detail. They were becoming a team.

One more hit to the classy paper cups, and the wine bottle was ready for the recycling bin — which was nowhere to be found. They had also finished the excellent salamis, the hard-to-pronounce cheeses, and the scrumptious baguette. They saved the yogurt for breakfast.

Joshua had come across a corner café where the following morning he would subject himself to scornful and derisive looks from patrons and proprietors by asking for two coffees to go. The French were condescendingly clear about which nation looked favorably on ordering takeout coffee: It lay about thirty-seven hundred miles due west.

They removed their plates and filled a plastic garbage bag that would be taken with them upon their departure. They would leave nothing behind.

It was approaching 11 p.m. Nightfall crept up on them, and both felt the tension and focused planning of the day take a toll on their bodies. Leora headed for her bedroom, yawning, and wished Joshua a pleasant sleep. Joshua said he'd be heading in soon. He wanted to review a few items before turning in.

In truth, Joshua was too wound up to sleep. He was so looking forward to ending Abu Yusalem's terror career. He moved to the living room, collapsed noisily onto the comfortable quilted loveseat, and began another review of every step of the next day's challenges.

Leora's bedroom door opened about ten minutes later, causing a slight creak that he hadn't noticed earlier.

"I see you're about as tired as I am," Leora said. "Mind if I join you?"

"Of course not." She interrupted Joshua's review of the plan, but the interruption was worth it. Wearing a white, virtually diaphanous cotton sleep shirt, she dropped into an armchair directly across from him. Her firm, ample breasts were youthfully arched, and her erect nipples stood tantalizingly against the cotton. Leora sat, legs crossed, wearing only panties under her translucent shirt.

"Leora, what's this?" He gestured at her clothing. "We may not live through our work tomorrow, and less than half an hour ago you were lobbying for my early acceptance into a retirement home. So why the scanty night clothes?"

Leora was taken aback. Despite Joshua's good looks and great physique, she thought of them only as partners on a mission. She'd paid little attention to her sleep outfit. Who thought about appropriate night clothing when packing for a kill assignment?

"Sorry. I may have felt too comfortable and dressed too loosely."

She may not have been coming on to Joshua, but he sure took note.

How can I dredge up an old joke at a time like this? He thought. But there it was, racing through his mind as a deflection from his real thoughts. To defuse the suddenly awkward atmosphere, he began in a determined voice, "Three women from a nearby kibbutz are walking on a beach in Tel Aviv. They come across a sleeping man lying nude on his back, a newspaper covering his face to protect his eyes from the glaring sun. The first woman looks him up and down and says, 'No, that's not my husband.' The second woman looks carefully at the sleeping man and says, 'You're right, that's not your husband.' The third woman looks him over and says, 'He's not even from our kibbutz.'"

Leora moaned, "Which part of your creaking memory bank did this come from?"

Despite his controlled arousal and recollection of the days of casual sex in the young country's kibbutz living, Joshua was convinced that any follow-through with Leora was wrong. Perhaps, he thought, excavating that tired Israeli joke about free sex in Israel was an unconscious, if paradoxical, attempt to break the mood.

The two times he'd been unfaithful to Anat, he'd been racked with guilt, a feeling that he didn't want to intrude into his dedication to eradicate Abu Yusalem.

His focus remained riveted to the next day's work.

20
A Shot at Abu Yusalem

Five days to Rosh Hashana. Less than a week before Israel would launch its preemptive strike. Operations to hit the attack sites beyond their borders were moving ahead.

Neither Leora nor Joshua showed any discomfort after the previous evening's close call. They were focused on their assignment. The cool, blustery weather and light rain made little difference to them; they weren't there to sightsee. Inclement weather would affect pedestrian traffic, which even in pleasant and sunny conditions was sparse on this out-of-the-way tree-lined street.

They'd meticulously scanned their apartment for papers, glassware and any other items they'd brought in. While the apartment was rented to Bradbury and Associates, they couldn't be sure whether an inquisitive tenant had a duplicate key.

Leora's bag was folded into Joshua's leather briefcase, leaving him just enough room for his rifle. Leora carried only her chic pocketbook with the pastel floral designs, just roomy enough for her Beretta and five 15-round clips. Joshua had tucked the other Beretta into the waistband of his dark business suit.

It was almost noon. After a final run-through, Leora left the apartment for what appeared to be a leisurely stroll. Once again, high-heeled shoes hurt her feet as she neared the corner of Rue Lacharriere, Abu Yusalem's street.

At 12:50, Joshua locked the apartment door behind him and breathed a sigh of relief, as no fourth-floor tenant seemed to be lurking in the hallway. 8200 no doubt had a dossier on his three immediate neighbors and would have avoided renting a Mossad apartment where busybodies might patrol the hallways.

Leather briefcase in hand, he jogged up the nine steps to the roof, careful not to grip the banister. Slowly, he opened the door. He'd oiled the rusted hinges with olive oil that had come with their dinner order. The door opened with barely a sound.

Joshua assembled his weapon. The MTAR-21 could be broken into components that were easy to piece together and disassemble rapidly. He mounted the telescopic sight that he hoped had been perfectly calibrated by the colleagues who had delivered their weapons. Mossad agents relied on collaboration.

He opened the tripod so that it just cleared the four-foot guard wall. The light rain was no bother, but the sporadic wind gusts would present a challenge at a distance of more than 800 yards. There were no second chances; a miss and the quarry would hit his rabbit hole and disappear.

Joshua screwed on the silencer and fiddled with the range-finder. At 1:20 he was satisfied that his scope was as good as he could get it with no practice shots. The wind gusts concerned him, and he muttered that he'd have to aim a millimeter to the left to compensate for the breezes. He placed his leather case on its side and kneeled on it with his somewhat sore left knee. He braced his rifle on the tripod and made a final scope adjustment.

His heart was pounding; the day of reckoning with his nemesis was at hand. Images of the devastation and mayhem of the Budapest massacre raced through his mind. He worked hard to suppress distractions.

At 1:25 a sleek black limo pulled to the front of the house. If Abu Yusalem were true to character, he would emerge at precisely 1:30. The five-minute wait was an eternity.

The front door to the luxury apartment on Rue Lacharriere opened at straight up 1:30. First out was one plain-suit guy. The Armani hand-tailored suit and the $500 silk tie followed him. Bringing up the rear was another off-the-rack guy. They all seemed relaxed and in no particular hurry. The brown berets tilted at rakish angles on all three men surprised Joshua.

He put the gray silk tie in the crosshairs of his scope, moved a millimeter to its left, held his breath, and fired two quick and virtually silent rounds. The first shot penetrated the tie about a half-millimeter to the left of where Joshua wanted to place it. Where the second hit didn't much matter; the hollow-point shell did its damage. He could see the blood spurt through his scope. No one could have survived that hit.

One of the guards drew his weapon and looked for a target. Through the scope Joshua saw Leora at the front of Yusalem's limo. She'd been waiting at the corner to cut off any escape route if the long shot missed or only wounded their target. It paid off. The driver was sprawled, seemingly lifeless, over the steering wheel. Leora hit the guard with his weapon drawn and almost separated his head from his torso with two shots from her silenced Beretta. The second guard had already retreated into the apartment. There was no value in pursuing him, as the real target lay sprawled on the rainy sidewalk.

Joshua flew down to the building entrance; weapon disassembled and back in its case. He'd made sure to collect the two spent cartridges from his rooftop perch. He jumped into their Ford Escort and turned the corner where Leora was waiting, having calmly returned her weapon to her floral handbag.

As Joshua pulled alongside the gory mess, Leora was snapping cellphone photos of the silk-tied cadaver. The other two corpses were unrecognizable. The inclement weather had kept the street free of pedestrians.

Leora slid into the blue Escort. "Quite a shot, Mr. Retiree."

"Frankly," Joshua answered, "I think your Beretta shot was harder."

They pulled away and drove three blocks to Rue Ternaux. Joshua turned right into the small side street.

"Did you use the 9mm clips with the Russian markings?"

"That's why I left all the shells on the ground," she answered, annoyed that he questioned her.

He parked the car and carefully wiped the steering wheel,

removing fingerprints. Leora followed suit in the passenger area. They stepped out of the Escort and into a waiting white Renault. As planned, a local agent was waiting near the new car. Joshua handed him his briefcase, which now contained both Berettas and the remaining clips.

A brief nod and a handshake to his Paris-based colleague, and they were off on the 300-mile drive to Amsterdam. It would be too risky boarding a flight to Israel at the Paris airport. Staying within the speed limit, they merged onto the A1 highway, heading north toward Belgium and eventually to Schiphol International Airport in Amsterdam.

Alan and Cynthia Benson of Chicago were booked on Lufthansa Flight 645, Amsterdam to Tel Aviv, departing at 9:18 p.m. Joshua would discard the Richard and Marla Tyler passports in a safe and undetectable way.

"What are our new names?" Leora smiled as she asked.

"We did it," Joshua blurted out as he patted the sweat off his forehead with his blue-checked handkerchief. "Great job, Leora. We rid the world of a global threat that most people never even heard of."

Leora wasn't listening. She was reading an encrypted text that had just come through on her phone. The Office had responded to her forwarded pictures of the silk-tie, Armani-suited assassin.

She read the message aloud: "Nice job, you just bought the wrong product. The pictures don't match up. See you soon. Have a good trip."

"Holy shit." Joshua slammed his hand against the steering wheel, swerving into an unwanted lane change. "I knew I should have kneeled down to ID the guy I shot. The berets they were wearing fooled me. That cat has more than nine lives. How the hell did he know? He must have been the guard who ran back inside. How did he disappear? How could I have missed him again?"

"Joshua," Leora placed her hand gently on his shoulder, "I see what you've been saying about this phantom. We'll get him yet.

As planned, I made an anonymous call to the police about the bomb factory on Rue Beccaria. I warned them about the sarin and radioactive material. Our agent is hanging out near the entrance to ensure that the police arrive on the scene. So let's say that this was a partial success."

A scowl greeted her "partial success" comment.

She patted his shoulder, ignoring the glare, and lowered her arm. "The French police," she said with a dose of sarcasm, "will take credit for foiling an attack on Paris and dismantling a bomb-making factory in the heart of the city. I don't see how Israel can be implicated."

She looked out the car window and at the road racing by. "Intel assures us," she said, "Ibrahim Ashrawi and the twenty-four Quds guys in Paris are still a go in five days."

Joshua lifted his face heavenward and peered through the wet windshield. Almost as if uttering a mournful prayer, he said: "I promise to avenge all six of you and the others murdered and injured at the bar mitzvah in Budapest. I won't rest for a moment until we've killed this bastard who escaped once again."

Leora was thinking about what their failure could mean. She feared that the Quds Force, soon to be spread out in Paris and heavily armed, would be hard to beat within five days.

21 Operation Never Again Begins

Dolphin-1 swung westward at a depth of about 500 feet. It could dive to 3,000, which was a risk Captain David Bargal, a veteran submarine commanding officer, wasn't prepared to take in that sector of the Mediterranean. The Balearic Sea off the coast of Spain was still relatively calm, although November and December would find it less welcoming.

The captain ordered Lieutenant Markov in the navigation center to adjust the hydroplanes, bringing them up to about 150 feet. Captain Bargal kept a close watch on the inertial navigation system that monitored the sub's motion and gave him constant updates on its position. The sub's shallow depth was necessary to navigate the narrow Strait of Gibraltar. He activated the electric alternators of his engines and silenced its three diesel engines. The state-of-the-art sub would glide through the passageway unnoticed by even the most sophisticated sonar detection systems.

Headquarters had maintained a strict silence on the scope and goal of the mission. The captain knew only that he was to head to the Atlantic toward the U.S. and that his ten passengers of the elite Shayetet 13 commando unit spoke of a major operation in the works — somewhere.

He and his three lieutenant commanders were headed to the captain's private quarters to receive an electronic briefing. It was unnerving to be at the front end of a major offshore military operation without knowing the details. He surmised that his destination was somewhere on America's East Coast.

Captain Bargal followed his senior staff and the commander

of the strike force into his cramped quarters. The ubiquitous Israeli coffee machine was revved up, with strong blends in pods pretty much the only selection available.

"Yossi," the captain asked, addressing his tech officer, "will you set up the necessary equipment for our televised transmission? These devices are so temperamental."

Yossi grinned. "But you're trained and equipped to command a $1.5 billion war machine with the lives of over thirty-five soldiers in your hands?"

"That's why I have you guys around, to keep me from making mistakes."

The friendly banter helped break both the monotony and tension of days spent in the cramped underwater metal tube. Captain Bargal invited friendly exchanges. His successful wartime exploits were known to all the crew and read like a Jane's book of maritime credentials. He was neither threatened nor offended by criticism and humor aimed at him personally.

His approach to military command and discipline stressed initiative and independent decision-making in real-time warfare. He, like many Israeli commanders, believed that excessive focus on a rigid military hierarchy was counter to developing the teamwork and esprit de corps that were hallmarks of the country's military.

"You know my rank," he'd announced to his crew on the first day as the sub's commanding officer. "I don't need it repeated every time you want to talk with me. My name is David."

The familiar crackle of an encrypted transmission interrupted the banter. The fifty-inch screen brought the fatigued face of the prime minister into focus. The defense minister, the chief of staff, Lavi of Aman, and Levi of Mossad were sitting beside him.

"Good afternoon, gentlemen," the PM began. "I hope that all is well and that you're experiencing smooth sailing. Can one say sailing when you're moving under the surface?"

Captain Bargal attended the same counter-terrorism training as the PM. They maintained a friendly relationship.

"Eliezer," he answered, "you're the PM, so you can say what you please."

"Ah, a new and most welcome policy," Simcha responded. Without pause, he began the briefing. "David, we and Diaspora Jews are facing a threat that is primed to hit us on Rosh Hashana." The PM ran through the details of the mission and a rough overview of the responses to other challenges. "Your passengers constitute one arm of our response. We expect that you'll arrive off the coast of Alabama, in the Southeastern U.S., on the evening of September 5."

There was a collective gasp when the destination was mentioned.

"You'll surface, and your passengers will make their way to shore on the rubber Zodiac Milpro launches loaded onto your sub. They'll be met by Mossad agents to be transported to their staging ground in the suburbs of Birmingham. Three Mossad agents will drive vans labeled 'The Baptist Church of Our Lord' of New Orleans, Louisiana.

"It's unlikely that the vans will be stopped by any American highway police, but if they are, don't protest too strenuously. We have the U.S. president's personal approval, as well as the FBI's involvement as backup. They can call us on their encrypted phones; we'll be in our command center around the clock until our successful defense is complete on all fronts.

"The force will proceed about 285 miles to a house that we have in the neighborhood of the Quds base."

Captain Bargal, his officers, and the commando captain had a slew of logistical questions.

As the PM prepared to sign off, he added, "Gentlemen, I want you to know that all military plans of action have been vetted by 8200. We'll stay in very close communication with you. Good afternoon." The screen went dark abruptly. Transmissions were kept, brief lessening the chance of interception.

The PM's mention of 8200 was important to the officers. The spy agency's assessment of Israel's plans was important. They rarely handed out gold stars that were undeserved.

The men sat stunned. An Israeli attack on American soil and with its government's knowledge and possibly even complicity? Sammy, the sub's lieutenant commander and executive officer, asked the two-part question that was on most officers' minds: "David, did you know of this mission before we headed out to sea? America's FBI is competent, so why allow us to take on this action?"

The captain's response to the lieutenant's questions about prior knowledge of their destination and actions would be repeated in three other submarines about to embark on their missions. Their orders would be conveyed to them once they were well out to sea.

"I had no advance knowledge of our orders, Sammy," Bargal said. "We all learned of our mission at the same time, about ten minutes ago. I concluded that our course would bring us to the U.S. East Coast. I had no idea why, although we all knew it was not to sightsee at Disney World.

"Second, I have no idea what kind of a deal was struck to allow Israeli soldiers to act on American soil. My best guess is that we're to perform a duty that America would love to accomplish but sees as too politically difficult.

"We've just heard of the threats to the Jews of Birmingham, Alabama, by Iranian terror squads. Maybe our PM convinced the Americans that we'd be performing a service to the world, one that they can't manage at this time."

Dolphin-2 completed half of the 3,600 miles to the Strait of Gibraltar by September 1. Once through the strait, it would swing north after clearing Spain and Portugal and surface in the Bay of Biscay just off the coast of Le Havre, France.

The captain received a transmission similar to the one sent to Dolphin-1. He and seven senior and junior officers had been at sea for two days with no battle plans, no identified mission, and no knowledge of their final destination. Headquarters thought it too risky to provide orders to even their most trusted officers. Once out to sea, the chances of a communications slip were virtually nil.

Commanding Officer Eli Kochba was a twenty-year veteran of Israel's rapidly expanding naval force. His keen mind and navigational skills won him the admiration of even his most wise-assed junior officers. What was missing was Kochba's sense of humor.

Several of his officers approached the captain. "Sir," joked Ehud, the chief navigator heading the group, "since we've charted a course toward the Strait of Gibraltar" — STROG was the identifier used by sub navigators — "maybe we should attack Gibraltar and the Iberian Peninsula. They've got a civilian population of 30,000 and no army. This way we can claim an immediate victory." The group laughed.

Captain Kochba wasn't amused. The PM's talk shortly afterward dampened the crew's levity. Within minutes after receiving the message, they focused on the difficult mission ahead of them.

The ten commandos now had a handle on their complex assignment. They'd wondered why they were traveling by sub. Despite their training in diverse battlefield theaters, this was the Unit's first exposure to the cramped and claustrophobic conditions of a submarine.

They relieved the pressure and boredom by alternating between intense blackjack games and detailed reviews of battle plans once they hit Paris.

Avram, the Mossad agent who infiltrated the Quds unit in Paris, joined them. He requested to return as part of Israel's strike force. It seemed that Ashrawi bought the *Le Monde* article about his demise at the hands of "kidnappers." The newspaper's Page 3 picture of him lying bloodied and lifeless in the hotel corridor clinched it.

Set to arrive the night of September 5, less than two days before the planned attack, Dolphin-2 was to position itself two miles off the Le Havre port. Using Zodiac rubber launches, the force would hit the shore. Mossad agents, colleagues of Avram's, would meet them in three Regional Discount Airlines vans displaying the company's colorful logo. The drive was about 125 miles to Paris' Eleventh Arrondissement, where the Quds Force was based.

Dolphin-3 slid out of its berth, aiming for an Italian arrival at nightfall September 5. Mediterranean maritime congestion called for artful maneuvering as the sub steered clear of Russia's *Admiral Kuznetsov*.

The electric alternators kicked in early as the boat dived to 750 feet to avoid detection by its protectors: several destroyers and guided missile cruisers that would serve as escorts for the aircraft carriers of America's Sixth Fleet.

The captain mused how ironic it would be to be hunted by the destroyers that were arriving to back Israel. The sub's underwater signature, however, was virtually undetectable. They headed west through the Mediterranean, switched back to diesel engines, rose to a depth of about 400 feet, and prepared to swing north at the Tyrrhenian Sea toward Rome.

The sub was to come within two miles of Fiumicino, Italy, by nightfall. Ari, the lead Mossad agent in Rome, would be at their landing site. They'd drive the twenty miles on the A91 in three Euro Sports Association vans. The short ride would bring them to the Trastevere District near Isola Tiberina, command center of the Quds Force. A large studio apartment had been readied for them.

The ten commandos looked anything but fierce as they sat around the captain's dining table and traded bad, tired jokes. The area was one of the few open spaces in the sub. They squeezed in for a detailed briefing in T-shirts and shorts. Getting used to the cramped sub quarters under a couple of hundred feet of sea wasn't easy.

Dolphin-3's commanding officer was an anomaly in Israel's

navy. Most high-ranking naval officers were Israeli natives. But Captain Boris Lertov immigrated to Israel from Moscow twenty-five years earlier. Within a year of his arrival, he began his mandatory military service. He rose rapidly through the ranks. Three years into his career, he requested a transfer to the nascent naval force. In less than four years he commanded a Sa'ar 4.5-class missile attack craft. The captain, as he preferred being addressed, remained formal in his relationship with his crew.

The captain and five senior officers joined the commandos at the twelve-foot-long dining table. They pulled up chairs and squeezed in. They had spent a day and a half together. Commandos and crew had developed mutual respect, each appreciating the complexity of everyone's individual assignments. The journey was relatively short, but, still, the tight quarters generated personality clashes.

"We'll be arriving at our assigned location in — how long, Captain?" Yehuda, the lead commando, began the briefing.

"A bit over twenty-four hours," Lertov responded.

"So here," the boyish-looking officer continued, "is what I heard in the PM's message. The bad guys are on a small island in the middle of the Tiber. It's narrow and only yards from the southern shore, our base. The northern shore, where Rome's Great Synagogue is located, is about the same distance from the island.

"The Quds unit is made up of twelve snipers and explosives experts. Their plan is to attack three of Rome's principal synagogues, kill as many people as possible, neutralize the Italian police guards, and become martyrs if necessary."

He shifted in his seat. No one else moved.

"Two bridges link the island with both shores. The Iranians have been based in an abandoned warehouse. They're about thirty yards from a hospital that serves women and the elderly. They're sure to have sentries on each bridge. Our attack is timed for 0100 Zulu, when other actions we heard about will occur." There was a collective gasp as the commandos and crew reviewed what was planned on American soil.

"The timing is critical because Russia and Iran have tons of airpower in Syria ready to bomb Israel at 0300 Zulu. Our guys will hit their fighters on the ground — their ground. Timing and surprise are critical. We don't want to spook any of their forces so that they'll act prematurely.

"The Mossad guys who'll meet us as we land know the city well. They've been in Rome for over a year. Ari, their team leader, will guide us to our apartment, where our gear will be waiting for us. They'll be our eyes and ears in Rome and will make sure that our return to our taxi ride home will be uneventful." He eyed the men around the table. "Questions?"

Dolphin-4 left its Haifa mooring and headed south along the Mediterranean coast fully surfaced. As the calendar had just turned from August to September, the Israeli public was focused on preparations for Rosh Hashana, just days away.

Bathers paid scant attention to the surfaced sub cutting through the choppy sea. It never occurred to the beach revelers that this sleek war machine, now visible from any coastal city, might be carrying enough nuclear firepower to reduce the cities of a neighboring country to ashes. The sub was armed with turbo cruise missiles capable of hitting targets with great accuracy at well over 1,000 miles.

For Israelis, viewing the nation's military might was not unusual. Too often convoys of flatbed trucks transporting tanks north or south snarled traffic on highways. F-35s roared through Holy Land skies with regularity as the country was introduced to the new arrivals from America. Viewing the much-heralded Dolphin 2-class submarine, built in Germany, was hardly unusual.

Arik Golan, Dolphin-4's commanding officer, was a cool, levelheaded sailor well known to the Israeli military establishment. As a lieutenant commander, he'd led complex strike-force and hostage-rescue missions. That he was an unflappable decision-maker made him an easy selection for this dangerous and politically volatile assignment.

When IDF Chief of Staff Tzion described the operation to Golan, he gave him a clear directive: "Arik, you will be provoked, I'm sure, but you must keep your fingers away from the launch button. Your officers have been singled out carefully; you and your crew are sure to be tested."

"I'm honored and appreciate the confidence in us. You know, I'd like nothing more than to level the bastards, but count on me. The consequences of knee-jerk responses are clear."

Dolphin-4 cruised southeast on the surface of the warm waters of the Mediterranean toward Port Said. From there it would head to the Suez Canal. The sub was not the first Israeli warship to seek Egypt's permission to navigate the 125-mile-long canal. Israel's Foreign Ministry had requested that its warship have access to the Red Sea to participate in war games.

The Convention of Constantinople allowed safe passage through the canal for countries not at war with Egypt. The government did, however, demand that their cruisers escort the surfaced vessel at a speed not to exceed twenty knots. They stayed to the port and starboard sides of the sub until they reached the mouth of the Red Sea.

As the warships of both countries reached the end of the canal, sailors waved and saluted. Once implacable foes, the two countries proved they could maintain the cold peace between them.

They reached the open sea and dived to 450 feet. The next leg of their 1,300-mile voyage would take them to where the Red Sea merged with the Gulf of Aden. They would head north through the Arabian Sea to the Gulf of Oman, where they would surface — exposed to Russian and Iranian satellites.

In battle, their ballistic missiles could be fired from a depth of fifty feet, avoiding early satellite detection. The game plan, however, was to surface in full view of the enemy — and avoid testing that capability.

Captain Golan and his crew of thirty-five believed that a confrontation of who blinks first awaited them. They understood the importance of America's support and the positioning of its Sixth Fleet off Israel. Their backing, Golan maintained, would lessen the possibility of the unthinkable.

The captain had requested that four of the ship's twelve cruise missiles be armed with conventional warheads — just in case.

22
Preparing for The Northern Front

Tzion and Lavi headed out of Jerusalem on the morning of September 4. They'd return later that afternoon to meet with the PM and other Cabinet members. The chief of staff and Aman's director were to meet General Ron Karni, the head of Israel's air force, at Nevatim Air Base near Dimona in the Negev Desert.

Tzion generally rejected the luxury of a driver, considering it elitist and a waste of scarce resources. Today was the exception. Yarkoni had no qualms about the convenience and security of a trained driver-bodyguard. He convinced them that Menachem, who had guarded him for three years, should drive them to their desert destination.

Menachem pulled into the sprawling base having completed the 100-mile journey down Route 6 in just under two hours. The coating of sand and dust blanketing the black Mercedes after their desert jaunt offended his Germanic DNA. The limo generally shone under his meticulous upkeep.

They passed through two checkpoints on their way to base headquarters. Only five or six fighter planes were visible on the tarmac; the F-35s and most of the F-16Is and the F-15Es were parked well below the desert sands in acres of underground bunkers.

Tzion didn't wait for Menachem to get his door as they pulled into the reserved parking area. But he did make a point of holding the door open for the less agile Chaim Lavi.

General Karni was waiting in the front vestibule of headquarters. He greeted them warmly and guided them down a narrow hallway.

Karni, a fiftyish veteran of the IAF with a considerable paunch, complained to anyone who would listen that he was losing hair at an alarming rate. As no officer in the base wore a cap, his problem was on constant display.

"Great to see you both." His voice had a harsh, grating quality, although he would proclaim that he never touched a cigarette. "Yitzik Schneider, you know, the PM's aide, was here early this morning to brief me and a couple of others. So I'm up-to-date — unless things have changed since then."

In the most sensitive military communiqués, if face-to-face reporting was possible, it was preferred.

Tzion responded, "The situation is fluid, but I think you got the latest."

Lavi knew the IAF commander well. Karni had flown missions in his F-15 squadron about twenty-five years earlier. "Ron, will we be meeting with all the pilots you've selected for the mission?"

"Affirmative, Chaim. I knew that you and Igal wanted personal contact with each pilot."

Pilots' views about impending and past missions were important to the commanders. Israel's air force placed heavy emphasis on frontline feedback and field command decision-making.

Karni led them into a high-tech briefing room that looked more like an American movie theater than a military briefing venue. The seats were plush and comfortable, with a steep rake to allow for uninterrupted sight lines to the fifteen-by-fifteen screen. Seating capacity appeared to be about fifty, although only forty of the seats were occupied — by some of the finest fighter pilots in Israel.

Tzion whispered to Karni as they entered, "Wow. I'll have to speak to Meron about reducing budgetary allocations here. Look at this." He raised his eyebrows in faux astonishment.

"I knew I shouldn't have invited you guys here," Karni answered in mock defensiveness.

As they moved toward the front of the briefing center, Karni snapped, "Good morning gentlemen. Say hello to Chief of Staff General Igal Tzion and the director-general of Aman, General Chaim Lavi."

All stood in unison. There were polite shouts of *good morning* from many of the pilots.

"Good morning," Tzion began. "Chaim and I are here to talk and to listen. I know you've been briefed, but we'll hopefully add to that. Basically, we're here to go over the challenge ahead of us. Iranian pilots have been training with Russia's 34s and 35s for about a year and a half. That makes them good, and some of them may have even reached 20 percent of your abilities."

The laughter came quick and loud.

"Don't exaggerate their skills," one pilot called out.

"Several issues we want to emphasize," Tzion continued. "Russian pilots may be planning to fly some of the planes. Make no distinction between them and Iranians; take them out too. We may"—Tzion stroked his brow for emphasis—"have caught a bit of good luck. Most, if not all, of their planes are sitting above ground because of the recent thunderstorms in Syria. Their underground bunkers flooded."

A pilot in the front row, who looked about as old as a college freshman, called over his shoulder, "Gentlemen, someone upstairs is looking out for us."

Tzion cracked a smile. "They plan to attack us at 5 a.m.; we'll hit them at 4. We know"—Tzion anticipated the question from a pilot raising his hand—"that the Russians are aware of how often you've peed this morning. They track our air movements across the country. We'll rely on our stealths to fly under their radar and satellite detection. We'll camouflage our real direction until it's too late for them to respond."

Tzion stopped to address the pilot's question, which had to do with engagement with Russian pilots.

When he finished, Karni pointed to Lavi with admiration, "Before you sits one of Israel's legends. Some of you may know that Brigadier General Chaim Lavi led the squadron of F-15s that took out Syria's nuclear plant just before it was to go online."

"Yes," Lavi said, "but that was when I could see straight and didn't have prostate complications."

Laughter rippled through the room.

"Friends," Lavi began, brushing the wispy graying hair off his grooved brow, "perhaps as never before, we face a threat to our country and the Diaspora Jewish community as well. As we speak, three of our submarines are underway to locations in Europe and America. They are transporting troops from Sayeret Matkal and Shayetet 13 to preempt attacks on Diaspora communities in three allied countries. A fourth sub is headed for the Gulf of Oman to send our Iranian friends a clear message. Not since our independence have we been called on to act internationally with conventional — or almost conventional — force."

The general paused to allow the ripple of whispers to die down when America was included as an attack destination. The "almost conventional" comment was lost on no one. The Q&A session afterward would certainly deal with those surprises.

"The airpower to our north is formidable. We know all about their 34s and 35s. We also know that you guy are among the finest pilots in the world." Lavi's passion revved up. "We've worked long and hard on evading and jamming Russia's S-400 and 300s. Our 35s and 16s will be able to fly sea top up to Syria and turn inland near Latakia to hit our targets.

"We know that Russia's *Kuznetsov* is offshore and may think about sending help. You've been instructed to be aware of this. I can tell you that they and the Caspian Fleet headed our way will be cautious about any adventure, as America has agreed to help us by moving their Sixth Fleet into our backyard."

The last comment brought a buzz and a virtually uniform "kol hakavod," the Hebrew equivalent of "way to go."

"Before we take your questions and hear your thoughts, one additional point. Hatzerim air base will put its fighters on high alert to guard against any mischief coming from south or east."

He looked around the room, nodding at the pilots.

"Good luck. Our country is fortunate to have such skilled guardians. We're here for as long as you have questions and comments. Finally, we hope you won't be insulted that we've blocked all electronic and telephonic communication into and out of this base. We know that you understand why. Your next outgoing messages will be the afternoon of Rosh Hashana to tell your loved ones all is well."

The generals and pilots sat glued to the giant screen showing live satellite pictures of the air base in Syria. The next hour was spent answering questions and viewing simulated air combat. The generals led discussions about attack strategies, weapons selection, and air-to-air combat tactics.

The return ride to Jerusalem featured lively exchanges between the generals about strategies and armament choices. Menachem joined the discussion. Karni had invited him into the pilots' briefing session.

"We know," Menachem offered, "that the world's response to our preemptive attacks in Syria and abroad will be one of shock and condemnation. In my humble opinion" — which was not so humble — "Israel should do what we need to do. The fear of condemnation shouldn't drive our actions. We've been down this road before."

Kahan, of Shin Bet, had referred to Masada at a Cabinet meeting. Israel's poor image on the world stage amplified its self-reliance and continually put an apocalyptic scenario at the forefront of its collective consciousness. Existential threats inevitably resulted in a Masada-inspired narrative. Defeat was never an alternative.

23
A Warm Welcome to Beirut

Christina Marlowe and Ryan Williamson passed their British passports to the clunky, bored-looking officer sitting in the cramped immigration control booth. Christina admired her passport picture as she opened the document. Black hair becomes me, she thought.

Beirut-Rafic Hariri International Airport was a veritable Hezbollah headquarters. Heavily armed soldiers of the terror force were everywhere. The Hezbollah flag even flew above the national flag of Lebanon. It was as if they'd landed in the country of Lebanon-Hezbollah.

"What is your business here in Lebanon?" the passport control official asked Ryan as he glanced over his left shoulder wistfully, as if wishing the clock would move faster.

"We are a BBC news team. Christina and I have been on a worldwide assignment reporting on global warming."

"Why do I not hear a British accent?" the officer, perking up, asked in passable English.

"You will note, sir, that I was born in Kansas City, Missouri, in the USA. I am an immigrant to Great Britain going on twenty years. My colleague is Argentinian born, as you can see from her passport."

In excellent Spanish, the official, now dialed in, asked Christina a number of questions, which she answered to his satisfaction. He stamped both passports and said, "I'm sure that you will find it quite hot here."

Once through the control booth, they strolled to the Budget Car rental booth. The clerk's English was excellent as they arranged, as ordered, to rent the least expensive Toyota available. Ryan handed the agent his BBC credit card, which was validated and returned. They needed the car, Ryan requested, for two days.

Christina and Ryan maintained their false identities until safely inside their gray Toyota, which reeked of cigarette smoke. Their Mossad counterparts had warned them to remain locked into their borrowed identities while on airport grounds. The Office had reported that both terminals and the airport perimeter had a slew of strategically placed listening devices.

Only when their windows were closed and the noisy air-conditioning unit was switched on did they address one another as Joshua and Leora.

"The passport control guy's Spanish was pretty good," Leora said, feeling her throat getting irritated from the cigarette smoke odor.

"Can't say the same about his English," Joshua noted, "but the car rental lady's English was great."

They sat in the Toyota in the unrestricted arrival area and waited for EGYPTAIR Flight 462, originating in Paris and coming from Prague. "Hope we've timed Abu's flight right," Joshua muttered more to himself than to Leora. "8200 has been sending messages to my phone. They keep telling me they're on top of the endless escape hatches this Houdini has at his disposal. We'll see."

The most recent text put about an 80 percent probability on Yusalem meeting with Naswalah al-Din, the military head of Hezbollah, at the Golf Club of Lebanon. It was an unusual choice for a meeting place for the terrorists, the very reason they were to meet there. The club also had a veritable small army as its security force.

Leora was busy computing time and distance: "The ride to the club from the airport is about six miles. With no traffic, we could get there in ten to twelve minutes."

"Programming complete," Joshua said after checking his texts. What he meant was that an Israeli Predator drone, hovering about twenty miles off the attractive Lebanese coastline, had been remotely programmed to arm its six Hellfire missiles.

Leora nudged Joshua. "Check out the two black Lincoln Navigator SUVs that just pulled up, over there by the arrival doors."

Rather than wave off the limos, which were defiantly parked in a restricted area, the guards cheerfully greeted the drivers. A Lebanese Army soldier, AK-47 slung casually over his shoulder, sauntered over to the lead car, rested his left elbow on its roof, and appeared to be enjoying his conversation with its driver.

Within five minutes, the double arrival doors swung open, and three burly security personnel stepped through and scanned the area. Leora, poking Joshua in the ribs, almost shouted, "Check it out; so far, looks like 8200 is a bull's eye. Three more guys are coming out behind that first group." Three mean-looking men, very much the bodyguard types, wearing sport jackets and carrying cloth carry-on bags, almost immediately followed them. The trio sported full black beards, white *taqiyas*, scowls, and deeply furrowed brows that even their sunglasses couldn't hide. This was no ordinary arrival.

A moment later a dark-blue Armani suit, a $500 silk tie, and blindingly bright alligator shoes emerged, stylishly wrapped around an energetic Abu Yusalem. Joshua trained his pocket binoculars on Yusalem and appeared mesmerized as he studied his nemesis. "Definite ID," he muttered to Leora. "No mistake this time."

"No way one could look that rested and unwrinkled flying coach," Leora complained. "Joshua, talk to Levi. He yells at us about the expense of checking luggage."

Yusalem entered the second limo, and both black chariots took off.

Joshua pulled out of the public lot of the arrival area while Leora texted the models and colors of the two cars to military headquarters. They would soon be on Beirut-Saida Highway, heading north toward the golf club.

They followed the limos at a distance of about a half-mile.

When they were two miles from the club, it was clear that it would be the meeting place. Leora said in an excited, overly loud voice, "I just texted our conclusion to drone control center, Northern Command, in the Golan Heights. I think we'll get the bastard this time."

She soon added, "It's a go. Just got the center's response."

Joshua made a slow, easy U-turn at the next intersection and headed south, away from the club.

They stopped about three miles south of the airport at the deserted shoreline at Khalde, where an Israeli cutter flying Hezbollah colors would meet them, and got out of their soon-to-be-abandoned rental.

They were relieved to see the Israeli patrol boat about a mile out. A commando was guiding a rubber Zodiac to shore, their ride to the waiting cutter.

"Better than Budget Rental," Leora said. The rented car would be retrieved by Lebanese authorities and traced to a dead end, as would their credit card charges.

Two Israeli F-16s roared overhead, having met no resistance as they entered Lebanese airspace. They were a noisy insurance policy that no resistance would be encountered. The attack on Yusalem, the Israeli military concluded, would appear unrelated to the Rosh Hashana attacks. The IDF and its terrorist adversaries were involved in perennial cat-and-mouse actions. These sporadic military forays often seem minor when compared with the splinter group infighting within Hezbollah, Hamas, or Islamic Jihad. Yusalem carried a target on his back, even with his allies.

The roar of the fighter planes paled in comparison with the earth-rattling explosions when two Hellfire missiles from the Israeli drone virtually disintegrated the two limos as they turned into the ornately gated entrance to the posh club. It remained to be seen if even Houdini could have escaped those blasts.

24
Moving Into Position In the USA

Dolphin-1 cut through the Atlantic just east of Cuba and entered the Gulf of Mexico the evening of September 4 — right on schedule. She completed the final 600 or so miles and arrived about two miles offshore the evening of September 5.

The commandos had prepared their gear, which included sidearms. Automatic weapons and explosives would be waiting at their destination. It was unusual for them to begin any mission without their heavy weapons, especially one this dangerous.

The sub surfaced as night set in for real. The shimmering lights of Gulf Coast hotels and casinos appeared on the horizon like a pale-green patina. The crew lowered the inflatable Zodiacs — held fast to the sub by knotted towlines — into the warm Gulf water.

The tropical breeze and its subtle pine fragrance caressed Captain Bargal as he stood on deck. He forcibly exhaled the stale air that had irritated his bronchials for days. Being confined in close quarters with forty-five soldiers for a week and a half was no picnic.

"Yaacov, the Mossad guy, will be waiting on the beach to guide you to vans that will take you to Birmingham. After your successful mission," Bargal continued, "Yaacov and his team will drive you back to Orange Beach, where your launches will be waiting. Good luck. Remember, we'll remain submerged until your nighttime return."

The two launches slid away and swung hard right toward

shore. Within five minutes of push-off, the sub slipped below the surface.

Each Zodiac held five commandos with little room to spare. They made their way in the smooth Gulf waters in surprising quiet. Israel's navy techs had muffled the launch motors used by its commando forces. They could be detached from the deflated Zodiacs and loaded onto the sub with relative ease.

They reached shore close to where Yaacov guided them with an electronic device similar to a GPS. After brief introductions, they stored the boats in a rented metal unit, the kind used by Alabama beach regulars.

The team slid into three white church vans, each driven by a Mossad agent. Fifteen minutes after arrival, the vans were headed north on the highway. The 285-mile trip was less bumpy and faster when they reached Interstate 65 near Mobile. Yaacov drove the lead van and used the almost-four-hour drive to brief Eli, the unit's commander.

"We should be in Birmingham in about three and a half hours," Yaacov began. "We rented a house about three blocks from the Quds unit's base.

"They have two houses but will come together in one before their attack to pray, confirm plans, and check arms and explosives. How they managed to amass automatic weapons and explosives is a matter left to the American government; we have enough to deal with. Eli, I know that there's much to coordinate, so stop me at any time."

"Thanks, Yaacov." Eli's voice was surprisingly deep given his boyish features. "Let's hear the basics of your plan. Before we crash for the night, you can go through the operation with the full team in Birmingham."

"Sounds good to me," Yaacov said, suppressing a yawn. "OK, here goes. The time difference between Birmingham and Israel is eight hours. That is, we're eight hours behind Israel. It's critical that we coordinate our actions so that not one terrorist escapes to sound the alarm. Israel will attack the Russian planes in Syria at 4 a.m. Israel time. Here in Birmingham, that is 8 p.m. the night before. We'll coordinate our attack using Zulu time.

"That means tomorrow night is the start of our operation. We've arranged with the help of the American FBI, who are, believe it or not, with us every step of the way, that beginning at 7 p.m. there'll be a massive regional outage of all satellite and cell phone communications. No one in Russia or Tehran will receive word of our operation until it's too late. We have to be 100% sure that we do nothing to blow America's cover. Their involvement with us, if made public, will cause a big stink."

Yaacov was surprised that Eli remained riveted and alert despite the late hour and their ten-day journey in a submarine. "Let me know when it's too much, too late.

"The FBI got the power company to evacuate two or three homes across the road from the Quds house, claiming a dangerous gas leak. The families have been temporarily relocated to nearby hotels. We have automatic weapons, hand grenades, and a supply of TATP in our facility. With the help of my tech guys, we also developed a drone on wheels.

"The façade of the drone looks like a big, flowering bush common to this region. We'll program the drone to roll slowly toward the bad guys' house, carrying enough TATP to blow up the house and ensure that there are no survivors.

"We created a drone for each of the four sides of the house," Yaacov continued, as if he were describing building rather than demolishing something, "ensuring total destruction. We should be able to make our way close to the Quds house unnoticed, since the neighbors have been moved to hotels. With the people across the road away, we'll avoid collateral damage. We'll have to take out only one or two sentries."

"These drones roll toward the house?" Eli asked with an almost boyish fascination.

"Their small motors can easily be programmed for direction and speed. We'll arrange for them to take an hour to inch up to the home so that they arouse no suspicion. That should give us enough time to be one hour back down the highway and on the way to the sub. We'll set off the charge by cellphone, which will, we hope, work at just the time we need it."

"I like it," Eli said with admiration. "I heard that you were a technology geek, but this may exceed even that description. Like a rolling drone? Sounds like a Bob Dylan song."

The others in the van moaned their disapproval.

"One more question," Eli asked. "Where's the Stormfront headquarters? I know it's in Birmingham. Several of us want to pay it a brief visit." He grinned. "Extra duty, you understand."

The vans pulled into the three-car garage of their Vestavia Hills rental just past midnight. The split-level ranch would easily accommodate the temporary tenants. They were eager to unload their gear.

They welcomed the sandwiches and cold drinks arranged on the kitchen counter as well as the bedroom's cache of automatic weapons, hand grenades, and explosives.

The unit's joker, Erez, asked, "Are the sandwiches made with organic produce?" That he could joke after ten days cooped up in a sub and a four-hour van ride had Yaacov and others shaking their heads.

Yaacov and Eli stood at the center of the bare living room and laid out in detail the plan that Eli was briefed on during their journey from Orange Beach. At about 2 a.m., both teams crashed, hoping to sleep for four or five hours.

September 6 was spent reviewing plans and contingencies so they would be clear even in the fog of battle.

At 6 p.m. Rosh Hashana eve, a "Baptist Church of our Lord" van pulled into the Stormfront headquarters parking lot. The 10,000-square-foot former printing complex housed its lone tenant in an otherwise deserted industrial park on the outskirts of the city.

The bright summer light waned as the Alabama sun dropped behind a line of Leyland cypresses and a dazzling array of birch and red maples. The deciduous trees hadn't begun their autumnal color show. The Stormfront signage was a stark contrast to the pastoral vista surrounding the bleak industrial park.

The banner that hung over the front entrance read "American Front for White Rights." Just under it was a second poster: "If You're WHITE You're Welcome." The smaller letters underneath read: "Muslims, Black Folk, and Jews Not Welcome."

Roni, a twenty-four-year-old unit member, said, "Hey, we're not welcome. Damn. Ima always said I'd be barred from the finest establishments if I didn't mend my ways." He mimed wiping away a tear.

About twenty-five pickup trucks were parked outside the building.

"Yaacov's briefing," Eli whispered to his team, "pointed out that the front door is double-plated steel. We'll have a greeting party of heavily armed guys who know how to use their automatic rifles. Avoid gunfire exchanges — we fire only if fired on first."

The thin veneer of claiming self-protection would not fly with the American public; notwithstanding the admiration for Israel's self-defense, an elaborate FBI whitewash would be indispensable. The plan presented to the American president described only the destruction of Stormfront's headquarters. No green light had been given for gunfire aimed at American citizens, irrespective of their crimes.

Yariv, their Mossad driver, pointed toward the rear entrance. "Just behind the garbage bins," he whispered, "that door will be double-plated as well."

In his best attempt to speak quietly, Eli said, "Let's send a message to these anti-Semites."

The team members spread out and slowly made their way toward both entrances. When the force was within five yards of the building, the alarm system was tripped. Floodlights flashed, and a screeching siren pierced the air.

They raced to both entrances and blew in the doors with satchels of TATP.

Six armed Stormfront guards, stunned by the explosions and blinded by smoke grenades, fired their automatic weapons blindly in the direction of both entrances. Other Stormfront members groped for their weapons. Within seconds, the deafening din of their gunfire reverberated throughout the headquarters.

The commandos waited for the order from Eli. With bullets pinging all around them and the smoke from the grenades dissipating, Eli gave the command to return fire.

In less than five minutes, silence prevailed. The unit entered the headquarters wearing gas masks that within moments were no longer necessary.

A careful search found four Stormfront corpses. Eighteen of the racists had escaped through a maze of basement passageways. Israel would have a lot to account for, despite having performed a community service for Alabamians. Deadly force, justified or not, would surely be condemned — even by a supportive American administration.

Israel had taken a step to warn racists worldwide that there were consequences to terrorizing Jews anywhere. But, at what cost?

Eli took a photograph out of a small leather case hanging from his belt. He moved from corpse to corpse, matching faces with the picture. Hazian wasn't among them. Neither was Richie Larkin, Hazian's nemesis. Richie, the embedded Mossad agent, had notified Tabor that he was unavailable that day.

One commando knelt next to a satchel and adjusted the connected timing device. He called out to the men who'd begun sweeping the floor for spent cartridge casings. "No need for that. In a few hours nothing in here will be recognizable. I've set the timer to blow and burn the place at 7:50 p.m. We should be on our way back to the sub by then. Yariv, don't forget to inform your FBI contacts not to enter the building before then."

To no one in particular as they made their way out, Eli said, "Convenient that their headquarters was in a remote business area. The morning mailman will be in for a big surprise."

They returned just in time for a final briefing before the attack. As they filed through the garage entrance, Eli announced: "Plan B didn't go exactly as we mapped it out. We were involved in a firefight we didn't want. And, to boot, Hazian wasn't there.

The real challenge for us is the next stage. As much as we would have liked counting Hazian among the recently martyred at Stormfront HQ, we have a shot at getting him with our attack on their base."

Yaacov reminded the guys now gathered in the living room that the FBI had arranged for a regional blackout of all cellphone service beginning at 7:10 p.m. "The time may seem unusual," Yaacov said, "but it's planned that way. The Quds sentries rotate every three hours, but they check in with their commander every hour on the hour.

"That means they'll call at 7. We're hoping that when we help the sentries become martyrs at 7:05, no one inside will become suspicious. They text Tehran regularly in what they believe is an indecipherable code. That communication will also be impossible soon after 7." News reports would soon state that the gap in service was caused by a satellite glitch.

Yaacov grinned as he said, "There shouldn't be any suspicion that the interruptions were linked to an Israeli military action 6,000 miles away from home."

They loaded the vans with weapons. The four "bushes" were gingerly placed on folded-down seats. At 6:55, the three vans pulled into the deserted target neighborhood. The gas leak ruse was in effect. They hoped it wouldn't arouse suspicion in the Quds headquarters.

Their base of operations was a 7,000-square-foot antebellum mansion set back about 100 feet from the road. A gently sloped, well-maintained lawn made the attractive home even more distinctive. It easily accommodated the full force gathered for final planning and prayers.

Two fluted columns framed the elegant eight-foot oak front door. The deep porch extended across the front of the brick building. Two rocking chairs flanked the entrance. It looked idyllic and quintessentially Southern.

Night hadn't set in, so approaching the home would be difficult. Yaacov would need to get within 100 feet of the target with his drones. At 7, Eli directed two snipers to cover those who would inch up through shadowy areas. Silencers would muffle their shots.

At 7:05, the right front sentry caught a .45 round in his left temple. The sniper used his MTAR-21 Variant fed by an Uzi magazine. The weapon's rapid-fire capability wasn't needed. As the guard fell, branches crackled under his limp body, alerting the second sentry. Finger on the trigger of his AK-47, he called out to his partner in Farsi, asking about the noise. The snipers had no shot until the guard turned the corner.

Receiving no response, he hurried toward the front position, cell phone in hand. A muffled shot from a sniper's rifle took half his head off. The area was now very quiet. Yaacov's rolling invention was about to make its debut.

Yaacov moved with purpose. "Yariv, Arnon, help me remove the firecrackers from the quilted valise. Unless you want to make a premature noise," he joked, "be gentle as you place the packets into the cushioned pouch at the back of each drone."

Each parcel had an external timing device coordinated to detonate by a single telephone signal at 7:55 p.m., five minutes after the resumption of satellite communication service and minutes before the air force's preemptive strike on the Russian-Iranian fighters in Syria.

Yaacov had created four rhododendron facsimiles complete with white blossoms and leaves. The artificial foliage concealed the small wheels. Each drone could be independently controlled, but all were set to deliver a massive explosion with the signal. The amount of explosives in each device would make it unlikely that anyone survived the blast. A sentry assigned by Eli confirmed that no one had left the building the past couple of hours.

TV reports would claim that the powerful blast seemed to be linked to the gas leaks — an investigation was underway. The FBI's scripted text would praise local officials who thankfully had organized the evacuation of neighboring homes when the leak was detected. Unfortunately, not every home took the emergency order seriously, the script read; there were casualties.

With the sentries martyred, several commandos and the Mossad agents placed the drones at the four sides of the home.

Eli warned, "Careful not to activate the motion-sensitive flood lights. Stay clear of the zone. We've been through this once today."

They signaled to Yaacov to start the motors. He fiddled with the third drone, which was uncooperative and required reprogramming.

It was getting dark fast. They gathered their gear, relieved that they were not drawn into another firefight; a second shoot-out on American soil would further complicate an already complex picture. They piled into their vans and headed south to Orange Beach. Mossad agents would remain in Alabama to deal with the three vans and the rental house.

The ride south on I-65 toward Mobile was uneventful. They passed a number of Alabama State Patrol cars on the lookout for speeders. They stayed well within the limit.

The Israeli caravan was about twenty miles outside Birmingham, having just passed an exit sign for Hoover, when a muffled explosion was heard over the rattle of the lead van's air conditioning. Thirty seconds later, a less powerful blast was heard.

Eli joked, "We'll have to get better about synchronizing our timing. It sounds like the interruption of Stormfront's community services was off by thirty seconds. We'll know how successful we were when we're on our underwater taxi ride home; they'll have the satellite data that monitored our movements. Kol hakavod. I can only pray that the other missions have been successful."

"Israel is fortunate," Yaacov said, "to have guys like you — who don't snore at night." More soberly, he added, "The world has become a more complex place. Not just for Jews, for everyone. But, especially for Jews. Our guys face similar challenges in Paris, Rome, and Syria. The next days are critical."

25
European Action

The port at Le Havre, France, was a heavily trafficked maze of freight ships heading north to the British Isles and south to other European destinations. Midnight to 4 a.m. was slack time for maritime activity.

Dolphin-2 surfaced at 12:30 a.m. on September 6, about two miles offshore and a mile beyond the port's protective barrier. Avram and his Paris Mossad colleagues estimated that the force would land just north of the Avant Port section of the sprawling shipping complex.

The commandos would hit shore at the darkened André Malraux Art Museum. The popular art center was closed to the public after 6 p.m. The parking lot would be free of cars except for three freshly painted vans and a small truck, all advertising "Regional Discount Airlines" with a Dublin, Ireland address.

Avram and the unit reviewed plans for their return the following night. The sub would resurface about two miles farther north to avoid contact with early morning freighter arrivals. They would fly the colors of the French flag. French warships frequented the Le Havre port. Israel had gambled that flying the French colors would be sufficient to mask that France had no submarine that remotely resembled Dolphin-2.

Just as in the U.S. operation, the force was equipped only with sidearms; their heavy weaponry awaited them in Paris.

Two Zodiacs eased away from the sub and headed northeast. The offshore breeze taxed their motors, and a stiff current had them drifting southward. Still, the muffled motors were barely audible despite the extra horsepower required. The guidance system operated by the land-based agents kept them on track.

Fifteen minutes later they made landfall, and the commandos connected with the Mossad agents. Hugs were traded as Avram reunited with the team he had worked with while monitoring and eventually infiltrating Ibrahim Ashrawi's network.

They hauled the Zodiacs out of the cold bay water and guided them up a ramp into the eighteen-foot truck parked in the museum lot. The markings of the popular discount airline would minimize suspicion should a night watchman spot the truck.

Captain Eyal Marcus, a sinewy, tanned thirty-year-old veteran, joined Avram and the lead Paris agent in the first van.

"Welcome, Captain." Benjamin, aka Beni, had taken over the lead Mossad position when Avram returned to Israel with Leora after the near miss at the St. Etienne hotel. He shook Marcus' hand. "Avram, great to see you. Looks like you gained a few pounds."

Marcus grinned and added: "Hard to believe, but that clever killer Ashrawi bought the hotel burglary thing. The article in *Le Monde* about the robbery and murder was convincing, pictures and all. How'd the newspaper get pictures of you lying dead of gunshot wounds?"

"Thanks for reminding me," Avram moaned. "I owe the reporter his monthly retainer. Talk to us, Beni. Captain Marcus is sick of hearing me after a week together under 500 feet of saltwater."

"Let me first make sure that I don't miss the entrance to the toll road toward Paris. We have about 125 miles to go on it. We won't use the same road on the way back."

"For budgetary purposes?" Avram asked.

"We all know how cheap the boss is," Beni said, "but that's not it. I want to avoid any possibility of being ID'd by tollbooth attendants. Every booth is manned. It's like jobs in France trump automation. You know all the international bullshit that'll be coming at us after this."

All agreed.

"Here goes," Beni began once he'd turned onto the toll road. "The bad guys are really bad. There are twenty-four Quds fighters in three apartments in a building in the Eleventh Arrondissement. The building has four apartments, with the one used to store their heavy weaponry and explosives.

"Four vans they've been using regularly are parked in the building's lot; they've been in these quarters for over a month. Their day is spent coordinating plans and reconnoitering access and exit points. Teams of four leave daily to scope out the Jewish neighborhood and commercial enterprises and customer shopping patterns on Rue des Rosiers. They want maximum casualties.

"One team has studied the police presence at synagogues as Rosh Hashana approaches. These fuckers are good, ruthless, and prepared for their eternal martyrdom."

Avram pounded on the glove compartment. "We're here," he said, smirking, "to expedite those martyrdom wishes."

The two-hour ride to Paris passed quietly. At 3:15 a.m., September 6, three Regional Discount Airlines vans pulled into the inner courtyard of an abandoned warehouse scheduled for demolition.

Fourteen figures emerged silently and entered through a rear door. The Matkal visitors were pleasantly surprised at the temporary layout of sleeping bags, hot and cold drinks, and sandwiches. They were especially impressed with the array of weaponry, including laser-guided RPG launchers.

"Before we relax too much, let's go over a few points," Beni said, gathering them around a folding table. "Bring your drinks and sandwiches; I'll be brief." He unfolded a five-by-five-foot street map of Paris, taped it to two columns, and aimed one of the dozen or so generator-powered floodlights at the map.

With a sandwich in his right hand and a cola in his left, Beni pointed to the map with his drink hand. "This is the street map that you reviewed on the sub." He took a long swig. "Here is where we are now, Rue Gambey in the Eleventh Arrondissement.

"About two blocks away, the Iranians' base is in a building just off Avenue Parmentier." He pointed to the east of Rue Gambey. "They're the only tenants in that private building.

"Our most recent inside intel came from a relatively reliable source, even though he is mostly Arab." He pointed to Avram seated to his right, referring to his Egyptian birthplace. "A man who risked his life on a daily — no, hourly — basis, having infiltrated the Quds Force months ago."

There was brief applause, and a ringing "kol hakavod" was shouted out.

Avram, embarrassed, called out, "Keep going, Beni."

Beni was interrupted by the familiar crackle of a televised transmission. The laptop set up on a folding table six feet to their left had been logged on upon their arrival. The group turned toward the computer as a familiar voice spoke.

"Hello to our brave warriors" was the greeting from the prime minister. "While you loll around in the lap of luxury in Paris, we've been sleeping in our command center in the Knesset. I'm here with Chaim Lavi of Aman, Igal Tzion, Zvi Levi, and Moshe Yarkoni."

He waved a hand that moved in and out of the screen. "Only Moshe is happy to be here, because he says the sandwiches that we've been living on are better than his wife's cooking. We've called to wish you good luck and to let you know that we've been observing all movement of the enemy on our satellite transmissions.

"Should there be any reason to notify you prior to your moving into action, we'll call you immediately. Get some rest, and we'll see you back in Israel in a few days."

The screen fell silent as abruptly as it had come to life. Communications were kept brief.

Beni joked, "I bet their sandwiches are better than ours, though so far I haven't heard any complaints about the cuisine; everyone must be tired. Captain Marcus, will you continue with the plan and timing of the attack?"

Marcus popped up with surprising agility, given his fatigue and the inhospitable accommodations of his six-day underwater experience. With military terseness he laid out the operation.

"We're coordinating our plans in Paris with military actions in different parts of the world. It's important that we execute efficiently so we don't tip off the enemy in those other places.

"Our information, from 8200 and Avram, is that the enemy numbers twenty-four Quds soldiers. We must ensure that there are twenty-four Quds martyrs when we exit Paris."

There was a murmur of agreement.

"We'll leave here at 1:15 tomorrow morning, which I remind you is Rosh Hashana. We'll take all of our gear and weapons as we won't return. The enemy is only a few blocks from us in a private stand-alone apartment building. That's lucky; we'll plant enough TATP to level the building with little chance of anyone walking out of there.

"We won't be around to know if there are survivors, so we'll leave that to you local guys or our satellites. We'll be en route to our ride home when the blast occurs. We've been instructed to plan the party for tomorrow morning at exactly 2:45 a.m. Paris time, so we'll use electronic timers and leave the site by 2:15.

"Chaim," Captain Marcus nodded to his left, "your team will work with Avram. Questions?"

The usual banter followed as the group headed toward their lap-of-luxury sleeping arrangements. The unit was accustomed to catching a few hours of shut-eye in harsh conditions. The usual jokesters made sleep more difficult by repeating old jokes and worn-out stories about sexual conquests that grew more grandiose and exotic with each telling.

The sputtering and coughing of a large truck pulling into their driveway just past midnight caused some alarm. Several fighters grabbed their automatic weapons. Beni assured the unit that it was the Paris waste disposal truck that they had secured.

"We may have been unclear about this, but here goes," Beni laid it out. "Our agents posed as movie producers filming scenes involving a garbage truck in the Eleventh Arrondissement."

Trash pickup in Paris generally occurred at ungodly hours in the morning to lessen congestion on the narrow streets. Parisians believed that the sadistic schedule was meant to cause maximum discomfort to Paris' citizenry.

"We hope," Beni continued, talking to the guys who hadn't dozed off, "the rented truck appearing about a half-hour earlier than the usual pickup time won't cause any suspicion. Paris's waste collection schedule's been a work in progress for seventy-five years.

"Nighttime pickup should allow sappers cover to get close enough to plant explosives at key spots in their building. Our satellite feedback shows no guards outside, but we need to cover our bases in case we missed something."

Final preparations were interrupted just before 1 a.m. September 7 by the crackle of a transmission on the laptop. All eyes were glued to the screen coming to life as Tzion began the communication from Jerusalem.

"We're observing, as I speak, six Quds loading a van, motor running.

"Our guess is that they're moving a part of their force into position to attack the Marais shops and institutions at daybreak or sooner. They appear to be loading automatic weapons and satchels that we assume contain grenades. They know that despite it being Rosh Hashana, most of the Jewish and Israeli shops will be open for business and unusually busy.

"They must be intercepted while the rest of the plan stays on track. They'll no doubt use the same route their surveillance units have taken in the past week. Avram and Beni, you'll be familiar with what I'm about to describe, and so the rest is up to you.

"They'll head west a few blocks and then south toward the Bastille. You can intercept them far enough away to take them out and coordinate the takedown with the banging of the garbage truck. It looks like they're minutes away from departure. I won't keep you." The transmission ended abruptly.

Captain Marcus looked to Uzi and Itai, his best marksmen, and snapped, "Get it together. We're out of here in two minutes. Avram, Beni, we'll need you with us. Gentlemen, we'll meet in twenty minutes at Avenue Parmentier to finish the job. Make as much noise as possible with the garbage truck without arousing suspicion. Uzi, Itai, bring the RPGs. See the rest of you soon."

They hurried to a waiting Regional Discount Airlines van and loaded their gear while Beni started the engine. The team headed south two blocks and shot southwest to greet the Quds van heading their way. Rue Boulle, about a mile and a half from the terrorists' building, was where they waited. They were a half-mile from the Bastille, where the Quds fighters would turn west toward the Jewish Quarter.

Marcus and company waited about ten minutes with no vehicle in sight. "Maybe they stopped to pray; they're so devout, you know," Uzi joked. No sooner had they finished chuckling than the headlights of a car appeared several blocks north.

Itai knelt about three feet from the van, aimed the rocket launcher, and waited until Uzi, using his infrared scope, confirmed it was the Iranians. A tap on his shoulder told Itai it was the Quds van. He squeezed the trigger.

Three seconds later, the van, now about two hundred yards away, was hit just under the front bumper and spun in the air, meeting the pavement in a ball of flame. A surprisingly subdued explosion followed. The real bang came moments later when the ammunition inside the van caused a secondary explosion.

A minute later, the Israelis were speeding north on a parallel avenue to their rendezvous at Avenue Parmentier. The sappers had planted enough TATP to level the Eiffel Tower. In the distance, fire trucks could be heard racing to the scene of what appeared to be an unfortunate car accident on Boulevard Richard Lenoir, near the Bastille.

"How did it go?" asked Eli, the lieutenant in charge in Marcus' absence.

"Looks like we got them all," Marcus answered.

"We're all set here," Eli whispered. "Timers set to go off at

2:45 local time."

"Follow our van," Beni said as he accounted for all of the commandos and agents. "I'll drive the garbage truck two blocks away and leave it in a parking lot. It can never be traced to us.

"From there, we take side streets at moderate speed; no need to attract a gendarme who may be nearby in his patrol car. I'll get us to the A13 highway until the exit just before the first toll-booth. It'll be parallel roads after that with little chance of detection until we're back in Le Havre. We should hear the result of our efforts about halfway to the port.

Marcus said, with a sigh of relief, "If we'd been in London, we might have needed better cover. Paris is behind a lot of European capitals with their CCTV cameras. Seems that London has cameras on every corner."

He nodded at the commandos. "Another precaution of our Paris team," he said, "was to arrange to have the Regional Discount Airlines signage peeled off in Le Havre. Each van will be labeled with the name of some food distributors from Belgium and the Netherlands."

The teams piled into the vans, weary but relieved that all seemed to go well.

Arriving at the André Malraux Art Museum at 4 a.m., the commandos found that their Zodiac launches had been carried to the shoreline by three new faces. Not surprisingly, the former Regional Discount Airlines storage truck was now identified as an organic farm produce distributor in Brussels.

The goodbyes were brief. The mission confirmed headquarters' belief that Special Forces could coordinate military actions with local Mossad agents with precision. Avram found it difficult to leave his colleagues again. But it would soon be dawn in France, and the sight of a sub surfaced just outside the port barriers—even one flying the French flag—might not be so well received.

They pushed off and headed for the sub two miles offshore. As they climbed aboard, crewmembers lifted the launches onto the deck, and the captain called out, "One hundred percent. Satellite imagery showed the target totally flattened."

He shook hands with each man as he passed him and said, "Let's say a prayer for the success and safety of our fighters now in the skies over Syria."

Breaking several moments of silence, Captain Kochba smiled and announced: "No one observed leaving after the blast and little collateral damage to nearby buildings — shattered windows and a sleepless rest of the night, maybe. Great job."

As the men loaded up their heavy gear to be stowed below, the lieutenant commander rapped Kochba on the shoulder — harder than he meant to — and said, "Captain, radar is picking up a French gunboat approaching starboard. Looks like a 68. They guard their ports, have plenty of firepower, and can really move."

"I knew it was too good to be true," Kochba muttered, shaking his head. "Get Alan dressed rapidly and up here ASAP. Ready torpedo turrets 16 and 18—conventional. Slow shift starboard; I'd like to face him when he gets here."

Alan was a lieutenant who had immigrated to Israel from Morocco six years earlier. He was a native French speaker and taught the language in Tel Aviv University's continuing education program. He was recruited for this mission, in part, for this ability.

"He's about three miles out and closing fast," the lieutenant commander said. Some concern in his voice, but not much more—yet.

Three minutes later Alan came topside in a neatly ironed French officer uniform, tassels and all. His leather belt was strapped across his chest, right to left, with the captain's braided lariat over his right shoulder. His firearm was holstered neatly across his waist. He waited for the French gunboat, sure to be joined by other sea craft momentarily. Three or four Israeli sailors in nondescript fatigues and T-shirts worked around him, seemingly paying little attention to the French vessel now alongside the sub.

Loudspeaker in hand, the gunboat's commander gruffly demanded, "What are you doing here? What's your business?" Seeing the "Captain" making his way down from the conning tower, his tone changed. "Apologies, mon capitaine; why are you out here?"

Alan responded in perfect and condescending French, "We are concluding our war games, which are testing the safety of our waters in general and our ports in particular. We were hoping that our 68s would respond effectively. You did."

Alan seemed to be enjoying this charade. "Please know I will personally report to the General de Division that No. 3864" — he read the numbers off the side of the gunboat — "should be commended for intercepting a vessel unknown to them. Now, sir, if you will move your 68 back a bit, we'll be able to submerge and complete our final test just north of here — which I will thank you not to divulge."

As the 68 commander was saluting the "capitaine," a French sailor emerged to whisper something in the commander's ear.

"Mon capitaine," he shouted, no longer using the bullhorn, "my officer says that the Defense Ministry has no knowledge of your war games."

In perfectly calm and accomplished French, Alan responded, "Of course not; that's why they are secret war games. We are testing port safety. Would it make sense to notify all of our arrival? You intercepted us out of professional duty. That is what we are after. That is what is to be commended."

Alan saluted the sailors, didn't wait for a response, and headed toward the conning tower and the lower deck. Latch secured, they slid backward and slowly submerged. He wasn't sure whether he'd left them smiling or furious. Now, it no longer mattered. They would soon be virtually undetectable and heading home. Captain Kochba, Alan and the crew seemed to be holding their breath as Dolphin-2 slid deeper and revved up its engines. Little attention was paid to the French flag still fluttering in the breeze just before they submerged.

The crew and its passengers sarcastically saluted in unison as Kochba said, "Nice work, *mon capitaine.*"

26
Commandos Visit Rome

The drive for Dolphin-3's commandos — from the landing site off Italy's coastal city of Fiumicino to Rome — was considerably shorter than those of the Birmingham and Paris forces. The three vans identified as "Euro Sports Association" had only to get to the A91 and then Via Aurelia for the twenty-mile trip to Rome.

But tension mounted as it became clear that the Israeli force would be more directly exposed on this mission than their colleagues were in Alabama and Paris. The twelve Quds terrorists were based in a warehouse on the narrow strip of a Tiber River island in the center of Rome.

Ari, the lead Mossad agent, was taken aback when he learned that Leora had volunteered for the mission but was redirected to another assignment. He was disappointed and hoped that her volunteering to return to Rome had something, anything, to do with him.

The Matkal force set up in a ground-floor apartment in the Trastevere district only blocks from the Tiber. Euro Sports vans were allowed to park on the sidewalk in front of the apartment. Mossad operatives posing as sports agents "contributed" a considerable sum of euros to ensure that the Italian police had flexible parking ordinances September 6.

Preplanning ensured that the cases marked "sporting equipment," delivered September 5, contained automatic weapons, explosives, and Ari's weapon of choice, which accompanied him to the medal award platform many times in sharpshooting competitions.

Ari gathered the unit for a briefing. Mossad and elite commando units had rarely combined forces for combat operations. Each sector had unique areas of specialization; they would be tested. The European and American actions required extensive on-site reconnoitering and planning that only Mossad could perform.

With coordination in mind, Ari asked that Yehuda, the commando unit's veteran commander, join him in the briefing.

"Here's an overview of our surveillance," Ari began as he unfurled a large street map of Rome. "Ishmael Al Fazzi — a killer known to you guys — and twelve Quds are in an abandoned warehouse on Tiberina Island — Isola Tiberina on this Italian map.

"The warehouse is only thirty to forty yards away from the Fatebenefratelli Hospital, which still functions as a hospital for the elderly and for women. Yes, I know that's an unusual combination. We'll complain to the government on our way out.

"There are two entry points to the island: the Cestio Bridge to the west and the Fabricio Bridge to the east. Our current location is here." He pointed to their apartment in Trastevere.

"Yehuda, take over. Let's go over the plan step by step. One thing for sure: We've got to cross back over the western bridge to our vans to get you guys back to the sub."

Yehuda laid it out, asked for comments, and handed out assignments.

"Knowing about Al Fazzi's paranoia, which helped keep him alive until now, there will be at least one guard on duty and maybe two at all times.

"Ari" — he turned to his Mossad partner — "we'll count on your sniper skills if we run into interference. We'd hoped to take the enemy out with TATP, but it's too risky with the hospital so close. We'll go with Plan B."

Yehuda concluded, "We've got to be back in the vans by 3 a.m. and hauling ass out of here."

"The terrorists have made this island their base," Ari added with a grimace, "because of how close it is to the Grand Synagogue, the Jewish shops, and the smaller neighborhood synagogues. We've been through this a bunch of times — let's get some rest."

September 6 passed without incident or police interference. The commando teams reviewed their assignments, checked their weapons, and played cards or complained that the local agents hadn't prepared elaborate pasta entrees.

By 2:15 a.m. on September 7, the heat of an unusually warm Rome day let up. The force moved into position just inside the Cestio Bridge. Only Ari remained on the bridge, ensuring that he had an unimpeded view of the warehouse and hospital entrance. He waited, his favorite automatic weapon with a mounted infrared scope and a silencer screwed into the muzzle, zeroed in on the Quds site.

The ambulance passing by his right shoulder, silent but with its emergency lights flashing was right on time. It pulled up to the entrance of the hospital. The driver and his partner jumped out and hurried to the back doors of the emergency vehicle. They lowered a wheelchair that held a patient who was hunched over and covered with a quilted blanket.

"One second, please." A Quds sentry positioned behind a column at the entrance of the nearby warehouse stopped them. In passable Italian he asked where the two attendants were taking the patient. The clearly visible AK-47 was all the authority he needed.

The patient's answer, in Italian, didn't convince the sentry. His suspicion sealed his fate. He approached the wheelchair and reached over to pull back the blanket. He froze as the silenced 9mm Beretta under the quilt sent two quick hollow-point shots into his chest.

As Yehuda suspected, Al Fazzi had a backup sentry. Maybe two. Aroused by the noise and curious about the flashing lights of the ambulance, the second sentry turned the corner from his northern guard position.

Alarmed at seeing his partner down, he raised his automatic weapon and aimed at the intruders. His errant shot rang out just as Ari took him down with one shot below his chin.

The guard's shot set the attack in motion. Like the operation at Birmingham's Stormfront headquarters, the front and rear doors were blown in. The Quds fighters didn't have time to get to their formidable arsenal. Still, a raging gun battle began in their warehouse base. Two commandos were hit.

Yehuda's wound came from a ricochet that grazed his right shoulder. Another commando was hit in the left thigh. Both were treated on the spot as the firefight ended. Ten Quds corpses lay around the central hall of the warehouse.

Yehuda matched the photograph from headquarters in Israel with the corpse lying no more than ten feet from him. He was ecstatic despite the searing pain in his shoulder: They'd ended the career of one of the world's most notorious terrorists, Ishmael Al Fazzi.

Ehud, the unit's techie, ensured all the bodies were accounted for. "I wish I had a better camera," he joked. "I hate to use a cellphone to get a picture of the famous Al Fazzi."

Yehuda barked, "Cut the bullshit and get pictures of all the bad guys. We've gotta get out of here ASAP."

They left the scene at moderate speeds, avoiding attention from the many Carabinieri speeding toward Fatebenefratelli Hospital, where reports of gunfire had just been called in.

Local authorities were notified in advance to expect that one or more Euro Sports Association vans might be crossing Rome's avenues several hours after midnight. They reportedly were heading toward their next sporting event.

As the vans made their way to the highway, Ari slowly got over his disappointment that his hesitation of a millisecond allowed the Quds sentry to get off a shot, setting off the fireworks. Leora's visit a few days ago in his hotel's Junior Suite 320 flooded his thoughts; it seemed like eons ago.

What had surely begun over Syria would affect his tiny homeland. Israeli pilots at that moment were probably dodging anti-aircraft missiles while trying to take out Russia's most advanced fighters.

27
A Visit to Arab Countries

On paper, the exotic destinations on Dolphin-4's route to the Gulf of Oman looked like an exciting tourist itinerary. The sub navigated the Suez Canal — fully surfaced with its escort of two Egyptian cruisers. Leaving the canal, the sub slid to a depth of 450 feet. It continued the length of the Red Sea heading for the Gulf of Aden, just north of Somalia.

Turning north through the Arabian Sea west of India, Dolphin-4 was positioned east of Muscat in the Gulf of Oman. It arrived ahead of schedule and remained submerged four hours longer than anticipated. Not many travel agents would have mistaken the fearsome battle machine bristling with nuclear-armed Turbo cruise missiles aimed at the heart of Iran with a cruise liner.

The defense minister had strongly recommended Captain Arik Golan. Yarkoni met with Tzion and made his position clear. "Golan is even-tempered, totally unflappable, and highly intelligent. He's a student of naval warfare. He's done his master's thesis on Hellenic sea battles. What Dolphin-4's commander has to do is finesse one of our most important and controversial battle plans. He'll have to be cool under pressure. You and I know he'll be tested. I think the Americans will be happy with him as our choice. Shit, he'll be out there totally on his own."

For decades, Israel's governments had neither denied nor confirmed that they possessed even one nuclear bomb, let alone over three hundred, including incalculably destructive thermonuclear warheads. Israel could deliver them over a distance of several thousand miles with astounding accuracy. America knew it. Russia knew it.

At 5 a.m. Oman time, 0100 Zulu Time, Rosh Hashana, September 7, Captain Golan was bringing his sub to the surface in hostile waters within 2,000 miles of Tehran.

If Russia had more carefully monitored the timeline, it might have questioned how America had sent an urgent notification that a nuclear-armed Israeli sub had appeared in the Gulf of Oman a full ten minutes before the actual surfacing. As it happened, the timing glitch was overlooked.

Golan's lieutenant called out, "Captain, radar just picked up two Iranian fighters — MIG-29s — scrambled from Hamadan. They're 155 miles out and closing sub sonically."

Dolphin-4 had no air or sea cover. They were on their own.

The lieutenant asked in a more measured tone, "Shall I activate the Stunners?" Golan's sub was armed with Israel's newest surface-to-air missile. Though not battle-tested, the system had proved accurate at a distance of 175 miles at the astonishing speed of Mach 7.5.

Golan responded, "My instinct is overruled by the political theater we have to play in. I'd love to teach the bastards a lesson." Reluctantly, he called out the order, "Prepare to dive to 300 feet."

It was hard suppressing his initial impulse, which was to blast the fighters out of the sky. This was precisely the scenario Minister Yarkoni envisioned when he pushed for Golan to lead the mission.

No sooner had the dive siren been sounded than they received a transmission from Tzion at Central Command in Jerusalem. "The Kremlin warned the Iranians of your presence in their backyard and made them back off. Thankfully, the Americans alerted the Russians, who were now aware of the weapons on board. The fighters turned back to their base."

Dolphin-4 bobbed on the surface, unchallenged in the warm Gulf waters, with eight nuclear missiles aimed at Tehran, Isfahan, and other major Iranian cities. Their conventional missiles remained untargeted for the "just in case" scenario.

Sounds in the Desert

The heavily reinforced portals of the underground silos at Palmachim Air Base slowly slid open. Israel's ultimate weapons were being elevated to the surface just before 3:30 a.m. on September 7. As in the Gulf of Oman, the plan was to have American and Russian satellites track their intended targets.

Israel's Jericho 3 intercontinental ballistic missiles were armed. They were capable of delivering nuclear payloads at supersonic speed up to 4,000 miles. Russian satellites would immediately plot their intended paths and determine that major Iranian nuclear reactors were in their crosshairs. Alon, addressing no one in particular, said, "I hope the intel we passed on to the Americans a few days ago will help them point out what others might miss."

Exposing the nuclear arsenal in advance of the preemptive attack in Syria was risky. The country's Iron Dome, David's Sling, and Arrow defense systems guarded the missiles. None had been tested in an all-out war. A squadron of F-16s at Hatzerim Air Base near Beersheba in the Negev was on full alert.

By 3:45 a.m., fourteen silos had been opened with MIRV missiles prepared for a launch all hoped would never occur. Each had payloads able to reach multiple independently targeted sites. Yarkoni uttered in a dirge like tone, "God willing, we'll never have to resort to the unthinkable."

The sub off Oman carried similar firepower. Not since the surprise attack in 1973, when Israel's existence was threatened, had nuclear weapons been readied for retaliation.

Russia's Awakening

Alarm bells sounded throughout the Kremlin. Their military analysts had put the pieces together. America's Sixth Fleet was on no more of a training exercise than was their Caspian

Flotilla.

At 3:50 a.m., the Kremlin's frenzied command center debated whether to abort the attack planned for just over an hour later. The general's call went directly to the president's encrypted line: "Sir, we see too many signs pointing to complications and intel leaks. What are your instructions? We are deeply troubled in command center."

The president's decision to cancel started working its way through their command structure. The order came too late.

The Pre-Emptive Strike

Russian and Iranian intelligence hadn't received status reports from their Quds teams in Alabama, Paris, and Rome. They would soon find out why.

At 3:52 a.m., Israeli intelligence monitoring the accelerated chatter at the Syrian air base reported to Central Command, "We're picking up lots of chatter and flight plans to pilots already in their cockpits. They're in Russian, Farsi, and Munhwao —the dialect spoken in North Korea."

With the prime minister sitting at his side in their all-night command center, Tzion joked about the multinational air force to their north. "A regular United Nations meeting. Thanks for the report." He called General Karni, the head of Israel's air force.

"Karni, Igal here in the command center in Jerusalem. Intelligence just informed us that it looks like some of the pilots in Syria are Russian and some North Korean; we're not certain how many of each. There may even be an Iranian pilot or two. We assume, as in the past, they'll all be part of the attack."

Karni interrupted him to say, "We were sure that this would be the case. We're prepared for all possibilities. How would you like us to handle it?"

"General," Tzion's voice grew louder than needed, "we treat them all as the enemy. Just as we discussed with your pilots at the briefing at Nevatim a few days ago, make no distinction between Iranian, Russian, and North Korean."

The PM chimed in, "We all agree on this, General. It's one enemy."

"Thank you, Prime Minister. That's what I wanted to hear. We're ready." Karni signed off.

"We're in situations we've never faced before," Yarkoni whispered to whoever would listen in the command center. "I'm not sure how many defense ministers have encountered such a range of dangers. Igal, Chaim, Zvi, I'm amazed at your planning and calm and determined approach to our challenges. OK, OK, you too, Mr. PM. I see that look in your eyes."

Yarkoni paused, waiting for some reciprocity about his own calming influence. None was heard — despite their admiration for his strategic approach to the confluence of politics and military actions.

"Where are we with respect to the American Sixth Fleet?" Yarkoni addressed the question to the group but looked directly at Tzion.

Tzion answered with a smile, "Our latest intel is that thirty of their forty ships are positioned 200 miles offshore. Three aircraft carriers, with 125 aircraft, are part of that battle group. Guided missile cruisers and destroyers are escorting them. The Americans have lived up to their promise. America hasn't announced any war games, so the Russians are certain to get the message."

"And the Russian fleet?" Lavi asked.

"They understand that they're no match for the U.S. Navy," Tzion answered, "and as a face-saver have begun their 'war games' just east of Crete. This leaves the *Kuznetsov* in our backyard. Karni will provide air cover should that battle-ax dare to intervene."

28
IAF Heads North

Had Central Command been closer to Nevatim Air Force Base 100 miles to the south, the deafening roar of the squadron of F-35s gunning their Pratt & Whitney engines would have drowned out the Cabinet members' discussion.

Ten conventional and twelve short-takeoff/vertical-landing fighters were lining up on one of the three runways. Twenty F-16s, the highly maneuverable fighters with sophisticated radar-jamming equipment, were in position for takeoff on Runway 3.

Israel's air force was taking no chances. The stealth fighters could fly directly to the northern border and remain undetected by Russian radar. But all flight paths took them south and then west over the Mediterranean before heading north toward Syria.

They had to avoid Russian detection. The radar scramblers led the way to confuse and jam Russia's batteries of thermobaric rocket launchers and highly accurate S-400, S-300, and SA-23 surface-to-air missiles.

A squadron of fighters at Hatzerim was pointing south and was considerably less noisy. The pilots were relaxing in the cockpit or standing on the tarmac near their planes, snacking. They would need only seconds to climb in and rev the engines.

Their job was to protect Israel's southern flank should Hamas calculate some military advantage in attacking from Gaza. It wasn't clear whether Hamas leadership was fully aware of the planned attack. Abu Yusalem had coordinated with Hezbollah, not Hamas.

At 3:30 a.m., an hour and a half before the expected attack, the fighters headed to Syria were lined up on Nevatim's three runways, the 35s and 16s facing south before their jog west and full throttle north. The lead radar jammers were armed with six air-to-air missiles and a nest of Sparrow air-to-surface rockets.

The stealths carried two missiles under their wings and four internal Delilahs. These had the unique ability to loiter in the air like a helicopter. Hovering allowed them to seek, track, and destroy mobile targets.

Nevatim's command center informed the prime minister they were minutes away from launching all aircraft. The PM, raising his voice to be heard above the din from the desert base, shouted, "Notify me when the fighters are airborne." He contacted Ambassador Sundblad at the American Embassy in Jerusalem and General Peterson in Washington with a status report.

The next stage of Operation Never Again was underway. Israel's commandos had concluded their assignments and were en route home. The preemptive strikes on Iranian and Russian forces were moments away.

At 3:57, Condor Squadron's commander called in: "Viper requesting permission to take off." The 35s' engines were roaring.

Control center responded, "T-minus-2, Viper. Stand fast."

Within seconds, Serpent, the commander of the twenty 16s in Talon Squadron, heard the control tower's commands: "T-minus-1, Serpent." Seconds later, command tower calmly conveyed the order: "Viper cleared for takeoff on Runway 1. Serpent cleared for takeoff on Runway 3. Godspeed to all."

At precisely 4, the desert air thundered, and the still-dark sky was ablaze with the afterburners of dozens of Israeli fighter-bombers. Within moments, back in formation over the Mediterranean, they changed course and gunned their engines, heading north toward Syria, the stealths a few clicks behind the jammers.

Central Command had intercepted orders being delivered in Farsi, Arabic, Munhwao, and Russian. The frantic Russian order to launch early had not yet reached them.

As a final check, Viper contacted Central Command: "How do we treat this United Nations delegation?" A similar question came from Serpent's cockpit.

The answer was clear: "When fired on by the Russian missile batteries, take 'em out. They're on Syrian territory. Try jamming first; they'll fire blind. If you or any of those in your command are in danger, your orders are to eliminate them."

"Understood. We're on it." The response came simultaneously from both commanders.

The lead jammers were about six minutes from the Syrian border and eight minutes from Khmeimim Air Base.

The Russian Sukhoi-35s and Su-34s were lined up on parallel runways facing south toward Israel. Their revving engines shattered the illusory calm around the Syrian base. At Khmeimim Air Base the IAF would encounter the massive array of Russian surface-to-air missile batteries.

The Kremlin delivered the frantic order to launch early at 4:02. Israel's Command Center disregarded it, considering it a possible ploy.

Israel spent months dissecting the excellent delivery systems of the S-400 and S-300 batteries. That homework was about to be tested. Three fighters peeled off to the west to guard against the possibility of the *Admiral Kuznetsov* launching its revamped MiG-29Ks. Backup for the IAF was on the way from Ramat David Air Base near the northern city of Afula.

A cloud of wildly inaccurate anti-aircraft missiles greeted the fighters diving to take out the temporarily blinded launchers. The IAF's jamming capability was augmented by Israel's satellite radar redirection. Israel had dedicated vast sums to develop an umbrella designed to block radar waves. It was also being battle-tested.

"Serpent to tower," Talon Squadron leader was calling in. "We're taking a shitload of 400s and 300s from all angles. They've got no visual, but they're coming at us hot and heavy. Snake and Wolfman are down. Both able to make it back to our territory." His calm voice belied the fury around him.

"You've got about seven minutes before they'll switch frequencies and come live again. Start counting." The control tower was terse but reassuring. "Viper, you there yet?"

"Just coming to the party," Viper responded. "We're here, Serpent, we're here."

Swooping in from the west, the stealths caught the Russian aircraft as they were scrambling to get airborne. The early wave had taken out much of this sector's protective batteries. The stealths were undetected by those still active. Their missiles announced their presence.

"Viper to tower."

"Go ahead, Viper."

"Looks like about seventy-five to eighty 300s and 23s crisscrossing the sky. The fog of these birds is worse than London's air. Oh, shit—looks like Tiger 1 is hit. Don't know if he can make it home."

"Copters on their way. See if he can make it back, even to Lebanon." Control's voice was measured and calm. "You've got under five minutes to blast them and get out of there."

Condor Squadron unleashed a barrage of air-to-surface missiles with internal guidance systems. They pounded the still-blind mobile batteries. Israel's new generation of guided munitions was making its debut.

Unit 8200 had identified Runways 3 and 4 on the Syrian air base as the only ones able to accommodate the state-of-the-art SU-35, which required a longer takeoff strip. Twelve fighters of Condor Squadron targeted those Russian fighters, which, when airborne, were challenges to be reckoned with. They destroyed the only runways that Russia's feared aircraft could use and systematically took out the grounded fighters.

Serpent, the Talon Squadron leader, in constant communication with Central Command, called in: "400s fired randomly hit Foxman and Snailman. Both ejected. Holy shit. What if these birds had eyes?"

Syrian airspace had become a deadly maze of Russian missiles launched despite their blinded radar.

"You've got under three minutes. Russians are scrambling to switch to alternate frequencies and reactivate. The battle has to end. These systems will be back in business soon."

Israeli fighters would find themselves in a gravely deteriorated battle theater if the batteries not yet destroyed came to life again. Even the stealths would be in danger.

Parachutes were seen billowing from the downed Israeli fighters. The squadron leaders gave headquarters the coordinates.

Central Command notified the squadron leaders that the *Kuznetsov* had just launched four MiG-29s, which were being engaged over the Mediterranean. A brief battle followed, with the Russian aircraft at a distinct disadvantage. Israeli fighters ambushed them as they took off from the arched and inefficient runway of the Russian carrier. The battle ended within moments. All four MiGs were lost. The Russians didn't launch additional fighters.

"Viper, Serpent, how are we looking?" The control tower had satellite imagery but needed close-ups. "You have about sixty seconds. Time to haul ass out of there. Percentage of destruction?"

Virtually in unison, both squadron leaders said, "About as close to total as we could come."

"Looks to me," Viper added, "not one of theirs is undamaged. We're out of here." As the squadrons signed out, they peeled off and shot southwest over the sea back to Israeli airspace.

Moments after reentry, central radar tracking in Tel Aviv issued an emergency communication to the PM at the command center in Jerusalem. "A frigate 700 miles out escorting the Caspian Flotilla," the officer reported, "just launched three Kalibr-NK cruise missiles at Tel Aviv."

The voice was tense but calm: "Sir, they appear to be conventional. We estimate that they're carrying significant payloads with a range of 900 miles and fair accuracy. We're in range.

Activating David's Sling and Arrow systems. Any other orders?"

"Thanks, captain, back to you ASAP."

The PM called President Trainor on his hotline. "Mr. President, the Russians just launched three ballistic missiles at Tel Aviv. We ask that you intervene with them and keep them from actions that may tip the balance in a way none of us wants."

"Eliezer, we just heard from the Russian Embassy that they were launched by a rogue frigate commander." The president's voice was tense as he added, "The Kremlin's aware that an attack on Israel by their navy would be considered an attack on an American ally. They understand what your missiles are armed with as well.

"As a warning, our cruisers plotted the trajectory of a number of sea-to-sea Harpoons at the lead ships of the Russian flotilla. Russia tracked this immediately. We also had fifty fighters take off from our carriers. So far, they're just sightseeing. We're on it. You're not alone."

Russia understood the warnings and repeated the urgent communication to the White House that the rogue commander who'd ordered the launching had been relieved of his duties and detained. They claimed that they'd failed to redirect or disarm the missiles headed toward Tel Aviv.

The country's air raid sirens had been wailing for at least fifteen minutes. Emergency radio stations warned the population that this was not a drill. This was war. The paths to shelters were unobstructed — the practice drills proved indispensable. Ari Kahan's Shin Bet air raid drills had been successful.

Three cruise missiles were headed toward the mainland. Israel's X-band radar reported incoming in the atmosphere 450 miles out.

Communication was taken over by Tzion. "Sir," direct contact was now with the ballistic weapons center south of Tel Aviv, "three Arrows away." Israel's intercontinental air defense battalion launched the country's long-range, first-line defense shield. The Arrows were designed to knock out rockets at an altitude of over ten miles.

Tzion, now the only Cabinet member in direct contact with the launch command center, demanded, "I want a minute-by-minute tracking of incoming."

"Two just intercepted by Arrows. Disintegrated 350 miles offshore," reported the clipped voice from the center.

"And the third?" barked a tense Tzion.

"Missed it, sir; launching two Slings."

The newly developed anti-missile system, designed to intercept medium- and long-range weapons, had never been employed in combat.

Tzion turned to the four others in the command center and warned, "I don't think we'll catch this one.

"Point of impact?" he demanded from the tracking unit.

"Center of Ashkelon, sir. Eighteen minutes out."

Levi blurted, "Ashkelon?" He caught himself and remained silent.

Kahan and the civil defense agencies had prepared for war to which unfortunately they were no strangers. Vans patrolled the streets with loudspeakers blaring warnings: The country was at war. The myriad bomb shelters that dotted Israeli cityscapes were filling rapidly with frightened and rudely awakened families.

Little attention was paid to the political fallout that would surely come after the battle. Opposition to the ruling coalition would certainly criticize the timing of the notification of Israeli citizens. Who knew what and when? But at this point, public safety was the sole focus of Kahan's agency.

Kahan, at his central office communication center, sent a text message: "All mobile patrols in Ashkelon, you are warned that you have ten minutes more to canvass streets. Ten minutes — no more. After that, all drivers are ordered to shelters. This is not a request. It's an order. It's clear that one missile got past our defense shield. Ashkelon is the point of impact."

At 4:45 on the morning of Rosh Hashana, Ashkelon boomed and shuddered as if the city center had experienced a major earthquake. The hundreds of bomb shelters that formed a labyrinthine network of connecting tunnels deep in the bowels of the city shook with unprecedented intensity.

The blast took out two square blocks of central Ashkelon, a major port city in Israel's south. Virtually every apartment building was leveled or sustained severe damage. The blaring sirens of ambulances and fire engines racing to the blast site struck an eerie harmony with the lower-pitched wail of air raid sirens.

"My God," the PM moaned, "I pray our citizens took the warnings seriously and got to shelters."

Tzion stood, paced angrily, glared at the PM, and virtually spat out, "I'd like to order Dolphin-4 to launch two conventional MIRVs at Shiraz."

A resolute prime minister answered, tapping the rickety table near him with an open hand, "Igal, I'm as furious as you are, but we've crushed the Russian-Iranian attack. We destroyed their vaunted airpower in Syria. Iran understands now that, if threatened, we might resort to massive nuclear retaliation. The Americans lived up to their part of our agreement."

The PM paced, hands stroking his graying and unkempt hair. "I don't believe we should take this to the next level. The hit on a major Israeli city is horrifying. We're still unclear about how bad it was. But I believe that if we take the next step, it could lead to global conflict." He stopped speaking and made eye contact with Lavi, Yarkoni and Levi. "Your thoughts, gentlemen. But I must tell you in advance that I'm convinced this would be the result."

There was no debate. They agreed that Iran and Russia had been dealt a significant blow. Iran's Quds Force terror squads had been annihilated in three far-flung locations. Lavi reminded them of the Yom Kippur War in 1973, when Israel, after taking a pounding in the opening days of battle, recovered and drove within sixty miles of Cairo, poised to strike Egypt and the entire Arab world a mortal blow.

Lavi continued, forever calm under pressure: "Kissinger, the U.S. secretary of state, pushed us to accept a cease-fire, believing that the Arab world could never forgive an Israeli invasion of an Arab capital. Their anger and humiliation would make peace in the future a virtual impossibility. Try to imagine" — he waved his hand emphatically — "Dolphin-4 traveling through the Suez Canal with Egyptian escorts, had we invaded.

"I don't believe that we'll have a peace treaty with Iran for decades — maybe ever," Lavi lamented, wagging his right pointer. "But missiles on a major city of theirs will bring all-out war."

"And Ashkelon bombed?" Tzion barked.

Yarkoni responded emotionally, "It was the Russians, and they were stopped by the Americans. They confirmed that the launching was at the hands of a renegade commander who has been relieved and is in custody. He launched them before the Kremlin could stop him."

The PM slowly scanned the drawn and taut faces of the men sitting in their cramped command center. Levi looked despondent as he turned his back on the other Israeli leaders. Simcha addressed his Mossad director, "What is it, Zvi? We're all totally drained, I know."

Levi turned toward the group, pale and shaken. "My son, Yehud, and his pregnant wife just moved into an apartment in central Ashkelon."

29
Security Cabinet's Conclusions

Seventy-two hours had passed since Operation Never Again ended. The Security Cabinet convened beneath the Knesset, all looking pale and disheveled.

The novelty of the PM's espresso machine had worn thin, and despite Israel's multifront military successes, there was no gloating or victory lap.

"One hundred thirty-three Israelis killed when the missile hit Ashkelon," the prime minister began. "Ari, if it weren't for your air raid drills, the loss would have certainly been far greater."

Tzion stood, focused and angry: "Five F-16s and two F-35s lost over Syria. A dozen more badly damaged; four pilots unaccounted for. We believe they're alive and held by Hezbollah. Who knows what the damage would have been if we hadn't blinded their missile systems?

"As expected," Tzion noted more calmly, "Dolphin subs played a big role in our military actions. Those who were the visionaries and fought for untested war machines *and* convinced guys like me who were doubtful about the appropriations, kol hakavod." Tzion looked directly at General Lavi as he spoke and thanked him with a nod. Lavi had lobbied aggressively for the outlandishly expensive subs.

"I'll leave the analysis to better military minds than mine," Alon cut in, leaning back in his chair. With unusual gravitas he continued, "But from my perspective, much has come clear." He tapped his pen on the conference table as if to announce he was about to begin his histrionics. But he stayed on point and seemed subdued.

"The Americans stood by us and risked military confrontation. They showed balls and commitment. Moving the Sixth Fleet battle group into position and cooperating in our military intervention in Alabama were invaluable." He raised his voice an octave and shook his head as if in disbelief, "Their FBI played an indispensable role in helping us eliminate the terrorists. So far, they have stayed hands-off when we sent Stormfront a message. It remains to be seen how pissed they'll be about our unavoidable firefight."

"*It also remains to be seen*," Tzion, still pacing, reacted in his usual clipped manner, "how Russia will respond. They lost a tremendous amount of military equipment. And, maybe more important to them, their bragging rights as the main player in the Middle East were exposed as hollow."

"As for Iran, who knows?" Yarkoni chimed in. "They'll remain an enemy for decades to come. For years I've argued that as a world power — saying that sounds strange, but it's true — we must protect the Jews of the Diaspora. History, *our history*, requires that we defeat forces that threaten the Diaspora, even if the Jews of Massachusetts or Brussels believe that their governments will protect them.

"I don't mean to become Western Europe's police force. I fully understand and respect you questioning our Diaspora role, Igal." He nodded to Tzion, acknowledging his reluctance to accept Israel's role beyond its regional theater.

"Vicious anti-Semites like the Jobbik party, Golden Dawn, and the endless stream of Jew-haters littering Europe must know that our commandos, our Mossad, will strike at them should they threaten Jews with violence anywhere in the world. I believe it's clear that they've got to look over their shoulders from today on."

Alex Meron, the laconic, penny-pinching head of the Finance Ministry, offered a rare observation. He scratched the bald spot that a few years earlier sported a mound of thinning brown hair. It was unusual for the reclusive but respected minister to offer a nonfinancial opinion.

"For years I've wrestled with the question: Are we our brothers' keeper? Diaspora Jews," his voice rising above his traditional monotone drone, "*are* our brothers and sisters. Perhaps we have the chutzpah to reinterpret passages of Genesis." He slowly scanned the room, pausing at each member, "We all studied how an aggressive and jealous Cain kills his brother Abel. When God asks Cain, 'Where is your brother?' Cain's answer is 'Am I my brother's keeper?' "

Meron continued his longest foray into unbudgeted territory: "The modern version of Cain's reply might imply an unwillingness to care for our brothers. We all saw what carrying this notion out to its most demonic end looked like when the Vichy government collaborated with the Nazis identifying and rounding up defenseless French Jews.

"We do have a responsibility to be our brothers' keeper." Meron sat back, pleased that the murmur was one of acceptance. Approval of his comments was rare, as his colleagues always bitched and moaned about his fiscal constraints and endless stream of Excel spreadsheets.

A visibly saddened Levi added, "Nicely said, Alex. I think that you've hit on what's in our hearts better than any of us could have. I want to add to Moshe's earlier point. We're not fighting to restrict free speech. The world will always have an abundance of anti-Semites." Levi shook his head ruefully. "Universities will for the foreseeable future be hotbeds of controversy and targets for anti-Zionist propaganda. Students need something to bitch about and advocate for or against. We're a convenient target."

Levi stood and began pacing and gesticulating with both hands. He pointed to his nearest colleague and asked rhetorically, "How many of us remember student demonstrations throughout Europe and the States in support of the Red Army Faction or Baader-Meinhof in the '70s? How many knew what those killers really advocated, what they stood for, as they carried placards in their support? They publicly promoted shaking up the status quo, with their sinister goals well camouflaged."

The PM cut off the discussion, bringing it back to the current reality. He focused on the commitment that he'd made to President Trainor.

"The agreement with Trainor, which he made clear was a demand, calls for us to move rapidly toward dismantling several settlements. We also need to take first steps toward peace talks with the Palestinians. I intend to adhere to that agreement." Turning toward Kahan with a barely disguised smirk, he asked, "That is, if it's OK with you, Ari."

Ari Kahan, the lone left-leaning Cabinet member, smiled and nodded, paying little attention to the PM's caustic tone. The comment about peace talks was a welcome and long-overdue position he'd fought for in the Cabinet.

Alon added, "I believe that we can now acknowledge that we may have gotten off lightly with the American demands."

"What do you mean?" Tzion asked.

"We desperately needed their support. Eliezer" — he turned to the PM — "I don't want to speak for you, but I believe that we would have agreed to almost any demand of theirs." He gently slapped the conference table, "Peace talks and a few settlements dismantled let us off easy. Yes?"

"We'll see." The PM responded, pursing his lips and tilting his head to the right. "I believe the demands have only just begun. Time will tell."

Kahan stood and walked toward Levi. He stopped near him and added, without his traditional sarcasm, "Getting back to your point about university campus vitriol against us — how much of it seems justifiable because of our perceived intransigence in entering peace talks with the Palestinians? I agree in advance," he held out both hands in faux humility, "so no need to yell at me, that maybe only 50 percent of the anger at us is justified.

"When we begin dismantling our settlements — yes, yes, not all of them — a good deal of the international and domestic rancor about our fifty years of occupation will dissolve." The usual *not again* moaning from his colleagues was absent. "Time will tell here as well."

He lowered his voice: "The pain of our losses in Ashkelon is great" — he put his hand on Levi's shoulder — "but having dealt Iran a blow while uncovering the Russian ruse on the world gives me some hope."

The PM nodded to Kahan. "I expect that we'll soon be on the well-worn path toward condemnation by the U.N. Security Council. I can already visualize," shaking his head and feigning a grimace, "the resolution censuring us for our preemptive attack on the peace-loving forces of Iran and Russia. No doubt Italy and France will have a word or two about our actions on their soil. I think we're prepared for that."

With a tremor in his voice, Tzion said, "We have too many heroes to acknowledge individually. Too many losses to bear. 8200 provided us with on target intel. Our fighter pilots performed with skill and valor. As expected, our 35s were indispensable for evading Russian radar, while our 16s were mostly successful in jamming the many Russian missile batteries."

Turning to Lavi, Tzion nodded and bowed slightly: "The professionalism and precision of our Sayeret Matkal and Shayetet 13 commandos was exemplary. As usual, your forces were outstanding. I can go on for much longer, but I know that Zvi wants to speak."

Levi, still unsure about the fate of his only son and daughter-in-law, Yehud and Rachel, composed himself.

"There are two persons who must be singled out. I've taken the liberty of inviting Joshua Canaan and Leora Bargal — now you know her name — to speak with us. It's important that we hear from them and that they're acknowledged by the Cabinet."

Nodding toward the PM, Levi waited for a thumbs-up. He walked to the mahogany door just behind the PM, opened it, and signaled for Leora and Joshua to enter. The loud applause embarrassed both agents.

"Zvi," Joshua began preemptively, "I'm still unclear how you convinced me to return to duty and how I survived the first two days after sharing my intentions with Anat."

The Cabinet members laughed, temporarily relieving the anguish over their losses.

Levi stayed focused. "What you and Leora accomplished is beyond what can be expected of even Mossad agents. You risked your lives and were never deterred from your mission."

Joshua took the initiative. "Our goals, and I stress the *our*, were mostly accomplished. Leora, my partner," he walked to where she sat and stood behind her, "is remarkable for her intelligence, strategy, bravery."

Leora blushed and fidgeted with the middle button on her white pantsuit.

Joshua continued, "First, she played a major role in foiling the Paris sarin-bomb plot. Next was Leora's extraordinary assessment of the three overseas military actions. We were focused on tracking and killing Yusalem while at the same time minimizing the probability of a Hezbollah missile attack coordinated with the air assault."

Tzion looked puzzled: "What's your assessment of why Hezbollah's barrage didn't occur? Northern Command was prepared for a rain of missiles. In your opinion, why didn't that play out?"

"It's chutzpah for me to offer military assessments, given those in this room," Joshua said as he scanned the faces of the Cabinet members. "But since I'm soon to re-enter retirement, or, as Leora would suggest, a senior citizen home" — she cracked a smile — "I'll offer my thoughts."

He stepped closer to the conference table. "Our drone hit in Beirut and our earlier action in Paris, when Leora and I almost killed Yusalem, may have made it too risky for Hezbollah's leadership to expose their tactics and launch sites to us. They're clever and want to maintain their stranglehold on Lebanon." He raised his voice and held out his right hand for emphasis. "I believe that Hezbollah's leadership understood what Russia and Iran failed to see: that we had cracked their codes and anticipated their actions.

"The time will come when they launch their missiles. This is no surprise to you, and we have no doubt about this. They'll choose the time — unless we preemptively strike them. The next confrontation with Hezbollah, in our opinion, is only a matter of time."

He nodded to Israel's leaders around the table. "It doesn't take a military genius to see what Iran is up to in Syria; with Russia's help, they're building bases for the future. They'll continue to develop a significant presence in Syria. Yes, Iran took a beating, but with Syria a broken state and Hezbollah as their proxy army, it's only a matter of time until they again confront us."

Tzion agreed, offering an additional thought: "Much depends on America. We've just experienced an administration that was unequivocal in its support. They stood up to Russia and Iran. Maybe the years of U.S. hands-off policy in Syria and with other neighbors of ours are over."

A loud rap on the door behind the PM interrupted Joshua and Tzion. An aide to the PM entered and spoke to him privately.

He returned after two minutes and asked that all Cabinet members and Leora and Joshua accompany him to the technology center down the hall. Two techies guided them to seats in front of the massive screen where the computer system was just booting up. All other screens were dark.

Joshua looked at Leora, who wore a puzzled expression. She shrugged in the universal "I'm confused" posture. Joshua arched his eyebrows and held both palms out, facing up.

As the screen came alive with a satellite video of Beirut-Rafic Hariri Airport, Joshua whispered to Leora, "Damn. Levi's going to publicly criticize us for renting too large a Toyota."

Leora poked him with her elbow.

The purpose of the interruption by the PM's aide soon became clear.

The satellite captured the arrival of Abu Yusalem at the airport on the day he was scheduled to meet with Naswalah al-Din, military commander of Hezbollah, at the Golf Club of Lebanon.

The video clearly depicted every moment of the terrorist's arrival and his entry into the second black Lincoln Navigator. The satellite cameras followed the vans as they pulled away from the restricted parking area outside the arrival gate.

The gray Toyota — with Leora and Joshua inside grumbling about the cigarette smoke — followed about two minutes later and turned west down a side street as a shortcut to the club. In that 120-second window, the black limo stopped parallel to a green Subaru. One man, wearing a straw Panama hat with a blanket draped over his shoulder, emerged from the Lincoln and jumped into the waiting sedan, which sped off east, away from the club.

"That," the PM said, looking directly at Leora and Joshua, "is why Lebanese rescue crews found only seven mangled but identifiable bodies, none of them Abu Yusalem. It appears that he escaped once again."

Joshua asked that the video be run two more times. "Three times I missed him."

Leora blurted, "Four, counting Paris."

Joshua glared at her. He pounded a coffee table so hard that two cups bounced up and crashed on the stone-tiled floor.

"How many lives does this killer have?" Joshua asked. "Is it cunning and wile and an uncanny premonition of impending danger? Or is it something else?" He approached the screen, where the image of a very much alive Abu Yusalem had been frozen.

"Could it be," Joshua asked, "that while we've cracked the encrypted codes used by the Russians and Iranians, our intel may have been compromised as well? Or, maybe worse than that, Abu Yusalem may have had help from another source that we'll need to identify."

Joshua held back his thoughts about a possible security breach. "Mr. Prime Minister and members of the Security Cabinet, are we more secure after this terrible period? I hope we are."

He gathered his thoughts, trying hard not to sound like he

was lecturing: "We've shown our people, the Arab world, our archenemy Iran, and the world's superpowers that we have the means to defend not only our homeland, but the Jews of the Diaspora as well. Unfortunately, we probably have many wars ahead of us. History, when it comes to Jews, does repeat itself."

Eliezer Simcha raised both hands simultaneously, signaling that he wanted to speak. He referred back to Joshua's frightening insinuation: *Does Abu Yusalem have a contact within Israeli security*? Was it simply preternatural instinct that continually extricated him from danger? "Joshua, you and Leora came so close to eradicating Yusalem. Yet each time he evaded you."

Virtually in unison, Joshua and Leora said the terrorist still represented a danger to Israel.

"I'm certain," Joshua lamented, "that Yusalem will drag me out of my second retirement as well. He poses an enormous challenge to us and remains a relentless and crafty enemy. His escapes from well-planned traps make me suspicious. The prospect of a leak poses a risk to Mossad agents and to our security forces. Should I be coaxed out of my senior citizens home" — he threw a mock frown at Leora — "I'll be committed and driven to end that scourge's life."

The PM slowly shook his head and with conviction said, "I'll recommend that our security agencies perform a comprehensive investigation into the possibility of an internal breach."

Joshua's mind was churning. He walked over to Levi and sat next to him, putting his hand on Levi's knee. He whispered that he prayed his family had survived the Ashkelon blast. He switched gears, ignoring the others in the room. With warmth and conviction he said, "Zvi, I'll help you find the leak. I can't stop thinking about the Russian beauty that you drooled over when you visited me at my apartment's swimming pool. How much did she hear? What about our Russian-born submarine captain? What did Cabinet members tell their wives about your prolonged and secretive meetings? How carefully vetted were the techies in our technology center? I remember hearing that the American ambassador has a trusted assistant, Jared, who has an Iranian wife. We have to dig deeply and unemotionally. I'll be with you if you want me."

Levi nodded, rested his hand on Joshua's, and thanked him silently.

Eliezer Simcha stood, "I'm exhausted and ready to close this meeting.

"We've risen to challenges time and time again. We're far from a Utopian society, but no one can question the courage of our response to the global threat to Jews." He sighed heavily. "We're bruised, but we stand, not only for ourselves, but also for our brothers and sisters worldwide.

"We're celebrating Rosh Hashana, a new year, and maybe a new role — one we may have been destined to play for years." He nodded to Meron, the laconic finance minister. "Today we turned from Cain's response and forged our own. We were and will be our brothers' keeper."

Author's Note

My Brothers' Keeper is a work of fiction. All characters and events are representations of my imagination, shaped by years of working and living in Tel Aviv and Jerusalem. Many locations have been renamed, some given new addresses. The existential threat to Israel imagined in this novel and the particular virulent anti-Semitism described herein, while recurring with monotonous regularity, are fictitious.

New York's northwest neighborhoods were post-World War II melting pots. Immigrant groups — Irish, Italian and Jewish — living in close proximity, all struggled for the elusive American Dream. My parents were part of that immigrant group. Their two-year escape route from the Nazi onslaught, through uncaring European capitals, brought them to Ellis Island and safety in the USA. They were reluctant to speak of the horrors of the Holocaust and anti-Semitism. It wasn't until I moved to Israel that this pervasive scourge became clear to me.

Six months on, an Israeli absorption center brought it home. The concept of the center is brilliant: Immigrants from many countries live on a campus, learning Hebrew and of one another's cultural experiences. More often than not, anti-Jewish sentiment and persecution influenced the decision to emigrate. And so began my visceral education of the in-gathering of Jews in a neighborhood replete with daily dangers.

The region's volatility and toxicity have been intensified by Iran, Israel's most potent enemy, sworn to the destruction of the "Zionist state." The events of this novel are imaginary concoctions, but the ingredients are too readily at hand.

The Boycott, Divestment and Sanctions movement, benignly referred to as BDS, is a prime example of a pernicious ingredient. Beneath the protest of Israel's settlement policy lies the insidious declaration that Israel must be eradicated. The infiltration of Iran's notorious Quds Force into the European BDS networks is purely a work of fiction. I have no factual basis to say this has occurred.

Similarly, while Stormfront is a vicious, hate-spewing, diabolical reality created by an Alabama Klan boss, it is, thankfully, only a cyber-reality. You will not find the headquarters in Birmingham or anywhere else, should you care to track Stormfront down. Neither will the adventurous Paris traveler find the Relais St. Etienne in the Sixth Arrondissement. Perhaps if Leora had visited the lovely Relais St. Sulpice, upon which I modeled the St. Etienne, she would have had a more favorable result.

With pleasure, I share that the exquisite Dohány Street Synagogue remains, as always, an inviting reason to visit Budapest's Seventh District.

Throughout the novel, I played geographic acrostics. Pensione Lucchesi, visited by Leora in Rome, is actually a Florence landmark. The Prima Kings Hotel is a vibrant, four-star hotel in the heart of West Jerusalem on which I modeled the Prima Prince Hotel, where the story's transitional U.S. Embassy would be moved from Tel Aviv to Jerusalem.

Ashkelon, the beautiful Israeli city on the shores of the Mediterranean, retains its charm and allure. I hope the city's Chamber of Commerce will not revoke my permission to visit, given my fictional attack on its center.

Finally, while the events that form the fabric of this novel are imaginary, the danger to Israel is real. Russia has been dealt the winning hand in the region after America's nearly total troop withdrawal. The continued chaos in Syria and the infusion of Russian air and land forces are not positive harbingers. Iran's strengthened positions in Syria and continued support of Israel's closest enemy, Hezbollah, are additional causes for concern.

ABOUT THE AUTHOR

Harry D. Stern

Harry Stern has written and lectured on Middle Eastern affairs and their impact on Israel's military challenges. Upon receiving his M.A. and doctorate from Columbia University, Stern moved to Israel, where he assumed the role of Director of Community Organization for Southern Tel Aviv and held faculty positions in Jerusalem. Upon returning to the United States, Stern held the position of CEO of several Jewish organizations.

He has published articles in numerous professional journals. Most recently, his memoir, "Anemone in a Desert Landscape," was published by REJA Press. Several of his experiences in Israel after arriving as a new immigrant are described in that book.

Stern lives in Atlanta with his wife, Aviva. They have three children and five grandchildren.

ALSO BY THIS AUTHOR

Anemone in a Desert Landscape

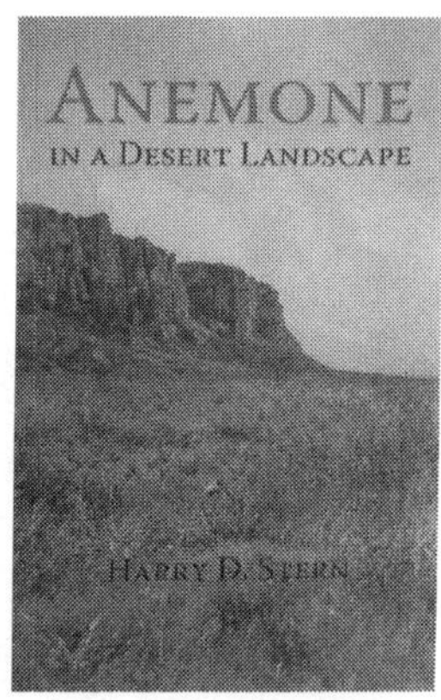

Growing up in the Washington Heights neighborhood of upper Manhattan, in New York City, in the 1940s and '50s, Harry depicts his struggle with conforming to conventional authority, with bittersweet and humorous biographical accounts. From a troubled youth in a neighborhood rife with a vibrant drug and organized gang culture, to achieving a doctoral degree from Columbia University and becoming the CEO of one of the largest Jewish Community Centers in the world, Harry Stern highlights the social, cultural and intra psychic challenges that he faced. His six plus years in Israel, provide insight into the attractions and challenges of living in a vibrant, developing country, fraught with societal deficits, but alive with infinite possibil-ities. His experiences as a new immigrant in many ways mirrored those of his parents, who immigrated to the United States having escaped the Holocaust.

Made in the USA
Columbia, SC
20 June 2020